CREVICE

JANICE BOEKHOFF

D1546068

WILD BLUE
PRESS

WildBluePress.com

CREVICE published by:
WILDBLUE PRESS

P.O. Box 102440
Denver, Colorado 80250

WILDBLUE PRESS is registered at the U.S. Patent and Trademark Offices.

978-1-942266-54-9   Trade Paperback ISBN
978-1-942266-55-6   eBook ISBN

Interior Formatting by Elijah Toten
Totencreative.com

Book Cover Design Kim Mesman
kmgraphics1.carbonmade.com

For Zach

May your adventurous spirit take you
places you have never dreamed possible

January, 1850
Jacob Waltz

It is a strange kind of misery to dwell on the last day I went to meet Ila. Most often, I refuse to let the memories come. But on my saddest days, I invite them, just to see her face in my mind one more time. Until now, I have never penned the account of that day, and I pray it will bring some release of the full control these events have over my heart.

On that day more than forty years ago, I climbed the rocky slope to our hidden cavern. As I neared the top of the small mountain, the late afternoon sun heated my back like a hot iron, and a desert wind blew dust in my face. I held my hat firm and clung to the side of the high cliff to guard against being blown off.

I was nervous, not just from the danger of the climb, but also because of my reason for the visit, so soon after my last. I planned to ask Ila for more gold to start my wood-carving shop. She had already given me plenty, but it was gone, given to a neighbor. I would explain how the woman had lost her husband to illness and had three children to feed, lest Ila think me greedy.

At the tall, narrow opening, I turned sideways to squeeze inside, placing my hands along the rock wall. Ila's dark hand reached out to pull me in. I stumbled into the small cavern.

It was shaped like an ax handle, long and thin. In one direction, it continued into darkness and in the other, the walls opened to the left—the head for the ax. The surfaces of the cavern were unblemished except for one perilous area directly across from the entrance. In the floor, a square hole, big enough for a man to fall through, dropped into the depths of the mountain.

As I regained my footing, I stood to my full height and looked up into Ila's ebony eyes. I reached out to caress her smooth, almond-colored cheek. Her beauty was primitive and timeless. I didn't know her age, nor did she. The one instance when I asked, she answered in the number of leaders her tribe had since she was a girl—three. I presumed her to be in her thirties, ten years younger than me, but I couldn't be certain.

Nevertheless, I'd loved her from the day she rescued me. I was in a desperate situation because my carelessness had resulted in a snake bite. She brought me to this cavern and nursed me until I recovered. Her kindness and gentleness were beyond compare.

Ila bent her head, attempting to get closer to my height. If only she could have seen herself as I did— lovely—but her tribe had convinced her of the contrary. In her younger years, Ila had begun to grow quickly. She kept growing until she was taller than every man in the tribe. Since no Apache man would marry a woman taller than himself, she had no marriage proposals. Eventually, her own father, the tribe's shaman, sent her to live inside this mountain, called the land of the "Thunder Spirit," saying a woman of her size should be made the wife of the spirit.

Though angered when I heard this, I did not speak ill of her father. Instead, I told Ila of my God who loved her without restriction, as did I.

Stretching up, I kissed her lips. A passionate kiss was all I would take from her. The Apache would never let her marry a foreigner, and I wouldn't defile her.

When our lips parted, she stepped back and examined me for a moment. Her eyes saw with a wisdom greater than most. She smoothed my beard and said I looked distressed. She spoke the words slowly, giving thought to each one. Although she had learned English as the daughter of a tribal leader, she had no one to speak it to in between my visits.

I remembered then the reason I had come, but asking for gold this soon after arriving would seem ungrateful. Looking into her eyes, I told her I had no care that couldn't be solved by gazing upon her radiant face. The custom of wooing was lost on her, but still I longed to say the words.

Near our feet, a tiny lizard ran from its hiding place. I bent down to lift him up, offering him to Ila. The little runners were her favorite. She said they kept her cavern clean and free from insects. While she was distracted by the lizard, I took the carving I had brought for her out of my pocket—a running lizard, my most detailed carving yet, made from white oak with pieces of silver tin used for the eyes.

After giving the animal a few strokes on the back, she lowered the squirming lizard to the ground. When she stood up, I handed her the wooden one. She smiled and took the gift, then stiffened as though it had offended her. She tilted her head toward the other end of the cavern, her eyes widening. It wasn't the carving—she had heard something. I had never come that way, but I knew there was another entrance down the tunnel.

I pulled the rifle off my pack, thinking it could be a prospector. Men searching for gold were capable of anything. But Ila pressed the barrel of my gun into the dirt and shook her head. Many in her tribe possessed guns. Even so, she would not want me to use it against another person.

She slipped the lizard carving into the folds of her tunic and led me around the corner to the ax-head part of the cavern, directing me to hide. I did what she wanted, crouching down behind the rock wall, but I kept my rifle in both hands.

As soon as Ila left me, light and quick footsteps came into the cavern. Steps so quiet could only belong to an Apache.

A low voice spoke to Ila in the almost musical language of her people. I listened silently from my hiding place without understanding. If anyone from her tribe were to see me, Ila would suffer for it.

When the one voice stopped, another began. From this angle, I could see her standing silent, but not the men who were speaking. Ila remained with her hands together in front, head down, her long hair hanging like a dark silk curtain.

When the second man stopped speaking, Ila lifted her head. It was her turn to talk, but her usually calm voice had a tone of fear in it. She only managed a few words before one of the men yelled at her.

She uttered an Apache word I recognized, one she had taught me. *Please.*

I tightened my grip on the gun, wishing I could see what the men were doing. But it wouldn't be safe to make them aware of my presence.

The men were silent, then Ila looked over at me, her face expressing desperation.

Something scraped along the rock directly above me. I looked up at the barrel of a rifle. Behind it, a pair of angry eyes stared at me. I should have realized they knew I was there the entire time.

The man with the gun kept his eyes on me, while another man, this one taller and without a weapon, grabbed my arm and pulled me into the main tunnel. Ila screamed and pushed herself between me and the two men. They backed away, but not far. I kept my weapon low, not wanting to shoot for fear of hitting Ila.

She spoke in hurried Apache, her voice pleading. The

short man yelled louder, moving his gun in unpredictable directions. Several times he referred to the Thunder Spirit. They must have thought she had dishonored one of their spirits.

I moved to step around her, but she held me back with one arm. Speaking again in her native tongue, she gestured at the short man, and I heard a name: Kuruk. It was a name that meant "bear," and the name of her brother.

Kuruk didn't answer Ila's pleas. Instead, he slowly raised the gun, pointing it at her.

I leaned to the side and started to raise my rifle, but Ila turned around quickly and pushed me hard with both hands. I stumbled across the tunnel toward the far wall, my feet sliding toward the hole in the floor. I swung my arms, trying to regain my balance.

My rifle slipped out of my hand and clattered away.

One foot slid from hard rock over to the empty black opening in the floor. My other leg shook as I desperately tried to keep from going over.

A loud blast sounded, echoing off the walls of the cave. A strong force propelled me forward again.

I screamed for Ila and twisted my body to face her, but gravity pulled me into the shaft. Darkness surrounded me. I continued to scream her name as I fell.

CHAPTER ONE

Like prairie dogs popping from their burrows, men in zippered jumpsuits went in and out of the Hearst Stone Mine entrance. Dust swirled around their feet as they headed for tunnels A and B, searching for a modicum of gold ore.

Standing near the entrance, Elery Hearst stared at the hillside opening where test tunnel C branched off from the other tunnels. No one had come out of there yet. She pressed the talk button on her walkie-talkie to interrupt the static—the signal for the supervisor to check in. A few seconds later, the static buzzed out, then immediately returned—Ron's way of telling her to be patient. What was he still doing in there? He'd been in the mine for hours with no report.

She walked through the parking lot and kicked the rear tire on her old Jeep, letting out a frustrated growl. There had to be something in tunnel C, and hopefully it was gold. If Ron and the other workers found nothing, she'd have to shut down Hearst Stone Mine for good.

Leaning on the bumper, she turned away from the entrance and gazed out at the mountains in the distance, a shadowed backdrop for the desert. She'd spent her whole life with these mountains, never once thinking of them as anything other than big hunks of rock. But today, as her crew struggled to find the ore that would keep the mine open, the mountains seemed to challenge her, as if expecting her to fail. Maybe the Spaniards had it right when they named the mountains Superstition.

She jumped at a tap on her shoulder. Pushing off the Jeep, she turned around, hoping to find Ron. Instead she looked up into her brother's chocolate-brown eyes. She smiled to hide her disappointment. "Garrick, aren't you supposed to be at school? It's almost midterms."

He shrugged and gave her a crooked grin. "I'll manage."

Of course, he would. College for Garrick was no different than high school. He had a habit of skipping class, yet somehow he managed to ace the tests and charm his teachers into letting him make up the written work. No doubt he was going for the record of lowest attendance while still graduating. At least, she hoped he'd graduate. "Why are you here?"

He opened his mouth to speak, but nothing came out. Pressing his lips together, he gave her a desperate look, as if she could wrestle the words out for him. He ran a hand through his jet-black hair, inherited, along with his dark eyes, from their dad's Native American ancestors. She would have gladly traded with him. Instead of exotic beauty, she got tawny brown curls and eyes that couldn't decide if they were blue or green, both from her mother's Polish side.

She watched him struggle in curious silence. A hint of sadness, or was it guilt, crept into his eyes for a second. But then it fled, replaced by a familiar glint. Obsession. She'd seen that look before. It meant trouble.

Garrick tapped his boot in the dirt. "There's this girl. I met her in class."

This was about a girl? Since when did he chase after girls? In his own words, he found most of them to be too pushy—Elery included. She kept her mouth shut, waiting for him to continue.

"This girl is a descendant." He opened his arms wide, as the words finally poured out. "An actual descendant,

El. She's related to Julia Thomas Schaffer. The woman who was with Waltz when he died."

There it was. The connection to Jacob Waltz and the Lost Dutchman Mine. For Garrick, it was always about hidden gold. If she tried, she could almost see a hint of yellow hiding deep in his eyes. So why didn't he seem to care about their working gold mine? "I'm dealing with real world problems here. I don't have time to waste on Dad's old bedtime stories."

He held up a hand as if putting her on mute. "Her name is Angela Harmon. Of course, she's related through marriage, not by blood. She's the great-great-great-granddaughter of Joseph Schaffer, Julia's brother-in-law."

Elery rolled her eyes. "Why are you telling me this?"

"Just listen, please."

"Garrick, you've been down this rabbit hole before. How many times? Let it go."

"Angela has a real lead. I'm close to finding it this time."

Like he was the last time. And the time before that. The search never ended. But Elery didn't have the patience for this. Not when she was needed at the mine. Her thoughts returning to tunnel C, she leaned around Garrick to glance at the arched entrance. Still no sign of Ron.

Turning back to Garrick, she opened her mouth to speak, but he cut her off.

"Please, try to understand. I'm doing this for Dad."

She rubbed a hand over her tightening chest. Her father's medical bills were piling up, and she didn't have the money to pay them. Neither of them did. "I know you want to help Dad, but searching for lost treasure isn't the answer."

"This is different."

"How do you know Angela's not lying? People are always trying to make money off the Dutchman legend."

"This information is real." His voice hitched. "I can find it this time. And when I do, I'll pay off all of Dad's bills."

She pursed her lips. "If it's real, why would Angela want to search for it with you instead of someone in her family?"

"Her family is in Texas. She needs my help, which means I need yours." He twisted his body to tap a hand on the vehicle behind her. "Can I borrow your Jeep so we can go farther into the desert?"

Her back stiffened, and anger bubbled up inside her. "That's what you want? You came to ask if I'd give you my vehicle to support your fantasy?"

He grimaced. "I ..."

Over Garrick's shoulder, she caught a glimpse of Chad Milner, one of her newest miners, coming out of the entrance. Her heart raced. He'd been in tunnel C.

Leaving a stammering Garrick behind, she charged toward Chad. "Where's Ron?"

"He said he'd be out in a minute." Chad grinned, grabbed her arm and gave it a playful squeeze. "Don't be so nervous."

She pulled away, glaring at him. Couldn't Chad take a hint? She'd been brushing him off for the last month. "Professional behavior, please."

He shrugged, still grinning at her.

Her disinterest certainly wasn't about his looks. His unruly golden brown hair and matching amber eyes gave him the carefree look of a surfer, but she didn't date employees. And even if he weren't an employee, he had two strikes against him. First, everything amused him. Life was a big joke, and he refused to take anything seriously. Second, he had the same gleam in his eyes that spoke of a sickness she knew all too well—gold fever.

Chad moved closer, dusted off one of his dirty hands and reached toward her face. Whatever he planned to do would likely be inappropriate. She took a giant step to the side. As she turned, she caught a glimpse of Garrick getting into his car. Hopefully, he wasn't leaving angry, but she couldn't support a hunt for phantom riches.

"Hey, Romeo." Ron Gremming's voice boomed from behind Chad.

She shifted to face Ron, her heart pounding in her chest. Finally, she'd get some answers.

Ron trudged over, his dark, slightly-too-long hair swaying as he walked. Streaks of black dirt striped his tanned face. He stopped next to Chad, standing a few inches taller. His eyes narrowed. He gestured at Chad with his thumb, pointing over his shoulder. "Your drool break is over. Get back to work."

A flush crept up Elery's neck. Winking at her, Chad took off for the mine entrance. She cleared her throat and pushed aside a curl that had escaped her ponytail. She waited until Chad was out of earshot to speak. "How are things in tunnel C?"

Ron thrust his bottom lip out, then looked down at his feet. "Barren mostly."

Her shoulders dropped. They had started digging in the tunnel two days ago, hoping to intersect the original gold vein farther into the mountain. "No sign of ore or evidence of alteration by hot fluids?"

"None."

Her hands trembled as disappointment drowned her. If the mine failed, she failed too. Only a year after her father had retired and given her the reins.

Ron shuffled his feet, causing red dust to circle around their boots. "I'm sorry."

Swallowing hard, she lifted her chin. This wasn't Ron's fault. "Keep pushing through. Maybe we'll find something."

He kicked her boot with his and gave a wry smile. "If you'd only pray to the Thunder Spirit, then maybe ..."

"Not this time." Although she had taken a chance and prayed, it looked like God's answer was no. She forced a weak smile. No way would she let the other miners know how bad this was for the mine. This was a burden she and Ron would bear alone.

She started to turn away from Ron, then froze. The ground under her feet shook, throwing her off balance. She tightened her leg muscles to keep from falling. A piercing whine shrieked out of the loudspeakers—the alarm.

Her gaze shot up to meet Ron's. His wide eyes mirrored the panic rising in her chest.

A cave-in.

She sprinted toward the entrance with Ron following close behind. Men in jumpsuits flooded from the opening, a cloud of dust pushing out with them. Several miners ran past her, gasping for breath. One held his arm tight against his side. Another wiped at a bleeding gash on his cheek. Her assistant foreman dashed out, seemingly unhurt, but covered in dirt from head to toe.

She grabbed Art Lange around the shoulders. "What happened?"

Art caught his breath before answering. "Part of tunnel C collapsed."

A wave of dread washed over her. Collapsed? They had equipment to guard against this. "Was the ceiling stabilizer in place?"

Art wiped dust from his weathered face. "Yes, but it tipped over with the cave-in."

She tried to swallow past the lump forming in her throat. "Is anyone still in there?"

"Don't know." Art blinked and rubbed at his bloodshot eyes. "I was running for my life."

She looked back at Ron. "Get a head count."

Miners continued to pour from the tunnels. Those from tunnels A and B looked around in confusion at first, then shock. The ones from tunnel C came out open-mouthed, smudged and smeared in black, many with wounds from falling rocks.

The mine had a strict rule of no more than twenty miners in a particular tunnel at one time. A head count wouldn't take long. Maybe everyone had already made it out. Elery gaped at the scene as Ron made the rounds. What happened? The machine was an older model and in need of replacement, but her mechanic checked it each night. And as soon as tunnel C had become profitable, she would have replaced it. The tight knot in her throat grew. Now, it was too late.

A long moment later, Ron approached her, his face a mask of distress. "The only miner unaccounted for is Chad."

All of the air rushed out of her lungs. She doubled over, putting her hands on her knees. This couldn't be happening. She sucked in shallow breaths. Chad had just been out here, talking to her.

The alarm continued to whine, reminding her of her responsibility. She didn't have time to fall apart. With a sharp intake of breath, she stood upright and steeled herself for what came next. Ron had moved closer to the entrance to help those with minor injuries. She swiveled to face Art. "Check the seismometer. See if the mine has settled."

Nodding his head, Art turned to go, then turned back. "And if it has?"

Elery fought against the moisture burning her eyes. "Start digging. We have to find Chad."

For a second, she stood in place, overwhelmed by the chaos. The alarm would have automatically alerted emergency personnel so the one fire truck and ambulance in Quartz Creek should already be on their way. They would tend to the wounded. She had to find a way to get to Chad. Heavy equipment would make it easier, but she'd have to borrow the machines from nearby mines. She dashed to her office trailer to make the calls.

Half an hour later, she joined her crew as they dug through the enormous pile of basalt blocking the way to Chad. In the center of the tunnel, a grinding machine worked to chew through the bigger chunks of rock, generating a grainy silt that covered everything. Sweat and black grime formed a cocoon-like paste over her exposed face and arms. She hadn't wanted to waste time changing into a canvas jumpsuit, so her work jeans and T-shirt were smeared with dark streaks.

A ceiling stabilizer, borrowed from a copper mine, kept its massive metal plate secured against the roof of the tunnel. This one was the same model as the one now buried in the tunnel, only much newer. It crept along behind their slow progress.

Hour after hour passed, every second a grain of sand dropping through the hourglass of Chad's life—if he was alive. Her crew rotated through as some men took breaks to eat or rest. She refused to leave, not wanting to give up even a moment that she could be digging.

Scooping up another shovelful of crushed rock, she tossed it in a rolling cart behind her. Had Chad been crushed by the initial collapse? Or was he buried alive and waiting for rescue? Twelve hours later, they still didn't know.

She returned for another scoop, then paused with the shovel in the air. The motor on the digging machine revved out of control. A loud clunking noise sounded through the tunnel. The drill bit had hit something.

Elery sliced her hand across her throat to tell Ron to cut the engine. She took her shovel and poked at the obstruction.

A layer of dark basalt fell away, revealing shiny

metal—the failed ceiling stabilizer. The machine had collapsed halfway onto itself, and then fallen sideways, drilling the flat support plate into the floor of the tunnel.

Despite the heat of the enclosed space, goose bumps rose on her arms. They had to be close to Chad. Now that the machine noise had stopped, she listened for a brief second. No voice calling for help. Was he unconscious? Or dead? The thought spiked her blood pressure.

"Hand digging with shovels only. Be careful, guys." She speared a chunk of rock with her shovel, scraped it away and tossed it backward into a cart. Repeating the same motion over and over, she and the other men scraped away the confining material.

Little by little, they exposed the back wheels of the machine, hanging in the air. A large mound of rock had fallen underneath. Elery speared another shovel of dirt. Twisted to throw it in the cart. Turned back.

She thrust the shovel in once again, then stopped. Something brown stuck out from the pile. The toe of a work boot.

Her stomach lurched. She fought down the nausea, sucking in short breaths full of dust. "He's here!"

Dropping to her knees, she frantically brushed away loose rock with her gloved hands. Several of the men used their shovels to move the rock surrounding Chad. Once exposed, his legs lay perfectly still. *Come on, Chad. Please, be alive.*

They continued chipping away at the mass of confining debris. Up to his knees, then his thighs. At his waist, the rock fell away in one slump, revealing a cavity. The collapsing roof slab had hit the machine, which acted as a break. The rest of his body lay in this small space, his eyes closed, his hands fisted over his chest. His hard hat, still snug on his head, had a hairline crack down the front.

"Chad." Elery scooted into the narrow space beside

him. Leaning down, she pressed the tips of her fingers into his neck. He had a pulse. She let out a relieved breath and turned to Ron. "Get Dr. Sallow and a stretcher."

Before she could turn back, Chad's hand clamped down hard on her arm. "Boss." His voice came out in a hoarse whisper.

She pulled the glove off her other hand and placed her hand on his. "I'm here. We'll get you out."

"I'm ... already ... out."

He didn't know where he was. She squeezed his hand. "You're still in the mine, but the doc is coming. Don't give up."

Another whisper came from his lips, too soft to hear clearly, but it sounded like "gone."

"No, you're not gone. Hang in there."

His eyes flew open, and his gaze shot everywhere at once, as if he just realized he was in the mine. He settled on her, focusing intently on her face. "You have to find it."

"Find what?"

He licked his bottom lip, moistening a layer of dirt. "The mine."

"You're in the mine. But we're getting you out. I promise."

"No ..." His hands traveled up her arm, pulling her closer. "It's in the shell."

The shell? He was fading, delusional even. She cupped his face in her hands. "Snap out of it. You're going to be okay." The lie burned her lips. One look at the rest of him and anyone could see he wouldn't be okay. The rocks had smashed his body from the pelvis down. He'd never walk again. But he had a chance to live.

A shower of marble-sized debris rained down. She hovered over Chad, using her arms and hard-hat-covered head to protect him. When the rockslide subsided, she leaned back and looked down. His hands had flopped to the ground. His eyes were closed. She picked up one of his arms. It hung limp. "Chad!" She patted him lightly on the cheeks. "Wake up!"

Dr. Chris Sallow pushed past her. She scooted out and moved to the opposite wall to make room for him, accidentally kicking Chad's legs in the process. His eyes never opened. The doctor placed his fingers on Chad's neck as he waved at two men carrying a stretcher. After a few seconds, Dr. Sallow glanced around, found her and gave a slight shake of his head. "I'm sorry, Elery. He's gone."

Her mind went numb for a second before kicking into overdrive. *No, this can't be happening.* Chad had spoken to her seconds ago. He couldn't die here. Not like this. He was so young. She clutched her arms to her chest.

The men lifted Chad's body onto the stretcher. His head rolled back, and his arm slid off the canvas material. Dr. Sallow placed Chad's arm back beside his body.

She coughed as she tried to swallow past her nausea. Tears rimmed her eyes. The men stared at her, waiting for direction.

"Go home, everyone. We got our man out." *Only the man was dead.*

She should probably pray or give some words of wisdom, but everything inside her had shut down. Her core had solidified into granite.

The men followed her orders and filed out with their shovels. Everyone left, except for Ron.

Elery unsnapped her hard hat and threw it to the ground, then she let her back slide down the wall, sinking to the floor of the tunnel. She pressed her fists against her temples.

Ron crouched down in a squat in front of her. "Death is a reality in mining. Chad knew the risks." He dropped one knee to the ground and touched her leg. "At the end there, what did he say to you?"

A lone tear escaped to wind its way down her cheek. She smeared it into her dirty skin. "He wasn't making any sense."

What did it matter anyway? Chad was dead. Killed by a machine she should have replaced. Her chin quivered, and more tears raced from her eyes. She couldn't apologize. She couldn't take it back. The weight of his death would rest on her shoulders forever.

CHAPTER TWO

"Jesus asks us for one simple thing." Pastor Miguel Arroyo held up one finger for dramatic effect.

Every church member, even her dad, had their eyes riveted on the man. Elery looked down at her feet. Normally, she tried to pay attention on Sunday mornings, but there wasn't anything normal in her life anymore.

"Belief," Pastor Arroyo continued. "That's all Jesus wants. Give Him your belief, and He'll take care of the rest. But that's harder to do than it is to say."

Several members of the congregation nodded. Elery looked up at the tall cross fastened to the wall. Had Chad believed? She hadn't known him well enough to say.

The door to the sanctuary swung open, letting in a warm breeze. She looked up as Garrick slid into the seat next to her. What was he doing here? He usually attended church on campus, and she hadn't seen him since Friday, the day of the accident. She'd assumed he had gone back to Phoenix after their heated conversation, but maybe he stayed somewhere in Quartz Creek for the weekend?

Ignoring her questioning glance, Garrick focused on the pulpit where Pastor Arroyo had turned the floor over to Michael Hinckle, who bowed in front of the crowd. Elery, along with all the other regular members, had heard Michael's story several times before. Once a year, he described how the doctors diagnosed him with permanent paralysis of the legs and how God had healed him after the pastor and elders had prayed over him. Was that what she should have done for Chad that night?

Could she have saved him if she would have prayed for him?

At the end of his short speech, Michael ran a victory lap around the church, giving high-fives as he went. She clapped politely, as did the rest of the congregation.

"You have not ...," Pastor Arroyo's voice echoed through the sanctuary as he paused for emphasis, "because you ask not." He walked down the three steps to the ground and gave Michael a high-five before Michael took his seat. "Jesus said nothing is impossible for he who believes." The pastor pointed to the crowd, but he might as well have been pointing straight at her. "Do you believe with an unshakable faith?"

"Unshakable" would not be the word to describe her faith recently. More like the broken and crumbled tailings left behind at an abandoned mine.

"Some of you in here have problems because you're not trusting God. He wants to take away what ails you. He can cure you, even of disease. The Bible says He wants to bless us more abundantly than we can imagine. Do you believe He will do that?"

At the word "disease," Elery glanced at her father. He sat straight-backed, staring at the pulpit. The thin, cotton shirt he wore hid the gauze from the bandages covering his back. On Friday, he'd been in Phoenix having the doctor remove more spots of malignant melanoma. How was he feeling? She hadn't even asked him.

On the other side of her, Garrick shifted in his seat, but didn't glance her way. A shock of hair hid his eyes.

"Whoever has ailments, let him be healed." Pastor Arroyo gestured wide with his arms. "Come and the elders and I will pray for you. You can experience healing, if you ask."

Again, she looked at her father. Had he asked God for healing? He certainly wouldn't ask the pastor or the elders. It was a pride thing for him.

The band played a slow song for the altar call. They all stood and sang, but no one made their way to the front. Pastor Arroyo and the elders formed a circle, praying among themselves.

After the song, the pastor dismissed the congregation, and they filed out like ants from an anthill. She stepped out into the sunny February day. The best time of year in Arizona was the winter when the temperature was warm, instead of blistering hot. Garrick ran down the steps past her, then stopped in the parking lot and reached for her arm. "Can we talk?"

She hid her surprise at the request. After her refusal the other day, she'd expected him to hold a grudge for a while. "Sure. Let's walk." She pressed the car keys into her father's hand. "I'll meet you at home."

After their father left, she led Garrick in a stroll down Main Street. They passed establishments with names like Gold Rush Saloon and Wild Bill's Grocery on placards of fake wood to mimic an old Western town. The underlying buildings were from the late 1800s, but tourists didn't want original Western towns. They preferred fake movie versions.

Garrick folded his hands in front. "I wanted to talk to you about Angela again. I thought now would be a better time."

In other words, he hadn't liked her answer from before or perhaps he thought he hadn't had enough time to convince her because she'd brushed him off to talk to Chad and Ron. Where had he gone after the cave-in anyway?

"I know you don't trust my judgment when it comes to the Lost Mine."

He had that part right. Garrick had driven out into the desert to chase every rumor about the Dutchman posted on the Internet, he'd searched every historical archive in five surrounding towns, and scoured countless auctions for anything Jacob Waltz might have possessed.

"I don't blame you. At times, I haven't exercised the most caution in my zeal to find the mine."

She kept walking, hoping he'd get to the point.

"So, I find myself in the position of the boy who cried wolf. Why would you believe I've actually found something?"

Coming to the end of Main Street, she turned left on Oak, making a loop back to her childhood home she still shared with her dad. "I'm with you so far."

Garrick gave a short laugh. "Angela is the real deal."

The earnest tone in his voice broke her heart. She held her tongue rather than continue a futile argument.

"I need you to believe in her like I do."

There was that word again—believe. It only mattered to him what she believed because he wanted her to change her belief. She glanced over at him. His head hung low, his back hunched over as he focused on the ground. "Okay, what do you think this girl has found?"

He looked up, and a tentative smile crossed his face, the look of a school-kid who couldn't wait to share what he'd learned. "When Jacob Waltz died, most of his stuff was kept by Julia, the owner of the boarding house."

It was a name Elery had heard over and over again. Julia Thomas had cared for Jacob Waltz, the Dutchman, when he was dying in 1891. Waltz had told Julia about his gold mine and supposedly how to find it.

Garrick shifted on his feet. "I found documents in the university archives about a package sent to Joseph Schaffer in Kansas, items owned by his brother, Albert."

"What does that mean?"

He spoke faster, diving into the rabbit hole with fervor. "Come on, think about it. When Waltz died, Julia kept his belongings. Then when she died, her husband, Albert, would have kept them. After Albert's death, a large package was sent to his brother, Joseph. It could have been Waltz's final possessions."

Not very likely, but the small possibility was all Garrick would need to start the chase again. She slowly shook her head. Garrick's obsession had started when they were kids. At bedtime, their father used to tell stories of the Lost Dutchman Gold Mine, his way of distracting them from their mother's absence at night. Many times they had tried to tease out fact from fiction, but the legends folded in upon themselves like some sort of origami art.

Garrick tugged on the hem of his T-shirt. "That parcel went to Angela's family. She has an original map. It could lead us to the mine."

He slowed and took an awkward sidestep toward Elery, his pronounced limp pricking her conscience like a sharp needle. She pushed the shame deep inside. No way would she fall down her own rabbit hole into that dark abyss of guilt. She took a deep breath. "And if it doesn't?"

His arms gestured wildly. "It will ... because she has everything ... all the stuff Waltz had when he died." Garrick tilted his head. "Well, almost everything. Some stuff went to Waltz's own sister."

She cleared her throat to stop his rambling. "You don't understand, Garrick. *Our* family's mine is in trouble. That's a little more important than an imaginary one."

He put a finger to his chin as if considering her objection.

"Dad thinks I might have to sell it." Voicing the words made them more real. She pushed her mass of curls behind her shoulders. "It was in trouble before the accident. I don't know what to do or even if anyone would buy it now."

Their house was just ahead. A two-story Victorian

painted pale green with old brown shaker shingles. It was the house they both grew up in. Would they have to sell it, too? She stepped into the street to walk across.

Garrick hung back a step. "Come meet Angela this afternoon. She'll convince you."

Elery turned and let out a soft grunt. Her brother's persistence was both admirable and frustrating. In that way, at least, they were alike.

"Really, El. This could save the mine." He tapped his chest. "Or you could start a new one with me as your partner."

She stared at him from the middle of the empty street. Her younger brother. His body had filled out in his first year of college. Now, he stood before her with the broad-shouldered form of a man, but in his eyes shone the innocent light of a dreamer. He'd always believed he'd find the mine.

Turning back toward home, she answered him over her shoulder. "Fine." Eventually, she'd have to try to reason with him again, to try to take his dreams away. But for now, it wouldn't hurt to meet the girl.

***

"So, you're Garrick's sister." Angela gave her a wide smile as she gestured for Elery to enter the tiny living room.

Elery took a seat in the armchair across from the couch where Garrick was sitting. Angela's apartment wasn't a studio, but it came close in square footage. The living room was crowded with a desk and several bookshelves resting against the plain white walls. Only half of the shelves were filled with books, the rest of the shelf area held figurines, many of them carved out of wood. The one in the center stood out—a pale bleached carving of a running lizard. Had the artist tried to create an albino lizard or had the wood weathered to that color?

Angela lowered her lanky form to the couch next to Garrick and eyed Elery. "You're not what I expected."

Elery raised her eyebrows. She could say the same. Angela had an expressive face framed by stylish blond layers. It gave her an unexpected openness, as if she would listen intently to all your life's secrets. No shifty-eyed con woman here.

"For someone who works in a mine ..." Angela waved a graceful hand at Elery. "You're lovely. Long hair, earrings, pretty blue eyes. Not at all butch."

Elery pursed her lips. Angela was definitely trying too hard to get on her good side. "I leave my butch at the mine. Thanks for noticing."

With an awkward laugh, Angela scooted to the edge of the couch. "Well, let's get to the reason you're here." Reaching to the coffee table in front of her, she moved a book to the side. A large map clung to the glass underneath. Angela peeled it off and handed it to Elery, laying it on her open palms. "Hold this for a moment."

Elery examined it carefully. The markings resembled those she'd seen on maps Julia Thomas Schaffer had made from Jacob Waltz's death bed directions. After Waltz took his last breath, Julia had found a box of gold ore under the bed, proof that the mine was real. But she searched in the mountains for years without success. Finally, to recoup her losses, she sold some of these generic maps to gold hunters. This wasn't anything new.

"I want you to compare this map Julia sold with the map I found in my grandfather's things." Leaning down, Angela pulled a cardboard box from beneath the coffee table. She lifted the lid off the box, her palm hovering over it, almost reverently. "My grandfather died last year, and this box was in his attic, covered in dust. As far as I know, no one else has looked at these documents for two generations."

Elery glanced at Garrick. His wide eyes were fixed on Angela as she reached into the box.

"Check this out." Angela extracted a flimsy piece of yellowed paper and placed it on top of the map Elery already held. "I've made a copy of this, but I want you to see the original."

The second map was almost see-through. Elery positioned the two so the symbols overlapped. "This looks like the one you just gave me and every other Lost Dutchman treasure map."

Angela's eyes lit up. "Because it's the source of all the others." She stood and flipped the map over. On the back, a date was written. October 10, 1891. "This is Julia Thomas Schaffer's handwriting." Angela flipped the top map back over and realigned them. "Now, search for the difference."

Elery hunched over, peering at the document. Several landforms were marked including a creek with no name and a trail labeled "Military Trail." Nothing unusual there. She traced the line of the creek to the far edge of the map. A small dot had "oro" written next to it, the Spanish word for gold. Also typical of a treasure map from the late 1800s. The dot supposedly marked the location of the mine, but without other clues for reference it could be anywhere.

Something near the dot caught her eye. Was it a smudge? She bent her head closer to the map. The faded image of a cross came into focus positioned directly next to the creek. She flipped the map up to check the one underneath. It wasn't on the maps Julia sold. "Are you talking about this cross?"

An exuberant smile spread across Angela's face. "Yes. I think it's a grave marker. Probably for Waltz's partner."

"See what I mean, El?" Garrick looked at Elery with a matching grin. "Julia left something off all the other maps. She kept a clue for herself. And now we have it."

Elery had to admit Angela had a unique map and an intriguing interpretation of it. Crosses appeared on many maps of the area, but they were usually thought to indicate an altar or possibly a location for a mine. And yet, it was possible this one could indicate a grave. The disappearance of Waltz's partner was well known. "You think Waltz buried his partner?"

"Yes." A shadow of uncertainty flashed across Angela's face. "Why wouldn't he?"

"Because legend says Waltz murdered his partner. Why bury a man you were callous enough to murder?"

Garrick shifted in his seat. He knew the legends even better than she did. For her part, Angela kept up her poker face. "A grave makes the most sense for the cross symbol. The only death associated with Waltz is his partner, Jacob Weiser."

Angela made a decent case for her opinion, but that didn't make it true. "What else came in that box?"

Angela swept a hand toward the corner of the room where a small bookcase with glass doors sat. Its shelves held the pictures and wooden objects Elery had noticed earlier. "All of the carvings and one picture of Jacob Waltz."

After laying both maps back on the coffee table, Elery walked over to the cabinet. The picture, presumably of the Dutchman, was faded and dull, showing a man with a mop of dark hair and a long beard. It was the standard picture of the man, thought to be taken in 1846 in New York shortly after he entered this country from Germany. The carvings were ornate, especially the one of the lizard she had noticed earlier. It was situated as a display piece on top. The feet looked like they could run away as she looked on. Had Waltz made these?

Garrick walked up behind her. "We have to follow this lead."

The note of urgency in his voice twisted her stomach in knots. She'd heard his desperation many times before, especially after she'd graduated with her geology degree. Garrick had begged her to make detailed geologic maps of his areas of interest. At the time, she thought hard data would convince him to give up the search. It only added fuel to the fire. He would never stop looking, even though the lost mine hadn't been found in over a hundred years and it probably never would be. She turned to face him, her arms crossed over her chest. "You don't know where this grave is, and even if you found something, how do you expect to start a mine out there? The Superstition Mountains are part of Tonto National Forest now. You can't make a claim on national land."

"You're right, but we have an answer for that. Only a few locations come close to matching the topography on the map. Two of them are near the border, but not on national land, which means we would be dealing with private owners. But if we find it inside the national forest boundary, we can make a case to have the boundary modified so we can purchase the land with the mine."

Elery twisted her lips. The idea of discovering a ton of gold on someone else's property, then trying to buy it before they realized the value, didn't sit right with her. But Garrick didn't need her permission to go after the treasure, and although her vehicle would be useful, he didn't really need that either. He was trying to convince her because he wanted her support. Unfortunately, she couldn't give it. Gold was more to him than just cold metal. It was seductive and dangerous. She wouldn't encourage him to indulge his obsession.

***

"You know we could do it," Angela said.

Garrick watched Angela pace the wood floor of the apartment with amused interest. Elery had just left, and he should be getting on the road back to his apartment in Phoenix, but he'd rather sit here and talk more about the mine. Finally, he'd found someone who cared as much about finding it as he did. So much that she'd rented an apartment close to where she thought the mine was, instead of one on campus in Phoenix. He loved her excitement, but had to temper it a little. Searching in the Superstition Mountains wasn't like a stroll on the beach. Oh, there was sand for sure, but it was in the form of jagged quartz grains that made climbing a mountain slippery. Also Angela needed to know about the razor-sharp cactus needles, the poisonous rattlesnakes, and the scorching temperatures.

She stopped and tapped a bare foot on the floor. "All we need to find the treasure is a pickax and a topographic map, right?"

Was she talking to herself or to him? With her, it was hard to tell. He answered her anyway. "That and provisions for a few days, maybe a week. I have a tent and sleeping bags, so really it's just food and stuff to help make fires."

"Do you have a gun?"

He cast her a sideways glance. She knew he couldn't keep a gun on campus in his apartment. "No. My dad has a few, but it's better if he doesn't know I'm going." He had enough to worry about. "So I'd have to ask Elery where to find one in the house, and I don't think that's such a good idea."

"Why not?"

"She's made it clear she doesn't support us going after the mine."

"So what? She can't stop you."

"True, but she probably won't help me." His jaw

clenched. Why couldn't Elery understand that he was doing this for their father? If he found the gold, not only could they pay off the medical bills, but they could send him to a better facility for treatment. Money was power, and sometimes that power could buy life. He rubbed the back of his neck. "If we involve Elery, she might tell someone else."

"Good point. She thinks the search for the Dutchman's gold is a lost cause, so she probably wouldn't mention it to anyone else, but it's better not to take the chance." With a grin, Angela grabbed both of his shoulders and shook him. Her hair flipped forward and whispered against his face. "We could really do this."

He matched her grin, but shook his head slightly. "Not right now. We've got midterms this next week."

"I know, but I don't want to wait until school's out for the summer." Her full lips lowered into a pout. "I'd rather not end up as an egg frying on the desert floor."

She was right. If they waited much longer the desert and the mountains would start heating up like a blast furnace, raising the danger of heat stroke and dehydration.

Walking in a slow circle around him, she rubbed at the tension between his shoulder blades. It was an intimate gesture, the first time she'd touched him, other than a pat on the arm. Maybe she wanted to move beyond the level of friends? Did he want that? Up to this point, they'd treated each other like colleagues working on the same project.

She leaned down and spoke into his ear. "We can always make excuses for why we shouldn't go, but now is the time."

He drummed his fingers on the couch cushion. Waiting until fall to test the accuracy of her map sounded unbearable, not to mention that even more bills would have piled up by then. And if they found the Dutchman's mine, he'd have no need to finish school anyway.

She dropped her hands and peered over his shoulder, tilting her head to the side to look at him. Her eyelashes fluttered and her face held a now-or-never expression.

He turned his head, leaning his forehead against hers. Elery's opinion didn't matter. Angela was right. They needed to go now.

CHAPTER THREE

The morning sunshine streamed through the office window as Elery sat at her desk, holding her pen suspended over the pressed paper of the sympathy card. She couldn't merely sign her name. It wouldn't be enough. But what could she say? *I'm sorry I killed your son, and I don't blame you if you hate me.*

This afternoon, she'd be at the Methodist church across town attending Chad's funeral. How could she face his mother? When she had called Linda Milner in Kansas right after the cave-in, Linda hadn't said much, except that she would drive down right away. But she didn't get here in time. She hadn't gotten the chance to say goodbye. She hadn't heard her son's last words.

At the funeral, Elery would meet her for the first time. By then, Linda should have heard how Elery's negligence had killed her son. No sympathy card, no words of apology, no expression of sorrow could bring him back.

The office door vibrated with a loud bang. It had to be Ron. Only he knocked like he wanted to break the door down. She slid the card under a notebook. "Come in."

"Hey, LB." She raised an eyebrow. LB stood for Lady Boss, a moniker some of the other miners had given her. Ron's use of it meant he was trying to make her smile, or more likely, trying to make up for being late. "What happened this time?" she asked.

He flopped into the tattered chair across from her

desk, his dark hair waving with the motion of his body. "You know how it is. I had trouble sleeping last night and overslept."

She frowned. How many times had he used the same excuse? At least half a dozen in the last year. Ron lived in Superior, a little town twenty minutes away, but that was no excuse for being late. Was this his way of telling her he had some sort of a problem? Maybe a drinking problem?

"I checked in with the men," he said. "Operations have resumed in tunnels A and B. Also, I've informed everyone that operations will stop this afternoon to allow each of them a chance to attend the funeral."

She nodded and looked down at the desk as nausea swirled in her stomach. How could she carry on like normal? A whirlpool of guilt and anger churned within her, the emotions bumping into each other, colliding and mixing until her soul felt like it had gone through a blender.

"Are you still thinking about Chad?"

Her stomach churned in answer. How could she not think about him?

"It's hard to watch a man take his last breath."

The certainty in his voice set her on edge. What did Ron know of death?

"Sometimes all we can do is honor their final wishes. Did Chad tell you anything important at the end? Something you could do for him?"

She focused on Ron again. "No. His words were off. He didn't even know he was in the mine. And he said something weird. Something about a shell."

"Sounds like hallucinations." Ron pressed his lips into a thin line and leaned forward in the chair. "I also came in to tell you something else. I've heard from the Mine Safety and Health Administration. They had questions for me as part of their investigation of the accident."

Why hadn't they contacted her as the owner? Was it because they were investigating her negligence? She pressed a hand to her forehead.

Ron scooted his chair closer and touched her arm. "You okay?"

Part of her wanted to suck it up and tell him everything was fine, but it wasn't. She looked up and met his eyes, expecting pity, but seeing only curiosity. "No, I'm not okay. I don't know how to handle this."

"No one does."

She tugged on her lower lip. Last night, she'd hardly slept. Every time she closed her eyes, the memory of Chad's pained, dirty face materialized. "Then, what do I do?"

Ron leaned back and crossed his arms over his chest. "If you want some advice, I can tell you how to get through it."

Even though Ron was only a few years older than she, he had more experience in mining. And she was ready to listen. She needed something, anything, to help her deal with the guilt. "How?"

"You have to compartmentalize. Lock the emotions in a box and throw away the key." His gaze turned hard, his dark eyes intense. "Otherwise, it will eat away at you, and you'll lose the best parts of yourself."

She shook her head. "I think I've already lost those."

Ron stood and slammed his palms onto her desk. She jumped involuntarily. "Not many women could run a mine like you, Elery. One of your best qualities is your ambition. Don't give that up."

He turned and left, letting the door slam shut behind him. He was right. She wanted to give up on all of it. To never see another mine, especially this one. But for now, she'd have to take his advice to get through the day. All her emotions needed to stay locked away.

***

Lucan Milner glanced up at the line of mourners stretching out the door, like a crowd waiting for a Broadway play. Except the only play in this church was a tragedy. He looked down at the person in front of him, nodding in agreement as another unknown face told him how horrible his brother's death was. They didn't know what else to say and really it didn't make a difference. The kind words, the sympathy, none of it would bring Chad back.

The scent of flowers and dust in the air overwhelmed his nose. He twisted to the side and sneezed. When he turned back, an attractive young woman with golden brown curls held a tissue out for him.

"Thank you." He took it and turned away again to blow his nose. When he turned back this time, the woman held out a bottle of antibacterial cleanser. She was completely prepared, some sort of funerary Girl Scout. He squeezed the clear liquid from the bottle. "Uh, thanks again. I must be allergic to something in here."

As he handed the bottle back to her, he gave her a curious glance. There weren't too many women here, mostly men from the mine. She kept her head down as if afraid to meet his gaze. Her black sequined dress was a little flashy, but not inappropriate, and ended just above the knee, revealing long, tanned legs. She tugged at the hem of the dress. Had he been staring?

This wasn't exactly the time to notice a woman, but all day his mind had been searching for any excuse not to think of the task before him—burying his brother. He stuck out his hand. "I'm Lucan Milner."

She finally looked up into his eyes. Her mouth dropped open, and she searched his face in astonishment.

He sighed. "You're not the first one to have that reaction today. Chad is my twin brother." Lucan winced. "I mean, he *was* my twin."

She finally took his outstretched hand. "I'm Elery Hearst, the owner of the mine. I didn't know Chad had a brother."

"Not many people did. We moved to town only a few months ago."

A quick nod. She opened her mouth, then clamped it shut again. Her lower lip quivered as she spoke. "I can't express how sorry I am for your loss."

"Thank you."

As he released her hand, she took a step back. Her gaze flew to the other mourners in line, then back to him. She gulped in a breath. "This shouldn't have happened. I try to prevent stuff like this. I do my best to protect the miners, but I should have replaced it. The equipment, the stabilizer, I mean." She bit her lip. "I never thought ... I mean, we've never lost a miner before ..."

Lucan's mouth tightened as the implications of her words sank in. What did it matter if this had never happened before? Now, it had. And what did she mean about the stabilizer? He stepped closer. "You said old equipment?"

She pressed her palm to her chest. "It was next in line to be replaced."

"Why hadn't you replaced it already?"

"I meant to. I just hadn't gotten to it yet."

"I understand." But he didn't understand at all. Her misty aqua eyes told him there was more to what happened. Had she chosen profits over safety? He waited for her to say more. When she didn't, he pointed to the rapidly filling pews. "You may sit anywhere."

After Elery, the line of mourners flew by in a haze,

requiring only half of his attention. The rest he spent turning her words over and over in his head. She said she cared about protecting the miners, but she also made it sound like Chad's accident could have been avoided. Which statement was the truth? Until the official report came out, he wouldn't know for sure.

Lucan shook hands with the last person in line, then walked to the front to check on his mother. She had lost a husband seven years ago and now a son. The grief she felt had to outweigh his own, but even so, losing Chad felt like losing a part of himself.

Bending down, Lucan placed a hand on her shoulder. "Are you ready to start, Mom?"

His mother's eyes focused on the coffin sitting on the platform before them. She reached up to Lucan's arm with hands that trembled. "Yes. Go tell them about your brother."

Lucan moved to the lectern, gripping the wooden sides with both hands. The crowd hushed to a whisper. "Thank you, everyone, for being here. It means a lot to me and my mother. This will be a short service, followed by a private burial." He sucked in a slow breath and blinked several times. "Chad and I were best friends. We talked every day, played basketball against each other and hiked on the weekends. We shared everything, even the same face."

That received a polite chuckle from a few people.

"And yet, we didn't share the same ambitions. Chad only wanted to be a miner. He moved here three months ago to realize that dream. I moved with him, mostly to keep him out of trouble." Lucan gave a sad smile. "But trouble usually found him no matter what I did. From bar fights to putting his truck in the ditch, he kept me busy. In his short twenty-six years, Chad lived more than most people do in a lifetime. He went after his dreams with passion. I'm grateful he died doing what he loved."

Lucan glanced over the crowd for a few seconds before his eyes locked onto Elery's. She seemed to recoil from his direct stare, but she didn't look away. What was he searching for? Guilt? Innocence? Or maybe just the truth?

Seconds later, he rubbed a hand over his face—the spell broken. "I hope that each and every one of you is blessed to have someone you love as unconditionally as I loved my brother."

He looked over to the coffin. Chad's hair was stiff, his pale skin made paler by the backdrop of white satin. The body lying there was merely a rough facsimile of his brother in life.

Shifting his gaze to focus on the audience again, a tear slipped out of the corner of his eye. He didn't bother to wipe it away. "A few people have asked to share their memories of Chad."

Lucan stepped back from the podium, motioning for two members of the audience to approach. One man recounted several practical jokes Chad played at the mine, including the time Chad had hollowed out the man's rock pick handle, causing it to split in half the next time he used it. Subdued laughter filtered through the church.

The second man told of weekends spent hiking in the mountains, hunting for clues to the Lost Dutchman Mine. He spoke of Chad's persistence, how driven he was to find the treasure.

After they finished, Lucan resumed his position at the podium. "Thank you, gentlemen." He faced the coffin again for a lingering moment. His next words would be the last he spoke to his brother. "Goodbye, Chad. Your life and your passion will not be forgotten."

He paused to give his mother a chance to decide whether she wanted to say something or not. At last, she shook her head, so he thanked them all for coming again, and concluded the service. With slow steps, he walked to the casket where he met his mother. They both stood and stared down at Chad for the last time. Putting his arm around her, he let her sob into his shoulder. His own tears ran down his face unchecked.

Several minutes later, he glanced behind to see the church almost empty. In one of the middle pews, Elery Hearst sat with her head down. She wiped at her eyes and got up to leave.

He whispered in his mother's ear. "I'll be right back." He wiped his own tears away as he hurried down the aisle. "Ms. Hearst, please wait."

Elery stopped and turned around, meeting his gaze with red-rimmed eyes. "Yes, Mr. Milner."

"I should have told you this before." Confusion and anger warred within him. The strain of the battle probably showed on his face, but he needed to do this. Elery had paid for Chad's funeral using insurance money given to Hearst Stone, and his mother had raised him to be grateful. With a stiff jaw, he said, "Thank you for your help."

She nodded, then walked down the aisle without looking back.

He watched her go, wondering if she paid for the funeral out of obligation or guilt. Either way, no amount of money could make up for losing Chad.

CHAPTER FOUR

Jayna Rowan wiped the sweat from her forehead as she approached the trailer that served as the main office for the Hearst Stone Mine. Although she was always excited to meet another female geologist, this would be a sensitive meeting for several reasons. First, she hoped Elery Hearst could give her some information. Jayna hadn't been able to track down a physical address for her new client, actually her first and only client. Hopefully, Elery had enough connections with miners in the area to help.

And second, news of the cave-in had reached Jayna only hours after coming to town. The mine had reopened two days ago, the same day as the funeral, but Elery was most certainly still reeling from the accident.

Reaching up to knock, Jayna almost knocked a woman in the nose when she opened the door. Jayna pulled her arm back. "Ms. Hearst?"

The woman wore jeans and a T-shirt with "My Pet Rock Is a Gold Nugget" written on the front. The woman's light brown hair, just a shade lighter than her own, was pulled back into a massive ponytail of bouncy curls. "I'm Elery. Can I help you?"

Jayna extended her hand. "Jayna Rowan with Rowan Geologic Consulting. You don't know me, but I wanted to come meet you."

Elery shook Jayna's hand, then held the door open. "Please, come in."

The rush of air conditioning cooled Jayna's skin as

she stepped inside. She tugged her T-shirt away from her sweaty body and wiped at the moisture collected at the base of her neck below her messy bun. Through a small window, the high peaks of the Superstition Mountains drew her gaze and a fierce longing filled her chest. It had been too long since she'd seen mountains. In a few hours, she would be out there hiking alone, free to explore at will, as long as she mapped for her client at the same time.

Elery walked behind the desk and sat, folding her hands on top. "What can I do for you?"

Tearing her attention from the mountains, Jayna sat in a well-used cushioned chair. The office held filing cabinets and a worn wooden desk. Nothing personal except a few mineral specimens—beryl, tourmaline and copper—sitting on top of the cabinets. No gold, but that was probably for security reasons.

Jayna met Elery's gaze. "When I travel, I make it a point to reach out to other female geologists. We tend to see life the same way and have the same struggles born from working in a male-dominated profession." She gave a friendly smile. "And you're the only female mine owner in this area. I applaud you on your accomplishment."

Elery frowned and glanced away. Was she thinking about the accident? "Are you a mine owner, Ms. Rowan?"

"Please, call me Jayna. No, I'm not."

"It's a heavy responsibility. Not only because of safety, but also because my miners depend on this income to support their families."

"Believe it or not, I understand."

"I don't see how you could."

The hurt in Elery's eyes radiated out and wrapped around Jayna's heart. The woman was torturing herself over what happened. Jayna lowered her voice. "I've been in charge of people who have died before." She closed her eyes briefly and offered up a silent prayer for strength. She hadn't expected this topic to come up so soon in the conversation, and the memories of her time in Hawaii still pierced her soul. "I do know what you're going through. This isn't your fault."

Elery bristled. "It *is* my fault if it's my responsibility to keep the miners safe." She gestured toward the mine entrance, visible through the window on the other side of the trailer. "I'm responsible for all of them."

Jayna nodded, the corners of her mouth turning down. So much for treading lightly around the accident. "Yes, you're responsible, but not everything that happens is your fault."

For a few minutes, the two women stared at each other. Elery didn't seem uncomfortable with the scrutiny, but the hard glint in her eyes said the subject of the mine accident was closed. "So, why did you come to Quartz Creek, Jayna?"

"Would you believe I was trying to escape the freezing February in Wisconsin?"

Elery gave a small smile. "You certainly accomplished that."

"My geologic specialty is volcanic rocks. A local client hired me to map the volcanics in a portion of the Superstition Mountains."

Elery tilted her head. "Who around here would have the funds to hire an out-of-town geologic consultant?"

Jayna pressed her lips together. This was the hard part. When the client had called, Jayna jumped at the chance to start her new consulting business with a fun week of mapping in sunny Arizona. She had arrived on site without doing any research on him. Now, she needed more information, but her client wanted to remain anonymous. Even so, she didn't like going into situations like this blind. "I'm sure you understand my client would like to remain as anonymous as possible for his own protection. I've been told how crazy 'Dutch

Hunters' can get about a geologic map." She swallowed hard. "But between you and me, I'd like any information you might have on this guy. If I tell you his name, will it stay confidential?"

"Of course."

"It's John Peralta."

Elery captured a stray curl near her face, twirling it around one finger. "Peralta? Like the Mexican Peraltas?"

"The what?"

"It's a legend that everyone around here assumes is true. The Peraltas were a Mexican family who supposedly found gold in the Superstition Mountains. They mined it, but before they could take it back to Mexico, the Apaches attacked, killing almost all of them."

Jayna wrinkled her brow. "This guy had dark hair and eyes, but I wouldn't say he looked Mexican."

Elery shrugged. "As far as I know, there aren't any Peraltas left in this area."

What did that mean? Had the man given her a fake name? Maybe he was serious about staying anonymous. "I don't like being kept in the dark, but I suppose I don't need to know who he is to map for him."

"As long as you're careful. Meet him in public places, get money up front, that kind of thing. I'm guessing this guy is looking for gold, maybe the Lost Dutchman Mine, but you're not the first to map those mountains. Most of the time, nobody finds anything."

Jayna winked at her. "Don't worry about me. I'm not looking for anything. I map the rocks, and my client can do whatever he chooses with the data." Jayna stood and offered her card. "It was very nice to meet you. Thanks for the information and if I can ever help you, please call."

Elery took the card without standing. "Nice meeting you, too. Stay safe out there."

"Will do." Jayna swept open the door and strode straight into the wall of heat outside.

Just great. Her first assignment for her new business and she didn't even know the real name of her client. She sucked in a long breath of dry desert air. It didn't matter. In a week, she would complete the geologic map, collect her fee and be done with Peralta, or whoever he was.

***

"Couldn't we have parked closer to the site? The less time walking in this blast furnace, the better." Angela's high voice rose another octave, dragging a razor blade over Garrick's already frayed nerves.

He continued through the narrow valley, refusing to answer her question yet again. She had asked some version of it a dozen times already. If not for Angela's complaining, there would be no sound, and that would suit him fine about now. This exciting adventure had turned into adventures in babysitting. They hadn't made much progress and were nearing the end of their third day of hiking.

Of the few areas they had identified as possible matches to the map, they'd eliminated only one so far. And his self-imposed deadline was looming. It was already Wednesday. If he didn't check in with Elery by tomorrow morning, she'd get his e-mail and have reason to worry. Even so, it would serve her right. This trip would have gone much faster with her Jeep to transport them to these remote areas. Then again, maybe he'd have good news tomorrow when he hiked out of the mountains and into cell phone range to call her. This site might be the one.

"Ouch!"

He glanced back. Angela held one of her fingers in her mouth. "What did you do?"

She extracted her finger and jabbed it over her shoulder. "That thing looked like a fuzzy tree."

Behind her, a cholla plant sat with its brown honeycomb underside and light green branches covered in barbs. The plants were everywhere. He was surprised it had taken her this long to touch one. "It's a cactus. Look closer before you touch."

Angela rolled her eyes. "Yeah, I got that. Thanks. Can you just help me out here?"

He grabbed her finger. A tiny brown dot on the side marked the site of the embedded barb. Placing his thumb and forefinger on either side, he squeezed her finger to force the barb out. She squealed in pain, but didn't fight him. Once he'd removed it, she snatched her hand away and put her finger back in her mouth. He shook his head and started up the valley again.

"I can't believe how hot it is." Angela folded the map in half and fanned herself with it.

"Give me that before you lose it." He grabbed the map, swinging it away from her.

"The only way for me to lose it would be if it floated away on the breeze." She wiped sweat off her brow. "Do you feel any air movement out here?"

He bit his lip to keep from matching her sarcasm. They'd talked about this. The valleys were always hot. Although today did seem especially brutal for February. On top of the already scorching temperature, a mist hung in the air, draping them like a heated blanket. It could mean an approaching storm front. "It will be cooler when we reach a peak."

"I don't know how you can wear pants out here."

Glancing over at her, he almost burst into laughter. Rather than push through the scrub brush and thorny cactus, she had to high-step over them, precisely because her shorts allowed the low plants to scrape her legs. She couldn't say he didn't warn her. "This is bearable at least.

It'll be much hotter out here in a couple of months when summer hits."

She stopped her crane-like gait to gape at him. "You mean, you've come out here when it's hotter?"

"Once. And I wouldn't do it again."

A glint of admiration shone in her eyes, helping him to remember to be patient with her. After all, she'd admitted that she'd never hiked more than a mile before. Clearly, she'd underestimated how difficult this trip would be, and he'd overestimated her abilities. No matter, once they found some evidence of the mine, Angela's attitude would change completely. "We're getting close to the second search area. Keep your eyes open. The sun is going down, and this mist is thickening."

Walking slowly, he scanned the ground as they approached the small river marked on the map. No evidence of a grave. Nothing except crumbled bits of quartz weathered from fallen granite boulders. The cliffs above kept a steady supply of raw material tumbling down. He checked the map again. It showed the cross right next to the river, a likely place for a grave since it was the only place around here where someone could dig deep enough to bury a person.

He swung around and made another pass, kicking at the ground as he walked. Still nothing, except silt and angled quartz pebbles. Surely, Waltz would have marked the grave somehow, otherwise why put it on the map. Maybe the grave was in the next valley over. The scale on the map was impossible to judge.

Shrugging off his backpack, he rolled his shoulders, then dropped the pack on the ground. "Let's camp down here for the night. Hopefully, the mist will burn off tomorrow and we can see more."

Angela gave an exaggerated sigh. He echoed the sentiment. Neither one of them had slept well last night. He'd rather not spend another night out here with her gasping at every animal howl. Not to mention her unreasonable paranoia over scorpions getting into the tent, as if the little critters could unzip the flap by themselves.

Still, he wouldn't let her antics dampen his excitement. This could be the trip where he found it. The lost mine might be just over this hill, or the next one. "Before we set up camp, I'm going to scout the hills nearby."

"Why do you call them hills?" She threw both arms out and spun around. "They're huge. All of them are mountains."

"Okay. You don't have to come."

Angela stopped and stared at him, her blue eyes wide with warring desires—come with him for more hiking or stay down here alone? He waited her out, secretly hoping she'd stay put.

Finally, she placed her hands on her slender hips. "I'll come." She swung the pack off her back. "But I'm not carrying this thing anymore."

Garrick nodded. He had no desire to put his pack back on either. Bending down, he pulled out a water bottle, then zipped it closed. They still had plenty of time to get to the top of this mountain and back down to make camp.

Holding the map in one hand, the water in the other, he led the way up the steep slope. The sound of their feet crunching over loose rock seemed to bounce off the cloudy air and back at them, surrounding them in a foggy haze. At least, Angela held her tongue on the way up. Maybe she was too tired for complaining.

Half an hour of huffing and puffing later, he paused to let their muscles rest. Sitting on a rock outcrop, he gazed into the cloudy mist. Too bad they couldn't see more, the view would probably be amazing. What were his fellow students doing in class right now? Certainly nothing as exciting as this.

Angela sat next to him, her blond hair flipping forward. She pushed it back with one hand and peered over at him. "How far up are we going?"

He snorted out a laugh. She'd only stopped complaining because she couldn't breathe. A good lesson to learn—keep her moving. "To the top. Come on, let's go."

She gave him a plaintive look, and he almost felt sorry for her. Almost. She'd have to toughen up if she wanted to find the mine. He brushed past her and continued up the slope.

The mist grew thicker as they ascended, like they were walking straight into a cloud. Garrick slowed his steps and squinted ahead. They should be close to the top, but he could barely see a few feet in front of his face.

He should probably turn back. At this rate, he could stumble over the mine entrance and not see it. But the thought of soon being stuck in a tent with Angela kept his legs moving.

"Are we there yet? Let me see the map."

The slower pace had given her the ability to speak. *Don't answer. Just keep going.*

She leaned into his back and grabbed for the map. He quickly swept it out of her reach. She lunged for it again. That was it. He'd had enough. He turned his head and opened his mouth, while simultaneously taking a big step away from her. But he never got a chance to voice his objection.

His front foot hit loose rock. The ground gave way, pitching him forward.

A scream tore from his mouth. The map fluttered out of his hand. He dropped the water bottle. It fell into empty space. He was at the edge of a cliff!

Shifting his weight, he tried to lean backward, but momentum dragged him over.

He reached for something, anything, to grab onto, but his hands clawed at the mist.

He plummeted through open space, twisting and turning as he fell.

Air rushed past him, stinging his face one second, whipping his hair so he couldn't see the next.

His right side slammed into rock, sending lightning streaks of sharp pain through his body. The impact snapped his neck back. His head hit, and everything went black.

***

"Garrick!"

The scream barely penetrated the fog clouding over Garrick's mind. Was that Angela? Why was she yelling at him? It hurt too much to think. He slipped further into the haze.

"Are you dead?"

Her voice pulled him out of the fog again. Was he dead? What a stupid thing to ask.

Sharp pain sliced through the back of his skull. The way his head hurt, dead didn't sound so bad right now. He opened his eyes to the hazy fog that existed outside of his mind. Trying hard to focus, he peered up and isolated her outline through the cloud. He could only see her torso, which meant she was kneeling at the edge. In a voice as loud as his pounding head would allow, he yelled, "I'm here."

"I can't see you. Where are you?"

Granite rock walls rose on both sides of him. On his left, the rock led up in uneven chunks to the cliff where Angela looked down. On the right, a deep crevice dropped into the mountain, buttressed by a short vertical ledge of basalt only a foot high. The water bottle had fallen with him and been trapped by the ledge.

"I fell into the top part of a crevice." He shifted his body, taking stock of the injuries—a sore shoulder, aching tail bone and of course there was his head which had a thousand drums thumping inside. He twisted at the waist, but his left leg wouldn't move. Reaching down, he tugged at his thigh. Nothing. His knee was caught between two boulders. "I'm stuck. My leg is wedged in."

"What do you want me to do?"

What *could* she do? His cell phone was in his pack, but it wouldn't work this far into the mountains anyway. And Angela definitely didn't have the skills to climb down the cliff to get him. "You'll have to go for help."

A momentary pause. "What if I came around to get you from below?"

He sat up and looked over the short rock wall. The mist wouldn't let him see far, but he could tell there was a sharp drop-off. "It won't work. I didn't fall as far as the valley floor." If he had, it would have killed him for sure. "I'm trapped partway up the mountain. I need you to hike out and get help."

He couldn't see her face, but he could imagine her horror at the idea of hiking out on her own. And why not? She had a better than average chance of dying out here, given her lack of survival skills.

"How about, I go get the rope and lower it down to you."

"Angela, I can't pull my leg out." His voice was laced with pain and irritation. He took a deep breath to calm down. He shouldn't be irritated with her. She wasn't the one who'd walked off a cliff. "Please."

"Fine. I'll be back as soon as I can."

He let his eyelids fall closed. Not even a minute passed before a loud baritone voice startled him. It came from the top of the cliff.

"Who are you?" the voice asked.

Pushing up on his elbows, Garrick squinted as he

looked up. The outline of another figure towered over Angela.

"My name's Angela. I'm so glad to see you, whoever you are."

"I'm Hellerman."

"Is that your first name or last name? Never mind, it doesn't matter. We need your help. I was hiking with a friend of mine, and he stepped off a cliff."

"Happens sometimes around here."

Garrick strained to hear every word. A random stranger showing up in the middle of nowhere could mean trouble. If only he could see this guy for himself.

"He's alive, but he's wedged into a crevice."

The outline of a tall person leaned over to look down. "That's unfortunate."

Unfortunate how? That Garrick was alive or that he needed assistance? Something in the man's tone raised Garrick's already skyrocketing blood pressure.

"Is there anything you can do to help?" Angela had sounded relieved since Hellerman had come, but now anxiety crept into her voice.

"If he's wedged in, the only thing that can help him is a rescue climber. I'm not one of those."

"Can you go get one?"

"We don't like them to come around here."

"Why not?"

"Boss likes his privacy."

His boss? What kind of employer did he have out here? As understanding dawned, Garrick's blood ran cold. Hellerman was an illegal miner. They had wandered into his territory. "Angela, run!"

"Garrick?" Her voice was panicked.

The two outlines disappeared from the edge. Bile rose up in his throat. Even if she ran, she wouldn't get far. Men like Hellerman didn't go anywhere without a gun.

With both hands he yanked at his leg again. It wouldn't budge. Slamming his head back to the rocky ground, he pounded his forehead with his fists. He'd led her out here, put her in danger, and now he couldn't do anything to help her.

CHAPTER FIVE

As Elery finished making her breakfast, she heard the floorboards creak on the stairs. Without turning around, she yelled over her shoulder. "Want an English muffin, Dad?"

The footsteps came down the hall and stopped behind her. "No, thanks. Candace promised me some homemade bread if I stop by for breakfast this morning."

"Ah, it's moved from Ms. Birch to Candace." She turned her head to flash him a smile. His budding romance had become the talk of the town. A retired mine owner who'd never remarried visiting the widowed church organist, ten years his junior. It qualified as a real scandal in Quartz Creek.

Her father pursed his lips, but said nothing.

Elery swung back to the toaster, grabbed the two sides of her flat muffin and dropped them on a plate. "So, have you heard from Garrick recently?" She tried to keep the worry out of her voice.

"Not in the last few days. Why?"

She searched for the butter in the fridge as she decided how to respond. Garrick hadn't returned her calls, not even the message she left giving him the details of the funeral. When he hadn't come to Chad's funeral, she'd driven to his apartment in Phoenix. No answer at the door.

If her dad knew, he'd worry and probably for no reason. Garrick was a free spirit who didn't bend to a timetable. Still, she had expected him to attend the funeral.

"I just wondered how midterms were going for him."

Her father had enough to worry about without adding Garrick to the list. Last night, he had told her that he'd bled through one of his bandages when he was at the grocery store. While trying to take care of it in the bathroom, one of the church elders had come in. Her dad quickly dismissed the wound as a scratch, and the man seemed to accept his explanation. It was a close call. If someone from Christ's Body Church discovered the extent of his lesions, he'd have to admit to having skin cancer, and he wasn't ready to do that yet.

Her father poured a cup of coffee into a travel thermos. "I'll head over to the church later to help with the garden."

"Okay." Their church cultivated a garden to feed the poor in Quartz Creek and in nearby Phoenix. He loved to help tend it.

"Are you going to the office?"

She heard the tension in his voice, the kind of caution used when approaching a skittish animal. His concern was valid. She still struggled to focus at work since the accident. No doubt, Ron had told him about the last couple of days, her swollen eyes and self-imposed seclusion. Men were again putting their lives at risk to dig out a profit for her. The miners handled the risk better than she. She'd rather give up on the whole thing. Not that it mattered. Without tunnel C, the mine would run dry in a matter of weeks. Then, she'd have to explain why she couldn't pay the miners. *Thanks so much for your years of faithful work, but now you're unemployed.*

She blew out a short breath. Until it was unavoidable, her father didn't need to strap on that worry. "I have paychecks to release on the computer and some other paperwork to finish."

He took a step toward the door, then turned back. "Do you know what your plans are for tunnel C?"

She sat at the kitchen table. "Not for sure."

It wasn't exactly a lie. She knew what she wanted to do, but Ron had a different opinion. He wanted to blast it closed. She thought they might be able to revive it. Part of the tunnel had survived the collapse. They could dig an offshoot tunnel a hundred yards in to see if they could find the rest of the original vein. She had to try something to find more gold. Fifty employees depended on the mine, not to mention her dad who drew a pension from the proceeds as part of his retirement, plus his medical bills. She couldn't let them down.

An hour later, she sat at her computer in her office trailer. The paychecks had been approved, and she was examining the report Ron had given her of the material they found in tunnel C. None of it looked worth pursuing.

With a heavy sigh, she decided to check e-mail instead. The first one was from Garrick. The date on the program said he sent it today, but inside the e-mail Garrick had typed in a different date. He'd written this on Monday, then set it up to automatically deliver on Thursday. Why?

As she quickly read through it, all worries about the mine were eclipsed by a new fear. This couldn't be right. She read it again, this time trying to blink away the words on the screen.

Elery,

Angela and I are going after the Lost Dutchman Mine. We know you don't want to help with the expedition so we're going in with the bare basics and only our feet to carry us. Once we've located some gold, we can then pay for our own mining supplies and transportation. I wanted you to know, just in case anything happens. I plan to contact you before this e-mail goes out, but if not, then you might consider looking for me.

Garrick

Seriously? Elery grabbed her cell phone, shifting it back and forth between her palms. Should she go after him? As an adult, he could make his own crazy decisions, although for this one he probably had a fair amount of help from Angela. And where the Lost Dutchman Mine was concerned, Garrick tended to lose all common sense.

Two years ago, on a solo hunt for the mine, he'd slipped and broken his arm. Rather than abandon the search, he tied his arm to his side and continued on. Several days later, he returned to the car to sleep. The following morning, she found him passed out in the car. By that time, his arm had started to heal, and he needed surgery to re-break it and set it. What if something worse had happened to him this time?

She tried Garrick's cell number. It went straight to voice mail. After leaving a short message to call her, she dropped the phone on the desk and again stared at the screen. She didn't have Angela's number. For several minutes, she tapped her fingers on the desk while she debated about what to do. The note, plus the fact she hadn't been able to find him for a couple of days, was cause for concern. Finally, she gave in and dialed the number for the sheriff. When it came down to it, no matter how irrational he could be, Garrick was her brother. If the situation were reversed, he'd go look for her.

"Pinal County Sheriff's Office. How can I help you?"

"Hi, Nora. It's Elery Hearst. Can I talk to the big guy for a minute?"

"Sure, sweetie. Hold on."

As Nora transferred her to Sheriff Rick Turner, she tried to tamp down her frustration with Garrick. Why couldn't he work at his studies, graduate, and get a job? Instead, he kept his head in the clouds dreaming of a treasure he had no claim to. They'd debated this dozens of times. In the end, Garrick always declared, in an amateur preacher's voice, that God intended to bless him mightily.

"This is Sheriff Turner."

"Sheriff, it's Elery Hearst."

"Hey, Elery. What's going on?"

A short knock sounded at the door and Ron came in. She put a finger up to let him know she was still on a call. "I'm not sure exactly. Garrick's out hunting for the lost mine. This time with a girl."

The sheriff grunted. "Not again. Is it a local girl?"

Ron raised his eyebrows at her. She motioned for him to sit in the chair in front of the desk. "Yes, although she just moved here. Her name is Angela and she commutes to the college in Phoenix."

"When did Garrick leave?"

She tucked her unruly hair behind her ears. "He sent me an e-mail dated on Monday."

"About three days, huh? That's not as long as he's been gone before. Any sign of the girl?"

"No. I don't have her cell phone number. I called Garrick and only got his voice mail."

Silence stretched over the line for several moments. The sheriff had a calm, calculating personality, usually an asset in his profession, unless you needed him to act quickly. It was a fifty-fifty shot whether he'd tell her to give it more time. She'd have to wait him out. Covering the receiver, she whispered to Ron, "What did you need?"

He lifted a stack of papers and shook them. "To go over these reports with you."

She twisted her lips to the side. "It might have to wait until later."

Ron nodded and left quietly.

A few seconds later, Sheriff Turner cleared his throat. "You know, I've been meaning to check out a report I got about a car parked on Hewitt Canyon Road on the south side of the mountains. Whoever would take a car down that rough road is pretty desperate. By the end, you'd be lucky to have anything left of the underside of the car. If it's his, that would be a good place to start a search. Why don't you meet me out there?"

Relief flooded through her. "Okay."

"Oh, and give me that girl's address if you have it. I'll check there first before I head out."

She gave him Angela's apartment address.

"Try not to panic, Elery. Hopefully, this is like the last time."

Except the last time, when she'd found Garrick sleeping in his car, he said he was getting ready to call her. This time he'd left a note. A note he knew she'd get today. So if everything was fine, why hadn't he called? She blew out a breath. "The car is a good starting point, but in case he's not there, do you know anyone who can track missing persons?"

The county had lost their emergency response technician last year to retirement. With tight budgets in a small town, sometimes people didn't get replaced.

The sheriff didn't hesitate. "Don't you worry. I've got the perfect guy."

***

Lucan's truck bounced over the rocks and ruts on the Hewitt Canyon Road. As he came to the turnout, he slowed and parked a car-length away from the other vehicles. He wouldn't contaminate the site where his dog needed to pick up the primary scent. He'd told the sheriff many times not to park so close, but the man talked more than he listened.

A wet nose smacked against Lucan's cheek as his spunky Labrador retriever tried to get a look out his window. "You ready to go to work, girl?"

At the word "work," the dog glued her rear end to the seat and stared intently at him. He grabbed his pack and tucked a leash in his pocket, but left her off lead.

"Good, let's go."

He opened the door, got out, then gave Sienna a nod to come out as well. They walked back to the sheriff's SUV together. The sheriff grunted as he forced his rotund body out of the seat. "I should have hauled the ATV out here. That road gets worse every year."

The pitted dirt road kept traffic through here to a minimum. Because of its remote access, more locals than tourists explored the southern side. Since Lucan spent much of his time tracking lost tourists, he hadn't explored this area as thoroughly. No better time than now. This hunt was a welcome distraction from sitting at home drowning in waves of grief.

Another officer exited the passenger side of the cruiser. The tall, muscular man with the shaved head and reddish goatee had the exact opposite dimensions of his boss. His name plate read Deputy Gene Hellerman. Lucan recognized him from the Sheriff's Office, but hadn't worked with him yet.

Lucan pointed a thumb at the car behind the police cruiser. "Is this my starting point?"

The sheriff nodded. "Yeah, it's Garrick's."

After wiping a layer of dust off the window, Lucan peered in. Empty, except for a box of granola bars in the back. Either Garrick hadn't brought any supplies or he'd taken them all with him.

Another vehicle crunched through the rocky dirt and parked behind the sheriff. Just what every missing person site needed, more company.

A woman jumped out of the Jeep as dust still swirled

around it. When the dust settled, Lucan got a clear look at her face. Elery Hearst.

He sucked in a deep breath and stopped in his tracks. The sheriff had told him the search was for Garrick Hearst, but he hadn't expected to see Elery here. The concerned frown on her face sparked his desire to help, making him want to approach her. But he couldn't move. Her words the night of the funeral echoed through his mind. *I should have replaced the stabilizer.* Had this woman been responsible for Chad's death?

Elery ran to Garrick's car, her loose curls bouncing with every step. She tried the door. Locked.

The sheriff shuffled slowly over to her. Hellerman hung back, a passive, almost disinterested, expression on his face.

She didn't seem to notice the sheriff's approach. Her gaze stayed focused on the car. The sheriff touched her arm to get her attention. "Elery, since Garrick's not here sleeping in his car, Lucan will start the search."

Sleeping in his car? Was this a regular occurrence? If so, Garrick could be someone who didn't want to be found.

Elery looked over at Lucan as if startled by his presence. In the sunlight, her eyes narrowed and flashed a teal blue color that matched the backdrop of sky behind her. Clearly, she'd rather have anyone else conducting this search. He echoed the sentiment. Too bad neither one of them had a choice in the matter. He and Sienna made up the only canine rescue unit in the county. "Do you know where Garrick might have gone?"

"He only told me it was somewhere outside the national forest boundary. I saw the map he wanted to follow, but I don't think I could recreate it."

"Okay, that's a start."

A flash of dark fur streaked past him. Sienna who had been sniffing the ground randomly had just now decided

Elery's arrival was more worth her effort. The dog ran straight for her and rudely stuck a nose between her legs. Elery gasped and pushed Sienna away.

"Sienna," he scolded. "Sit."

Sienna sat on Elery's foot, looking up at her with pleading brown eyes. The good dog act worked. Elery captured Sienna's head, rubbing behind her ears.

"She likes you," the sheriff said.

As if agreeing, the dog swung her head back toward Elery's private areas. Elery redirected her away.

Heat crept up Lucan's neck. "Sorry. That's her preferred method of saying hello. It's kind of a dog thing, but I'm trying to break the habit."

Elery cleared her throat. "It definitely felt more personal than hello."

Lucan snapped his fingers. Sienna ran to him with her ears and tail perked. "Time to work, girl." He looked up at Elery. "We're looking for your brother, right?"

She nodded and swallowed hard. "He's been out here for three days. And he might be with a girl named Angela."

The desperation in her eyes tugged at him. She was frantic to find Garrick, and he couldn't blame her. If it were Chad out there, he'd search until he dropped. But he'd never had the chance to save *his* brother. Tightness hardened his chest, and his stomach burned with acid. The person who could have done something for Chad stood right here, asking for his help.

Blame is not yours to parcel out.

The quiet voice from God caught him off guard, but it held no condemnation.

Condemnation. That was what he'd already given to Elery. Even though he had no idea if she truly deserved it, he wanted to blame her. He needed someone to blame.

He closed his eyes. *Lord, help me to put away all*

angry and vengeful thoughts. Give me strength to do my job.

Opening his eyes, he focused on the sheriff. "Since it hasn't rained, we have a good chance of tracking their movements. You know how spotty cell phone coverage is out here, but I'll report back every four hours if I can get reception."

Bending over slightly, he circled his fingers to Sienna, a signal for her to pick up a scent. The dog took off for the car, snuffling and snorting by the driver's side door.

Elery moved in front of Lucan. "I'd like to come with you."

Frowning, he shook his head. "I don't usually work that way." The look on her face said she wasn't convinced. He needed a better reason. But nothing came. He glanced at the sheriff, who merely nodded. Hellerman stood behind the sheriff with arms crossed, an amused smile on his face. If Lucan refused to allow the family member of a missing person to accompany him, it could affect his working relationship with the sheriff. This assignment just got a lot harder. He glanced at her jeans and boots. "Do you have a coat?"

"Yes."

"Water?"

"Yep."

Lucan took a deep breath, then blew it out. "Okay. Here are the rules. First, never interfere with Sienna when she's working. Don't talk to her. Don't pet her. Don't even make eye contact. Second, never leave my side. As we walk, we'll make our own trail. Too many will confuse her."

"Only two rules?" The question came out rude, and her surprised expression said she knew it.

Lucan gave her a sharp glance, but otherwise ignored her comment. He would act professional, no matter what, but still he couldn't escape the tragic irony. Three days after burying his own brother, he was looking for hers.

CHAPTER SIX

A hot desert wind blew in Elery's face as she trudged beside Lucan. They had followed Sienna for a mile down an unmaintained road, then into an upward sloping valley with mountains hemming them in on both sides. The slopes were littered with broken boulders, the peaks a series of jagged cliffs. Sienna trotted ahead of them with her nose six inches off the ground, weaving around all the different forms of cacti—tall soldier-like saguaro, beaver-tail cactus with branches like spiked paddle boards, and cholla with its honeycomb trunk covered in so many spines they looked like dandelion fluff. Sienna seemed to be happily following a strong scent. The only thing Elery could smell was the faint aroma of piñon pine drifting down from higher elevations.

After walking beside Lucan for an hour in silence, the sound of their crunching boots seemed to magnify with every step. What could she say to this man? "Sorry" wasn't enough, and yet she wanted to say it a thousand more times. Not that it would help. It might ease her conscience, but it would only make Lucan more uncomfortable. Still, she ought to say something. Ignoring each other only made this worse.

"What caused you to choose such a solitary profession?" Immediately, she could have kicked herself. It was a rude question, and the last person she should be rude to was Lucan. He probably wanted nothing to do with her, but instead of turning her away, he'd taken on the mission of finding her brother, a virtual stranger to him.

He glanced sideways at her, his expression unreadable. "I flunked out of fire-fighting school."

"Oh, I'm sorry."

The corner of his mouth turned up. "That was a joke, Elery."

"Oh." Of course, a joke. He was messing with her. Somehow, that tripled the awkwardness of this situation.

He didn't offer an actual answer to her question. And no way would she ask again. They walked on in silence, the only sound the scraping of their boots as they hurried to keep up with the retriever. For a mile or so more, they followed, stopping once for a water break to give Sienna a drink out of a collapsible travel bowl.

As they began walking again, the slope increased. They were heading up a mountain.

"Look." Lucan had kept quiet for so long, the deep baritone of his voice startled her. He sucked in a breath like he could keep it bottled up forever. He blew it out, and his shoulders slumped. "I'm sorry your brother is missing."

Such a simple statement, yet it spoke volumes. She glanced down at her feet. Dust billowed between her legs with every step. "Thanks. I'm sure you caught the impression back there that he'd done this before."

Lucan nodded, but kept his eyes on Sienna twenty yards ahead of them.

"It's not like it sounds. Garrick loves these mountains. He'd probably come out here all the time even without his addiction."

"His addiction?"

"He's a Dutchaholic. The lost mine has become his obsession."

Lucan halted, and she stopped next to him. His

brows pinched together. An expression of profound pain crossed his face in a flash, then left just as quickly.

Her heart pinched at the sorrow she'd seen on his face. "Did I say something wrong?"

"No." He resumed walking, picking up the pace to catch up with Sienna.

Was he thinking about his brother? She'd seen the same fever in Chad's eyes. Maybe she should change the subject. "How long have you had Sienna?"

"Three years."

She shaded her face with her hand to peer past the sun at the furry backside bobbing over the rough terrain. "How is it for a black dog in sunny Arizona?"

"She gets hot. I just have to make sure she drinks a lot."

"Did you get her as a puppy?"

He rubbed the back of his neck. "You know, you don't have to try so hard. We don't have to be friends."

Is that what she'd been trying to do, be his friend? To ease her conscience maybe? She opened her mouth, but nothing came out.

He shook his head, and a patch of brown hair flipped over his forehead. "I'm sorry. That was rude." He rolled his lip through his teeth. "Working is hard for me right now, but I can't sit at home thinking about Chad."

She had no right to ask, but she had to. "Do you want to talk about him?"

"Yes ... no." He panted out a breath. "I mean, I can't."

She nodded. He didn't want to talk about it with *her*. And she couldn't blame him. She glanced at his profile as he walked. Same square jaw, thin nose, and high forehead as Chad, and yet they looked different on him—less carefree, more intense. But even with his stony expression, Lucan had an air of peace that she'd never seen in Chad.

Up ahead, Sienna stopped next to the round opening

of a small cave. Had Garrick stopped here as well? It was barely big enough for a man to squeeze in and although it didn't appear deep, looks could be deceiving. The dog sat and waited for her master to give directions.

Lucan swung his pack off his shoulders and grabbed a flashlight. Crouching in front of the hole, he patted Sienna on the head. "Good girl. Wait here."

The flashlight beam cut through the dark as he duck-walked into the cavern. Elery bent at the waist and peered over his shoulder to get a look inside. Light bounced from the cave floor to the ceiling and back. Her geologic training kicked in. Something seemed out of place on the floor. Chunks of basalt were clumped all in one area. A man-made pile.

"Lucan." She leaned in and placed a hand on his shoulder.

He stilled. "What?"

"Back out slowly."

He moved only his head to look at her. "Why? I can see it goes back farther than it looks from the outside. Garrick could be stuck in there."

"He's not. Trust me."

"Okay, but you better tell me what's going on when I get out." After scooting out backward, he stood and faced her. "What's the deal? You asked me to come find your brother. That's what I'm trying to do."

She pointed at the opening. "It's a decoy."

Confusion furrowed his brow. "What do you mean, a decoy?"

"For centuries, Dutch Hunters have tried to keep others from looking for the mine. The best way to do that is to kill anyone who comes in the area after you. So they set up decoy caves to trap others. If another hunter goes looking in the cave, they are either killed or hurt badly enough they can't continue their search for the mine."

He looked at her sideways, skeptical. She motioned

for him to move farther away, and he followed, calling Sienna to join them. "The floor of that cave has a pile of basalt someone left there for a reason. There's probably a pressure pad under it." She picked up a baseball-sized rock. "Here, watch."

She turned and side-armed the rock through the opening, hitting the basalt pile dead on. A loud explosion sent a blast of dirt and rock plummeting to the floor of the cavern. A cloud of dust billowed out, reminding her a little too much of the day the mine tunnel collapsed. She tightened her stomach, pushing the upwelling emotions back down.

Lucan stared at her with his mouth wide open. At least he had listened to her warning, even though he didn't have any reason to trust her.

***

Lucan licked his lips and tasted dirt. In his few months here, he hadn't discovered a trap and no one had told him about them. It gave him a whole new appreciation for gold psychosis. To want to kill someone you didn't even know? Unbelievable.

Beside him, Elery brushed dirt from her jeans. She had saved him. This woman who likely bore responsibility for Chad's death had now saved his life. What was he supposed to do with that? Of course, he wouldn't even be out here if it weren't for her missing brother. He wiped a layer of sweat off his forehead and took a deep breath to calm his racing pulse. "Was the demonstration really necessary?"

She shrugged and pursed her full lips in a perturbed expression he might have found adorable in different circumstances. "You didn't believe me."

True enough. He'd thought she was a little off her rocker to assume it was a trap. "Okay. Anything else related to geology or a booby-trap, I'll believe you. Good?"

"Good."

He ruffled Sienna's coat to clean her fur and gave her the go signal. "Let's get back to work."

As Sienna continued to zig-zag in front of them, he watched her closely. Her nose plastered to the ground, tail straight up, she maneuvered between chunks of rock and skirted past the grasping spikes of cactus. She climbed up a low hill and disappeared over the other side.

He hurried to the top, uncomfortable with her out of eyesight. As he crested the mound, he heard a deadly sound. The rapid-fire tick, tick, tick of a rattler. He yelled, snapping his fingers at the same time. "Sienna!"

Sienna stopped and raised her head. Too late.

The rattlesnake's thick body flew through the air, its fangs aimed at her throat. She must have caught a glimpse of the danger because she turned away at the last second.

Lucan held his breath.

The snake missed Sienna's neck. It kept falling with gravity, finally sinking its teeth into her forelimb.

Sienna yelped, and he ran to her. Before he could reach her, she lowered her head and bit into the snake's body, yanking it off her leg. The snake scurried away, hiding under a nearby cactus.

Lucan grabbed her just as she collapsed to the ground. He lowered her down and knelt beside her. Sienna lay with one ear flipped up, her eyes closed. Stripping off his pack, he dug inside for his first-aid kit.

Elery knelt on the other side, raised Sienna's head and placed it in her lap. Sienna's eyes opened a fraction.

"It's going to be okay, girl." Lucan lifted the injured leg and wrapped a piece of fabric tightly around the shoulder above the bite. Sienna whimpered, but didn't open her eyes again. He brushed his hand over her ear.

Please, Lord, don't let her die. I can't take any more death.

Ducking back toward his pack, he grabbed a square, insulated container. He unzipped it, pulled out a needle and a vial. After piercing the membrane, he tugged on the plunger to extract the correct dose of medicine. He turned to Elery. "Hold her still."

Her eyes went wide at the sight of the needle, but she held Sienna tight by the shoulders.

He lifted Sienna's forelimb above the bite and stabbed the needle into the muscle. Pushing down the plunger, he released the antitoxin for the snake's venom. Sienna whimpered again. He patted her head. "Sorry."

After slipping the needle back into his pack, he focused on Elery again. Her eyebrows were raised in an unspoken question. "Antivenin," he said. "It will buy her some time, but we have to get her to the vet. Can you help me carry her?"

Elery pushed her hair behind her ears and nodded. At least she was willing to help, because they had miles to go to get back to the car. Thankfully, most of it was downhill.

"I'll take her front half because I'm taller. We need to keep the bite elevated."

He cradled Sienna's head against his chest, placing one arm under her rib cage and one though her front legs. Elery slid her arms under the dog's back end, and they lifted Sienna together.

Stumbling over rocks and brush, they hurried toward the truck. He couldn't lose Sienna, too. She made a difference, not just in his life, but in many others. In the last few months alone, she'd found half a dozen lost hikers around the county and two missing children from the neighboring county. Her career was impressive. But just as important, she gave him a reason to keep going. A job to do during the day. And at night, she curled up with him on the couch as he mourned his brother.

Shortly after they started, he realized Elery was struggling to keep up with his pace while holding half of a limp eighty-pound dog, but he couldn't slow down. He kept pushing on. To her credit, Elery didn't complain or ask him to ease up.

"How much time does it take for a snake bite to travel over the whole body?" she asked through panting breaths.

"Usually about sixty minutes, although the antivenin will slow that down considerably. Even so, we have to hurry."

"I understand."

His arms burned from the exertion. Hers had to be as well, but she held the dog's hindquarters close, rubbing along the back leg.

After a torturous hike and more than an hour later, the truck came into view. "Almost there, girl," Lucan whispered. "Hold on."

The last fifty feet seemed to drag on. He looked over at Elery once, surprised she'd made it the whole way back. She was a tough lady.

At the vehicle, Lucan balanced Sienna's head on his knee as he opened the passenger's side door. Then, he slid her front end in and took the back end from Elery's arms. After getting Sienna situated, he slammed the door shut, ran around the cab and opened the driver's side door.

Elery trailed after him. "Where are you taking her?"

"Moreland's veterinary clinic." He locked eyes with her. Granted, he wouldn't be out here if it weren't for her brother, but the trip back to the truck would have taken much longer without her. "Thanks."

He jumped in and took off, keeping one hand on the

wheel and one hand on Sienna's head. "It'll be okay, girl. Dr. Moreland will take good care of you."

Sienna opened her eyes once, then closed them and went to sleep. Was that a good thing or was she slipping away? It had taken them almost two hours to get back to the truck, and the vet was almost an hour away. Too much time. He stomped on the gas pedal, and the truck bounced on the rocky road with the extra burst of speed.

***

Lucan patted Sienna on the head one last time, then left her sleeping in the observation room. The vet said she should survive, although she wasn't out of the woods yet. They wanted to keep her for observation overnight, and probably for a few more days after that.

He shut the door and turned to walk down the hall. Looking ahead into the waiting room, he hesitated. Elery sat with her head bowed and hands clasped, praying. He hadn't expected her to come when she needed to be out looking for her brother, much less offer up prayers for his dog.

As he approached, Elery looked up at him, her blue eyes questioning.

"The vet thinks she'll be okay."

Her face relaxed. "Oh, good."

"Thanks for coming." He sank to the bench beside her. "And for helping to carry her so far."

"It's the least I could do. She got hurt because of me."

"Accidents happen." The double meaning of the statement brought his thoughts back to Chad. Was his death really just an accident? The skeptical look on Elery's face said she wouldn't let herself off the hook for either incident so easily. "I'm sorry Sienna won't be able to help search for your brother."

Elery shot him a surprised glance.

"Hey, I love my dog, but we still need to find your brother."

"I wish I knew where to look. The area is so large. He could be anywhere."

Lucan glanced out the glass front doors of the vet's office. "It's getting dark, so let's sleep on it. Maybe you'll have some idea of where to look in the morning."

His comment sounded more callous than he meant. How hard would it be for her to sleep knowing her brother might be hurt and waiting for help? But that wasn't something he'd ever have to worry about again. His brother was gone. He swiped a hand across his face, trying to wipe off the sweat and grime.

She nodded and rose to her feet. "Thank you for your help today."

Without waiting for a response, she turned and went through the double doors. He watched her get in her Jeep and leave before he considered going home himself. He'd rather stay here, but they wouldn't let him. After telling the receptionist he'd be back in the morning, he got in his truck and navigated the too-short drive home. He didn't like coming back to an apartment with no boisterous black lab to greet him.

He threw his backpack onto the couch, turned on the radio for some noise, and headed for a shower. The cool water cleansed away more than the dirt. He let his anxiety about Sienna flow down the drain as well. The vet said she'd be okay. That was what mattered.

However, Sienna would need some recovery time, which left him without a dog to help track Garrick. He'd talk to the sheriff in the morning about trying to borrow another dog from the City of Phoenix. There wasn't any other option.

Tell her.

The internal voice of God soothed him more than the cold water pouring over his head. "Tell her what, Lord?"

He imagined God wagging a finger at him. During their search through the mountains he'd heard God directing him to tell Elery about the journal pages, but he hadn't. He couldn't. No way would he go down that road.

I will go down every road with you.

Lucan lowered his head, letting the water pour down his neck. An image ran through his mind. Elery with her head bent in prayer. The woman was full of surprises. He wouldn't have guessed her to believe in prayer. Then again, that was probably an assumption he'd made in anger. She wasn't the heartless, greedy mine owner he'd assumed her to be after their first meeting.

Even so, the wound of losing his brother wasn't a week old, and God wanted him to scrape at it? "Why, Lord? The journal probably wouldn't help anyway.*"*

No answer came.

Probably because Lucan knew the answer. Last year, he'd come to a crossroads. A fork in the road of life where one path led to God's will and the other to his own. A friend had asked him to join a missionary team traveling to the jungles of South Africa. He'd longed for the adventure, for the chance to win new souls for Christ. That was the kind of treasure Lucan sought. But God had made it crystal clear. He needed to move to Quartz Creek with his brother.

Now that his brother was gone, some would say there hadn't been any point to coming here. But Lucan didn't see it that way. God had given him five extra months with his brother.

He'd chosen God's path then, and he would do it again. Even if he didn't understand it.

CHAPTER SEVEN

"Can't you do something?" Elery stomped her foot on the hard wood of Sheriff Turner's office floor. A little-girl kind of move, but she didn't care. "This is Garrick we're talking about."

He leaned back in his chair and folded his hands behind his head. It made him appear nonchalant, but she knew him better than that. He had to feel as useless as she did in finding Garrick. "I'm sorry, Elery. The only other dog scenting team near here is out of Phoenix."

She put her hands on his desk, leaning in close. "So get them here."

"The president is visiting Phoenix on Monday. The dog teams are spending the weekend scouting out all the potential sites he might visit. They're already working overtime and don't have the manpower to come down here." The sheriff moved his hands to rest on his massive stomach, rubbing it in circles. "Between you and me, they probably wouldn't have come anyway."

"Why not?"

"The Superstitions average dozens of missing people every year, usually outsiders. A few of them are never found. The counties surrounding us don't want to waste their time on what they consider crazy Dutch Hunters."

How could they turn their back on a missing person? Someone had to help Garrick. "Did you tell them he was local?"

"Yes, I told them. With the president coming, they still said they couldn't do it." Sheriff Turner let his chair pull him upright, then placed his palms on the desk. "I know what you're going through. I'm sick with worry too, but my hands are tied."

She straightened and spread her arms wide. "So, they're willing to say this is Garrick's fault and leave him to die."

The sheriff broke eye contact. Clearly, he thought Garrick was already gone.

No, she wouldn't believe it. "He's not dead."

Sheriff Turner met her gaze, his eyes full of compassion. His voice came out an octave lower. "You don't know that, Elery."

He was right. She kept assuming bad things wouldn't happen, but they happened all the time. People died all too often. Like Chad. But she wouldn't accept Garrick's death until she knew for sure.

"What about that volunteer group out of Phoenix that helps find missing people?"

"I'll contact them and have one of my officers coordinate with the volunteers." The sheriff picked up his phone. "But I'm afraid we might have to hope Garrick can make it back on his own. Even an army couldn't search every nook and cranny in the 150,000 acres of the Superstitions. Do what you can to dig up more clues to where he went. Give me somewhere to look."

"Fine." She stormed out of the office, slamming the door behind her. The sheriff had a point about not knowing where to look, but she couldn't give him any more leads to follow. If nobody else could help, it would be up to her to track down her brother.

***

Lucan sat cross-legged on the floor of the vet's office in front of Sienna's crate. She wagged the tip of her tail and made a small attempt to lick his hand, but otherwise, she lay still. The venom had taken its toll. She had another full week of recovery ahead of her.

Footsteps sounded on the concrete behind him. He turned his head expecting to see the vet's assistant. Instead, Elery came into the room, her hands stuffed in the pockets of her jeans, her shoulders hunched. Her eyes held traces of a long night, but even tired she looked somehow vibrant. Maybe it was her tanned skin and the streaks of blond highlighting the spirals of her brown curls.

She stopped several feet from the crate. "I wanted to see how Sienna was doing."

At the sound of Elery's voice, Sienna tried to lift her head, then quickly gave up, letting out a long sigh. He gave Sienna one last pat and got to his feet. "She's still wiped out, but that's normal. Thanks for coming by to check on her."

"I also wanted to let you know that I'm going to go out searching in the same area where we stopped yesterday." She shrugged. "So somebody knows where I've gone. I haven't told my dad Garrick is missing."

So, she had a father in town. Did she have any other family? Probably not a good time to ask. He gave a sidelong glance down the hallway before turning his gaze back to her. "Elery, do you think Garrick might have found it? The lost gold mine, I mean."

She tugged on her lip. "I guess he could have. Because of Angela, he had a map no one else had."

Was that why God wanted him to tell her? He sucked in a slow breath. "Can we talk for a minute in my truck?"

She puckered her eyebrows, but didn't protest. They walked in silence to his vehicle. He didn't speak until her door had closed. "I'm sorry about the secrecy, but you know how people get about the lost mine."

A rueful laugh escaped from her lips. It didn't surprise him. Her brother had been as crazy for the mine as Chad.

"I don't know if this will help, but I feel compelled to tell you something." He shifted in the seat to face her better. "I've only told a few people about this." He blew out a nervous breath. "Here goes. Seven years ago, my father died. He disappeared on a hike in the Superstition Mountains."

She tugged at a curl near the base of her neck. "I'm sorry."

He tapped his thumb against his leg. Talking about this with her was awkward. "My father was looking for the mine. When he didn't come back, my mother boxed up all his things and left them in the attic. Last year, we went through them and found a very old journal. A note attached to the journal had four different signatures associated with our family's history. Each ancestor signed the note as the journal was passed down through our family. A detailed family tree was drawn on the back of the note."

He paused, giving her a moment to process his story. Her eyebrows were raised like twin steeples, but she made no comment.

"The name of the author of the journal was written on the first page. My great-great-great-uncle." He cleared his throat and shifted in his seat. No telling how Elery would take this next revelation. "His name was Jacob Waltz."

Her mouth dropped open. When she stayed mute, he continued.

"I'm a descendant of the Dutchman." He put a hand on his chest. "I had no interest in chasing the mine. Look what happened to my dad. But Chad had other ideas."

She glanced up at the cloth roof of the truck. He could see the wheels turning. If only she would say something so he knew what she was thinking.

"Chad moved us here to Quartz Creek to pursue the clues he thought were in the journal."

Elery looked over at him and finally opened her mouth. "How do you know this journal is real?"

"My dad had the handwriting tested against artifacts containing the actual census signature of Jacob Waltz. As far as the experts can tell, the journal is authentic, although we haven't been able to figure out where it leads."

"Why are you telling me this?"

"If your brother actually discovered the mine, the best way to find him is to find the mine. Chad always suspected the journal held a clue to the mine that he couldn't decipher. He had the pages translated from the original German. I've never read the whole set of journal pages, only the first few, but if we read it together, maybe we could find something."

A glimmer of hope ignited in her eyes turning them into blue fire. "That's a decent idea. Where's the journal?"

"Here's the thing." Was he really about to ask her to go on a treasure hunt with him? God better have a good reason for this. He blew out another breath. "The pages won't be easy to get."

"What do you mean?"

"Shortly after we moved here, someone found out about the journal and threatened to take it—our cousin. Chad and I hid the pages to keep them safe."

"Where?"

"Several places, actually. We divided up the entries, each of us taking alternating ones, then we hid them in separate places. I know where the pages I hid are located, but not my brother's." Lucan swallowed the lump in his throat. Despite the dangers of Dutch Hunting, he'd never expected Chad to die. "We put clues on the bottom of the pages to help us find the next set. If we can find Chad's first set of pages, then I'm sure we can find the rest."

Elery's eyes clouded over, and she glanced out the window. The rocky peaks towered in the distance. She had to be weighing the alternatives. Wander around the mountains looking for Garrick like a needle in a haystack or spend time finding journal pages in hopes of locating a mine that's been lost for a hundred years. "Any idea of where the first page might be?"

"No, but I think he'd keep it close. We could try his apartment." Lucan's heart constricted until it felt as small and as hard as a walnut. Had he really just suggested they search through Chad's things? No way could he do that without breaking down. If this was God's way of making him deal with the pain, it was too soon.

CHAPTER EIGHT

Chad's apartment door creaked as it swung open, letting out a pungent odor. Elery covered her nose and held her breath.

"Sorry." Lucan took a step inside. "I guess that's the garbage. I haven't been inside to clean things out yet."

A twinge of guilt pinched her stomach. This situation forced him to confront his brother's death all over again. Standing in the doorway staring at Lucan, she could almost imagine Chad here in this apartment on his last day. Maybe reading the newspaper scattered across the coffee table or grabbing clothes out of the laundry basket in the corner of the living room.

"What?" Lucan asked.

She shook her head. "Nothing." He looked exactly like his brother, tall with wide shoulders, brown hair streaked with gold, shorter in the back, longer in front. No telltale mole or scar to differentiate them. And yet, Lucan had a different air about him. "Were you the older twin?"

His anguished eyes met hers, and she wanted to take back the question. "I was." He kicked aside a pair of dirty socks. "If you could see my apartment you'd know how opposite we were."

She could imagine Lucan performing spring-cleaning on his apartment three times a year. He probably organized his sock drawer by color. Older. Disciplined. Rescuer. Everything Chad wasn't. Maybe that explained why she found him much more attractive.

"I'll have to go through all of this eventually, so making a mess doesn't matter. Search for wherever he might hide papers." Lucan moved to the kitchen. He opened and closed drawers, rummaging through the contents. She glanced around the living room. How could she invade Chad's privacy like this?

For Garrick. She had to do this for her brother. Moving to the far wall, she rifled through some books on a bookshelf. The uncomfortable sensation of violating sacred space stole over her again. Maybe a little small talk would help take her mind off it. "You and Chad moved here from Kansas?"

"Yeah. When I realized I couldn't talk him out of it, I came to make sure he didn't find trouble."

Her assumption was correct. "You were an overprotective brother."

"Maybe. But I had other reasons for coming here."

"Like what?" She bit her lip. Why did she keep asking him such personal questions? It was nosy, rude even, and yet she couldn't seem to stop.

Lucan leaned through the rectangular peek-through opening from the kitchen. His amber eyes were as hard as a fossil. She'd managed to hit upon another bad memory. "I also came to Quartz Creek because I wanted to find out what happened to Dad."

She clamped her mouth shut just before she asked if he believed his dad was dead. She didn't have to ask. Out here, unsolved murders were the norm.

Lucan placed both hands on the kitchen counter and peered at her. His eyebrows were cinched tight. Why would he help her when this was obviously painful? But she couldn't ask him. She'd pried enough for one day.

She turned back to the bookshelves. Silence settled over the apartment as they continued searching. Even though it seemed too obvious a hiding place, she took her time looking through the myriad of Lost Dutchman texts. Chad must have owned every word written on the subject. From each book, several handwritten slips of paper fell out. Tapping her foot, she lifted the notes and scanned them. A collection of random ideas about the mine. No solid clues.

"Find anything?"

Lucan's close voice startled her. She thumbed through the slips of paper. "Not unless these notes mean anything."

"We can look at them later. Why don't we work on the bedroom? Chad has a desk in there that you can look through while I search the rest of the room."

"Okay." She placed the books in a short stack and followed Lucan down the hallway. Inside the bedroom, the sheets were strewn about the bed, papers balanced precariously on the edge of the desk and dirty clothes littered the floor. As was the case in the living room, the most organized space was a small bookshelf sitting in front of a window. She glanced at the objects resting on the bookshelf. The one on top stopped her in her tracks.

A cream-colored seashell as large as a shoe box leaned on its side, the curlicues laced with orange. The open portion of the shell pointed out the window behind it.

"What is it?" Lucan touched her shoulder. "Are you okay?"

"Your brother ..." Her eyes stayed locked on the shell. She swallowed hard as the memory swamped over her. Impulsively, she reached up and grabbed Lucan's hand, cradling it between hers. "I'd forgotten. I thought it was nonsense, you know, head injury and such." She gulped down a breath and met his concerned gaze. "Before he died, your brother told me to look in the shell."

The blood drained from Lucan's face, but he nodded solemnly. "Of course." He pulled away from her and walked over to the shell, touching the top with one finger.

He looked over his shoulder and gave a stiff smile. "We found this on the last vacation we took with Dad."

Lucan took the shell in both hands and lowered himself to the bed. With two fingers, he reached deep into the opening. "Something is here." He tugged until he extracted two folded over yellow sheets. Writing covered both sides of the paper. He unfolded the sheets and smoothed them.

Reality sunk in at that moment. Lucan truly was a descendant of the Dutchman, a closer link to the mine than Angela's ancestry. The pages in front of her were written a hundred years ago by a man with access to a fortune's worth of gold. It was a miner's dream. But all she cared about was finding Garrick.

Lucan handed the pages to her. "You might be tempted to skim the pages, but don't."

"Why not?"

"Chad followed all the obvious clues in these pages, and they didn't lead to anything. If there's a clue here to find, it's in a detail. Pay attention to the details."

Elery sat on the bed next to him and looked into his face. His earnest eyes held restrained tears. She fought the urge to put an arm around him for comfort. It wouldn't be appropriate given their relationship. Instead, she leaned closer, resting her shoulder against his as they read Jacob Waltz's words together.

The pages were split up on two different shades of paper, one buff-colored and one darker tan, as if written at different times. And yet, the date on the top of both pages matched.

Her pulse pounded as she read the front and back of the buff-colored page. Jacob Waltz and Ila were attacked by Ila's brother, Kuruk. A shotgun blast, then Jacob fell into a hole. What had happened to him? To Ila? Elery finished the page first, waiting anxiously for Lucan to finish. When he did, he flipped to the dark tan page, and they both resumed reading.

***

January 1850

I dropped through the shaft with my body bumping against the sides. Sharp rocks cut into my arms and back. My legs hit the bottom first, but they couldn't support the force of the fall. The rest of my body crumpled down as easily as a sheet of newsprint.

The back of my head hit last with enough force to cause me to lose all sensibility.

When I awoke, I was at the bottom of a narrow chasm. I couldn't determine how long I had been unconscious. Above the rock walls hemming me in, the first gathering of stars shone overhead.

I survived intact, although my muscles ached and my cuts bled. Ila had known the shaft would be my escape route. She'd protected me, but at what cost? I didn't even know if they had shot at her or me.

Getting slowly to my feet, I started to walk down the chasm. As I regained my balance, my steps quickened with the desperate need to find Ila.

The chasm widened the farther I walked, the walls seeming less like those of a prison and more like the fortification for a castle. Overhead, the stars came into their full glory and I saw glimpses of the moon. Finally, I came into the dry air of the desert. I circled around to view the rock cliff at a distance. I'd slid about halfway down the mountain to a flat mesa a couple hundred feet above the desert floor.

The only way to get back to Ila was to climb. I dug my boots in, grabbed for hand holds on the rough rocks, and climbed with only the light of the moon to guide me.

About halfway up, my head came above a cliff to another flat area. A small reflection drew my attention. A thin line of silver near the base of a rock formation that looked like twin fingers pointing to the sky.

I focused on the spot surrounding the silver item, and Ila's shape emerged. She lay face down on a large rock platform. Struggling up the cliff, I kept my gaze on her until I reached her unmoving form. The reflection had come from the inlaid eyes of the lizard carving I had given her. It was held firmly in her hand.

I crouched beside her and brushed her silky hair back from her face, whispering her name into her ear.

She didn't move. No breath came from her mouth.

Blood soaked her tunic on the left side near her waist. I lowered my forehead to her shoulder as the truth became clear. She was dead. They had killed her because of her association with me.

I reached for her hand, and the carving slipped from hers to mine. I tucked it into my pocket. Crawling to her other side, I touched her cheek, wondering if she had she died right away or if she had suffered as her attackers looked on.

Shifting to face her, I gave her a lingering kiss. Her lips were cold and slightly apart as if in a permanent gasp.

I pressed my cheek to hers, then sat up. Before I could think of what to do next, I saw movement to my right. I leaned out of the way as a boot swung past my face. The heel hit my forehead, propelling me backward.

I fell, then crawled along the ground to get away. Blood seeped from the wound and dripped down my cheek.

The man pulled his leg back for another kick. I dropped flat to the ground and the boot missed my head. As I looked up, I saw my attacker's face in the moonlight.

Kuruk.

Behind Kuruk, the tall man stepped out from the other side of the twin-finger rock formation. This time the tall man had the weapon, holding the rifle down at his side. He walked closer, mumbling foreign words as he came.

These men were intent on killing me, as well. They had killed Ila and then laid her out to draw me back. I had to do something, but there was nothing I could do. Except relent.

I was already on my knees, so I threw my arms out, and put my face to the ground, bowing before these evil men. I gave them an easy target, hoping they'd make it quick.

The mumbling and the footsteps stopped.

I glanced up. The two men looked at each other, clearly confused. I knew they didn't have any compunction about killing me. I wondered why they were hesitating.

Kuruk and the tall man were discussing me, probably wondering if I was a priest because of my high-collared shirt. Even the Apache would honor a man of the church.

The delay was an opportunity from the Lord. I would not waste it. I jumped to my feet, running at the man who held the gun. My shoulder hit him on the left side. He fell to the ground. I stumbled over him and kept running toward the desert.

They wouldn't be long in pursuing me. I needed to hide, but for that I was going the wrong direction. Even with only moonlight, I'd be easy to see and shoot in the desert.

A blast came from behind.

Chunks of rock fell around me. I glanced over my shoulder. One of the twin stone fingers at my back had been cut in half. I continued on, all the while thanking God for placing that rock there.

A few steps later, I changed direction and ran toward a small valley between this mountain and a neighboring one. On the way down, I had to slow my feet when the loose rock became too slippery. The tall man would need to reload, but even so, I was still in danger. No one could track like Apache men.

Fortunately, Ila had shown me a few things about this area. I passed through the valley and started up the other side at a faster pace.

Scanning the dark terrain ahead, I knew I was drawing near. The cliff I sought was halfway up the mountain and to the south.

I looked over my shoulder. The two men were about three wagon lengths behind me. I ran toward the edge of the mountain where a line of blackness marked the cliff. There, I stopped and looked down. Nothing, except darkness.

My stomach tossed and turned like a ship on rough seas. I looked over my shoulder again.

The tall man stopped and raised his gun.

I jumped before he could shoot me.

For the second time, my body floated in the air, before gravity pulled me down toward the unforgiving ground.

Air blew past my face and tears misted my eyes. I spun my arms to keep my body upright. Landing on my head would have only completed the job for them.

Something hard hit my left arm and flew away. A bat or perhaps a branch growing from the side of the cliff. Then, my feet hit the rock ledge and the rest of my body flattened like the bellows of an accordion, leaving me on my knees, gasping for breath.

I leaned back and pulled in large gulps of air until I could breathe again. My legs felt like all the muscles had been cut at the knees.

Up above, the faint outline of the two men was visible, bending over, peering down. They'd probably heard me hit the rock, much sooner than if I'd fallen to the valley floor. I didn't know if they could see me, but at least they didn't take the risk of jumping after me.

Even so, I couldn't stay there. By morning, all they would have to do is shoot me from the height of the cliff. Bending my legs beneath me, I crawled along the ledge to the front of another narrow canyon. This one was familiar. It led down to a sheltered archway where Ila and I had spent time gazing at the view of the desert below.

I wanted to stay there, to remember, to grieve, but I had to get far away while the shadows of night protected me. If I died, Ila's sacrifice would have been for nothing.

CHAPTER NINE

After they finished reading the first journal entry, Elery walked with Lucan to his apartment a block over to retrieve the next one. Although similar in layout, Lucan's apartment couldn't have been more different than Chad's. No food, clothing, or papers scattered about. Just a couch, small television, and one end table in the living room. Elery could probably put on her makeup in the reflection coming off the kitchen counters. Minimalist with a touch of germaphobe, except for the walls, where pictures in neat frames were scattered everywhere. Scenes of Lucan and Chad hiking, playing baseball, or skiing. Other frames held pictures of landscapes, dogs, birds, and even a close-up of a red fox's face. If Lucan took these, he had talent.

She walked over to the one spot in the apartment that had a painting instead of a photo. The portrait was an image of a man in his early forties with dark hair, high cheekbones, and amber eyes. The resemblance was uncanny. It had to be Lucan's father. "Did you paint this?"

He gave a short laugh. "No. My mother did. I can take pictures, but I can't create something from nothing like she does. It's of my dad."

"I thought so."

"She painted it about ten years ago." Putting his hands on both sides of the painting, he lifted it off the wall, turned it around, and set it on the carpet. An envelope stuck out of the bottom part of the frame.

Her heart rate jumped up a notch. The next set of journal pages.

Could she handle reading them? The vivid images from the last entry had yet to settle in her mind. Jacob Waltz embracing the lifeless body of his beloved. Murderous Apache chasing him. Jumping off a cliff to save his own life. What happened to him after that? She needed to know.

Lucan grabbed the envelope and rubbed it between his palms. When he glanced up, his eyes were deep pools of uncertainty. "Are you ready?"

It struck her that he might already know what the pages contained. "Have you read these?"

He nodded. "I've read this one and the first one Chad had, but not any of the others. Chad and I alternated the entries we hid so if anyone found one person's pages, it wouldn't lead them anywhere. I didn't read the other ones he gave me to hide because they wouldn't have made much sense out of order." Lucan cleared his throat and turned his back to her.

The magnitude of what he was doing hit her full force. She didn't deserve to see these pages, no matter how badly she wanted to find her brother. She looked down at her feet. "If you've changed your mind about this, it's okay."

"No, it's not that." He shifted on his feet before turning to face her again. "I didn't think about how this would affect me earlier. It's a secret Chad and I kept together. It feels wrong to share it with someone else." Dropping the envelope on the couch, he closed his eyes and pressed his fingertips against them. "But I know Chad would have wanted me to try to find the mine."

Tears seeped from behind his closed eyelids, wetting his lashes. She bit her lip to hold back her own tears. This man had lost so much because of her. He should turn her away. Instead, he held out an olive branch, inviting her into his pain.

A few seconds later, he opened his eyes and wiped away the moisture. He picked up the envelope, sat down and waited for her to sit next to him. With another inscrutable glance directed at her, he said, "Let's read."

She leaned closer and focused on the carefully penned handwriting.

***

September, 1863

I escaped from Ila's brother and the other tribe member, only to wander in the desert mountains without aim. I had little desire to sustain my existence. Ila had saved me, but without her my heart perished. Eventually, I left the Arizona territory to avoid both the Apache men and the memories of her. I traveled to the gold-laden state of California where I panned gold for the thirteen years that followed.

I worked for several different mine owners during that time. The last one was named Harrison Beaty, an honest man who paid a fair percentage of gold to each worker. It was dangerous work because of armed thieves, but they didn't scare me. I had already lost that which I valued most.

After I had been on Beaty's claim for a long time, I had saved enough gold to live on for a year, and I became restless. Prospering from another's claim had left me feeling dependent. I needed my own land. Finding it wasn't something I could do alone.

In all my time on the claim, I had made only one friend—Frederick Morse, a British man with unkempt blond hair and light blue eyes. The very opposite of me.

Even with my savings, I had no hope of changing

my situation until the day Fred returned from a journey to the Arizona territory. His sister's husband had been killed by the Apache, and Fred had gone to help with expenses from the burial. Upon his return, he found me while I was locking up the gold for the week.

We walked down to the river to talk. Fred spoke with compassion regarding his sister's sorrow at losing the love of her heart, though gold was the only love Fred had ever succumbed to. When he told of how the Apache killed the man, I trembled. In my night terrors, I still saw Ila's lifeless face. Even after all those years, her death held me bound in shackles of grief.

Fred must have noted the stricken look on my face because he paused for a time. No one at the claim, except Fred, knew about my history in the mountainous desert and even he couldn't fully understand. He had never lost true love because he had never found it—a situation far worse.

When Fred spoke again, he whispered the secret he'd been waiting to tell me. One of the Apache tribes had fought among themselves. During this struggle, the tribe's new shaman killed a warrior named Roaring Bear, who had been their leader for years.

At first, I didn't understand why he told me this, but then the name opened my memories. *Bear*. The Apache word for bear was "kuruk."

Ila's brother, the man who had murdered her, was dead.

I expected to feel some relief knowing this. I felt numb. No different than I had since she'd died. Kuruk would receive God's judgment, but this justice stirred nothing inside me.

And yet the event did mean something. I would no longer be fettered to a future in California. Just last week, Harrison had asked me to accompany a prospecting expedition east to the Arizona territory. I'd said no, but knowing Kuruk was gone would change my answer.

Thirteen years before, I'd seen a small portion of the amount of gold the Superstition Mountains held. Back then, I'd loved Ila more than the gold. This time gold was all I had.

CHAPTER TEN

Elery tossed and turned all night, tormented by dreams of her brother trapped in a dark cave. His face morphed from the youthful features she recognized to sunken cheeks with protruding bones, then to skeletal proportions with the skin stretched tight over the bones. She woke drenched in sweat, more desperate than ever to find him.

After hurrying through her morning routine, she left the house and walked toward Main Street. A long walk to Lucan's apartment would calm her nerves. She turned her face to the morning sun and let it warm her skin. A beautiful February day with temperatures promised to be in the 70s, not nearly as warm as the last few days. Good news for Garrick while the sun was up, but the swing to 40 degrees tonight would chill him to the bone—if he was out there somewhere.

She'd rather be out searching for him than looking for journal pages, except she didn't know where to look. If only the sheriff would try harder to get another dog tracking team. She kicked a rock off the sidewalk, and it rocketed across the street. No, the sheriff didn't deserve the blame. Garrick shouldn't have been out there on a crazy treasure hunt in the first place. Even so, he'd sent her the message, giving her the responsibility of finding him. Since outside help wasn't coming, her sole hope was to tease out possible leads from the journal. They had to find the rest of the pages Chad had hidden.

At the end of Main, she turned south. Lucan's apartment was three blocks down. Hopefully, he'd be awake and ready to continue their brainstorming session from last night.

"Elery?"

She spun around. Jayna strode across the street toward her. The eager expression on Jayna's lovely face gave her the look of a game show hostess about to hand out a prize. "Hi. Shouldn't you be out mapping?"

"Yes, but I'm glad I caught you." Jayna's expression turned serious. "I heard about your brother." She put a hand on Elery's elbow. "I want to help in any way I can."

"How did *you* hear about it?" Elery snapped.

Jayna removed her hand to push her ponytail over her shoulder. "The sheriff mentioned it."

"I see." Elery lowered her head and worked to tame down her attitude. Jayna hadn't done anything except be friendly. "Thanks. I've got a couple of leads I'm working on, but since you're going to be out in the mountains anyway, keep an eye out for him." She turned on her phone and showed Jayna a recent picture of Garrick.

"I will. I promise. And please let me know if I can do anything else."

Elery met Jayna's gaze. Her eyes were full of compassion. But not hope. Somehow, it made Elery feel like Garrick was already dead. She cleared her throat. "You can do something else. Don't tell anyone about his disappearance."

Jayna tilted her head. "Don't you want people to look for him?"

"I do." Elery blew a curl out of her face. "But I haven't told my dad yet. He's got some stuff he's dealing with. I didn't want to worry him."

"I understand."

Jayna turned to go, but Elery reached out to stop her. "Hey, you don't think this mysterious client of yours might know anything about Garrick, do you?"

"He hasn't mentioned anything to me."

The tone in her voice sounded like she had doubts. Elery stared at her, waiting for her to say more.

"I don't know what it is exactly." Jayna shifted on her feet. "The guy leaves me a little unsettled. It's nothing he's said or done. Just a feeling."

"But it could mean something." A Dutch Hunter might go crazy if they thought someone had encroached on their claim. Maybe this guy had done something to Garrick. "Did you find out any more about Peralta?"

"No. I met him once in the town park, right after I came to see you."

"Did he give you a check with that name on it?"

Jayna shook her head and her ponytail whisked across her shoulders. "We agreed on a fee over the phone before I came to Arizona. When I met him at the park, he paid me in gold, more than the fee. He told me to keep the change."

Elery tapped her foot, her suspicions rising. "Probably an illegal miner, which means Peralta isn't likely his real name."

Jayna's eyes widened. "I don't want to work for somebody like that. How would I find out for sure?"

"You could take a picture of him and show it around town. Someone has got to know him."

"True." Jayna tapped a hand on her hip. "But he did say he doesn't live in Quartz Creek."

"Where does he live?"

"He didn't tell me."

"That will make him harder to track down. I suppose you could ask him to meet you, then follow him. He might lead you to his mine."

Jayna punched her lightly on the arm. "I like the way you think. I'll try that."

Elery smiled, despite the circumstances. Obviously, she'd misjudged Jayna. The woman wasn't pampered or pushy, she had spunk. "Be careful, though. Miners will do anything to protect their claim. Especially the illegal ones."

"I'll watch out. Thanks." Jayna waved and walked back the way she'd come.

Elery continued on to Lucan's apartment. At his door, she knocked lightly. He opened it quickly, his eyes hazy with sleepiness, his sweatpants and T-shirt disheveled, and yet his caramel-brown hair lay in perfect order. "I'm sorry if I woke you."

"No problem. Normally, I'm an early riser, but I didn't sleep much last night."

Was it insomnia brought on by grief? She didn't dare ask.

"Come in. Let's work on the clue again."

She followed him to the couch and sat down. For an hour, they mulled over the cryptic clue Chad had written at the bottom of the first journal entry.

A deep place Jacob Waltz had never gone in his life.

So simple, and yet so hard to figure out. Probably the reason she had dreamed of a dark cave. Her subconscious was trying to work through the riddle. If they couldn't decode it, they'd never find the next journal entry. What could Chad have meant? Certainly not the lost mine, because Jacob had visited it often during his life. Some of the open pit copper mines had been around for a long while. Could Chad have meant one of those? But which one and where in the mine would they look?

Then it hit her. Chad wouldn't hide the pages in some random mine. Not when he had access to *her* mine.

Her mouth dropped open, and she turned to Lucan. His expression mirrored her own. Had they both had the same epiphany? "I think the clue refers to my mine. Where at Hearst Stone do you think Chad would hide something?"

He blinked, and his face went blank. "Nowhere. He wouldn't hide it there."

"Why not?"

Lucan didn't respond right away this time. When he spoke, his voice sounded strained. "Trust me, Hearst Stone is the last place he'd leave it. Other miners might find it. But I know what he meant. I know where to look."

She pulled on her lower lip. "Where?"

He hesitated before letting out a long sigh. "I'll tell you later. Just come back to my apartment after it gets dark."

After dark? This was getting creepy. Lucan didn't seem like the stalker type, but what if he had plans to hurt her because of his brother? Plus, it would waste another whole day when she could be out looking for Garrick. "Why after dark?"

"I'd rather not tell you until then. You'll have to trust me. Meet me here later tonight. Oh, and wear closed-toed shoes."

She expelled a relieved breath. If he wanted to kill her he wouldn't be concerned about her footwear. "Seriously, tell me what we're doing."

His voice held an amused edge to it when he spoke again. "Elery, you don't have to know everything all the time."

"Yes, I do." The words jumped out before she could stop them.

He stood and gestured at the door. "See you tonight."

The more she glared at him, the harder his face became until it was like chiseled granite. He wasn't going to tell her before he was ready. And he seemed to know keeping her in suspense would drive her crazy. She grunted her displeasure as she stood and turned to go. If she pushed him on this, he might stop helping her. He'd gone out of his way to share the journal pages. He deserved a little trust. But he'd better have a good reason for making her wait.

"Good to see you again, Mr. Peralta." Jayna shook his outstretched hand and took a seat next to him on the shaded park bench. The afternoon air had gone still, and she longed for even the driest breeze. She brushed a line of sweat off her forehead and reminded herself again the warmth was better than the snow now blanketing her home in Wisconsin.

"Jayna, please, call me John."

She stared at him under the cover of her sunglasses. A man with average features, dark hair and eyes, and the confidence of a mating bull. When she'd called him to suggest another meeting, he'd readily agreed, saying he meant to call her for the same reason. Could this regular guy have anything to do with Garrick's disappearance? Perhaps Elery was getting a little paranoid, fueled by Jayna's original suspicions. So what if he did have the name of an old mining family?

"Okay, John." Jayna tapped the topographic map he held in his hand. Thankfully, he hadn't asked why she'd wanted to meet him. "Did you come up with another search grid?"

"Perceptive." His mouth curled into a grin as he unfolded the map to a two-foot square. "I have a hunch the mine will be found in an area somewhere around here." He bit the cap off a red sharpie and drew a circle around three peaks on the southern side of the Superstitions. "I want you to map anything you find in this area."

She squinted at the location, suppressing a groan at the amount of territory—almost four square miles. "Isn't that inside the National Forest?"

"Some of it is, some isn't. That's for me to worry about. I'll be sure to establish the claim if the mine is found."

Slipping off her sunglasses, she tilted her head and

gave him a serious look. "Okay, but remember, I'm here to map. I'm a geologist, not a treasure hunter."

A sly grin crept across his face. "If I were you, I'd keep an eye out for treasure. Think of the publicity it would bring to your newly established geological consulting firm if you found the legendary Lost Dutchman Mine." His tone held the innocence of a dove's song, but clearly he was working her.

"Publicity or not, I'll do my job." She slid her sunglasses back on. "Give me three days for an area that large."

He nodded. After pushing off the bench, he leaned down and handed the map to her. "I'll see you in three days. Let's meet at the diner in Superior for lunch."

She watched his retreating form as he made his way to a brown pickup truck. Broad shoulders with a self-assured tilt to them and a tall, muscular build. Not that she was interested. She had a fiancé waiting at home. Besides, something about Peralta seemed unapproachable.

He hopped in and pulled the truck out amid a cloud of dust. She waited two seconds, then rushed to her rented Highlander. She couldn't let him get away.

Following at a distance, she trailed him along the streets of town. He weaved through several neighborhoods before finally turning onto the highway. She settled in behind him at a speed that kept her half a mile back.

Where was he headed? Did he live in another town? Superior, maybe? He'd communicated with her solely by cell phone and e-mail. As far as she knew, he could be living in his truck.

Several miles later, he slowed to a crawl and pulled over to the shoulder. What was he doing? She also slowed her vehicle and came along side of him.

The door of the truck flew open. He jumped out and waved at her. Busted. Now, she had to pull over.

After parking in front of his truck, she got out and

leaned against her vehicle, giving him a questioning look. Did he suspect she'd been following him?

He sauntered over. "Hey, I saw you behind me and thought I'd let you know the road you need is right there." Using one finger, he pointed back the way they had come. "You know, to get to the area we talked about."

His half-smile gave him away. He knew what she'd been doing, and he wasn't going to let her trail him.

Sighing, she opened her vehicle door. "Okay, thanks. Guess I missed it. I'll go check it out."

Her head held high, she swung the Highlander in a U-turn toward the road he'd indicated. She didn't look at him as she passed, but she felt his eyes burning into her. Her attempt at spying had failed. Nothing she could do now, except her job.

***

A swift breeze blew over Garrick's face, the wind racing fast beyond him and through the canyons. A gust blew one of the little lizards right off the rock just out of reach of where he lay trapped. He twisted, reaching for it until he couldn't stand the pain in his knee any longer. So much for his hoped-for meal of raw lizard.

The fine hairs on his arms stood straight up. The storm would be here soon. In the Superstition Mountains, thunderstorms were short-lived, but powerful. As long as lightning didn't strike him, this storm would mean survival. He needed water. He licked his chapped lips. Even with careful rationing, he'd drunk the contents of the water bottle by early last night.

The threat of the storm brought thoughts of Angela. Was she safe somewhere? What had Hellerman done with her? It had been almost three days since they had disappeared from the edge of the cliff. He hadn't heard any gunshots, and those would echo for miles, so he had hope she was alive. But if so, why hadn't anyone come for him yet?

For all he knew, she'd talked Hellerman into searching for the treasure with her instead. The same way she'd worked her charm on him. Who was he kidding? He hadn't needed much convincing. He'd come out here for the treasure, same as her. But was she desperate enough to get the gold that she would leave him to waste away in this crevice?

The first drops of rain began to fall. They stabbed like tiny daggers on Garrick's tender sunburned skin. He shoved his water bottle between two rocks, the open neck ready to catch fresh water. Spreading his jacket out on his chest, he held it like a tarp to capture the rain.

As the drops grew, he leaned his head back and opened his mouth wide, letting the fat drops splatter over his face. Water had never tasted so clean, so fresh, so life-affirming.

His jacket filled up. He folded it in half and poured the water into the bottle, using the bungee cord on the bottom to control the flow. The bottle was almost half full now.

He spread the jacket back on his chest as the deluge continued. Sheets of water poured from the heavens. He gulped down as much as he could until he retched. After vomiting, he wiped his mouth with a shirtsleeve, then rolled back over to drink in more.

The rain continued to pound the mountain. A loud crack exploded in his ears. Lightning?

Or something just as bad. Under the constant assault, the cliff had lost its grip on a large rock, letting the boulder loose to tumble down. It rolled end over end, crunching and breaking the cliff face as it went. Watching for a second, he tried to guess the trajectory, but the angled corners of the boulder kept it rolling in different directions.

He curled into a ball with his back to the cliff, his pinned left leg sticking out. It was all he could do, but depending on where the rock hit, it might not be enough.

The crunching sound filled his ears. He hunkered deeper into his protective huddle.

The impact shook his whole body. Pain knifed through his leg.

He waited for more pain. When none came, he uncurled and looked around. The massive rock had slammed into one of the boulders that had held his leg tight, effectively shattering the original rock. The debris, along with a thick spike from the fallen rock, covered his leg from knee to foot. The tip of his shoe stuck out on the other end. Not only could he still not move the leg, but he couldn't even see it.

He let out a growl and yelled up at the sky. "What's the deal, God? Are you just making sure I can't get out of here? It's not like I was going anywhere before!"

It dawned on him that might be the plan. He might die alone on the side of this mountain with nothing to show for his life except foiled attempts to find a lost mine.

No, he couldn't give in to defeatist thinking. He would get out of here. Someone would come for him. He looked again at the water bottle, it was full. The storm had blown over, and the punishing sun had reappeared, but at least, he'd have enough water to make it through a few more days. He could do this. He *had* to do this. His only job now was to survive.

CHAPTER ELEVEN

Elery turned away from the darkness rushing by the truck window and shot Lucan a glare. "Why exactly are we going to Phoenix?" He had convinced her to get in the vehicle by promising to tell her everything along the way. Up to this point, he'd failed to hold up his end of the bargain. And they were only a few miles away from Phoenix.

"To find the journal pages, of course." He glanced at her and his amber eyes twinkled with excitement. There was an adventurous side to him. Controlled, but still adventurous. Maybe this was a way to reconnect with his brother. It might be fun for her, too, if her own brother's life didn't depend on it. Fear burrowed deep into her stomach, intent on establishing a permanent residence. What if this was a waste of time? Assuming the journal pages would lead them to the mine, Garrick might not be anywhere near it.

Lucan didn't seem to want to share their destination, so she unfolded and refolded her arms to make a point of her frustration, then stared out the window at the suburbs dotting the outskirts of the city. Cookie-cutter homes full of regular people leading ordinary lives. Had she ever felt like that?

From her earliest memories, she'd worked the mine with her dad, tagging along as he inspected equipment, checking progress on veins, and even hammering at the rock. Those were the times she remembered as her happiest, swinging a pick next to him, feeling the dirt coat her skin. But he paid dearly for their mine excursions. Mom would yell for hours, accusing him of trying to turn her daughter into a boy.

He would calmly reply, "My dear, Elery is the first-born. It will be up to her to keep the mine going."

At which point, Mom would scream about how indecent it was for girls to play in mines. Then, she would give him the silent treatment for days. But he never gave in. They had fought about it for an especially long time the day Mom walked out.

No matter how many times her father tried to explain Mom's disappearance to Elery, she couldn't understand why Mom left. But she did know the truth of it—Mom left because of her.

A week later, Garrick had confirmed it, screaming that she had driven Mom away. The force of those words broke something fragile inside her. She had lashed out at Garrick intent on breaking him, too. It was a moment she could never take back. And Garrick had borne the consequences of it ever since.

The suburbs gave way to industrial buildings as the truck turned onto the exit that led to downtown Phoenix. Lucan bypassed several run-down buildings and a corner grocery store. The farther into the city they went, the fewer streetlights lit the way. What were they going to do here at night?

Finally, he pulled over near a set of railroad tracks on a city block that at first seemed empty. It was barely illuminated by a streetlight at the end of the block. A five-foot-tall iron fence surrounded the property. She peered through the window. Several arched iron gates towered over the center of the property like rusty sentinels guarding sparse blocks of granite in uneven rows.

A graveyard.

"What are we doing? Grave robbing or something?"

Lucan didn't answer. Instead, he jumped out of the truck and began rummaging around in the back end.

She got out and met him by the bumper. "Why are we here?"

He pulled two shovels from the truck bed, walked over to the iron fence, and pushed them through the bars. They fell onto the ground with a thud. Then, he grabbed two flashlights, handed one to her and smiled.

She took the flashlight. "We *are* grave robbing?"

"In a manner of speaking." Without turning it on, he circled his flashlight in the air. "Don't you get it?"

What didn't she get? They were standing in front of a cemetery ... a place full of dead people.

Of course. *A deep place Jacob Waltz had never gone in his life.*

His grave. She sucked in a breath of the cool, night air. They really were grave robbing.

She turned on the flashlight and shined it through the iron fence. For such a large space, few graves were marked with headstones. Most of the area lay barren, a mishmash of rock and debris. No wonder Lucan wanted her to wear closed-toed shoes.

In the nearest corner, sat two headstones, one was so low she couldn't read it and the other had a tall marker with the name George Petrash. Who was he? Behind the headstones, two low walls of stones traced man-sized rectangles in the sandy dirt.

She turned to Lucan, who directed her to stand on top of a fire hydrant near the fence. She climbed up with his help for balance.

"Up and over," he said.

Reluctantly, she reached out and climbed onto one of the granite pillars that were spaced every twenty feet apart as stability for the fence. Sitting on top, she swung her legs over. She dropped to the ground on the other side and moved out of the way as Lucan did the same.

He picked up a shovel, then walked over to the low granite headstone in the corner, shining his light on the carved words.

Jacob Waltz
1808-1891

A simple, square chunk of rock marking the final resting place of *the* Dutchman. The man who inspired an entire coven of devoted followers, all willing to die in search of what he'd found. Had Garrick already joined the ranks of dead Dutch Hunters?

Blinking back the morbidly unhelpful thought, she picked up the other shovel. She couldn't give up on Garrick.

Lucan spoke softly behind her. "I'm thinking Waltz is buried where the stones are."

"Who is George Petrash?"

"Research online said he was a friend of Waltz who buried him in their family plot." Lucan approached Waltz's headstone. "Chad wouldn't take the risk of disturbing the body, so that leaves three directions to dig. Left, right, and on the front side of the stone."

She tapped her phone to check the time. It was only 10:30, certainly not late enough for messing with people's graves. "What if we get caught?" She tugged on her lip. "I mean, what kind of sentence would we get for grave robbing?"

"Please stop using the word 'robbing.' We're not robbing. This is a search for my brother's property. Chad just happened to leave his property here, buried with Mr. Waltz." He cleared his throat. "I'm pretty sure it's near Waltz. Not in with him."

She grimaced. Hopefully, they wouldn't see anything gruesome. If Waltz wasn't inside the stone rectangle, he had to be in a coffin or something, right?

"I'll start digging on the right side." Lucan hefted the shovel up and drove it into the dirt. Wow, this was definitely a different side of Mr. Responsible. Was he embracing his brother's reckless ways in honor of Chad?

She pushed her shovel into the dirt on the left side of the grave marker. The dry soil was surprisingly easy to dig through. She turned over shovelful after shovelful, while Lucan did the same. Night had brought cooler temperatures, but with the exertion, sweat soon dripped down her forehead. She swiped at it and kept digging.

They had turned off the flashlights to conserve the batteries, allowing the bright moon to bathe the cemetery in milky light. Although grave robbing hadn't made it onto her bucket list, she'd definitely never forget this experience.

"Five feet down." Lucan had dug faster than her. "Nothing here." He placed both hands on the ground, pushed himself up and climbed out of the deep hole. "I'm going to stop here and fill it back in. I don't think he would have buried it deeper."

She had gotten only half that far down, but also found nothing. What if Lucan was wrong? What if the pages weren't here? Then, they'd wasted a whole day.

He went to work replacing the dirt, while she continued to dig. She thrust her shovel in for another scoop and flipped the dirt behind her, piling it in a haphazard mound. Turning back, she jammed the shovel into the ground.

Thwack.

She'd hit something. A dull smack, not metallic, more like plastic.

Lucan walked to her side of the gravestone and knelt beside her, peering over her shoulder. His breath brushed across her neck, at once cooling her sweat and firing up her insides. She shifted away and slipped down into the four-foot-deep hole. Planting her feet on opposite sides of the mysterious object, she scraped dirt off the top, moving her shovel along the sides to clear out space.

She pulled on the sides of the square shape. It wouldn't budge. She scraped around it some more, then tried again. No luck.

"Here, let me." Lucan leaned down and offered her a hand to help her out of the hole.

As her skin touched his, the rush of electricity surprised her. She tried to pull away, but he reached down with his free arm and circled her waist, lifting her up and out until she stood on firm ground, her body pressed against his. Her heart pounded at triple time. He kept her close for a few seconds, then relaxed his grip and let her slip away. Had he held her near on purpose? He could have helped her get out with just one hand.

Lucan dropped to his knees and lowered himself into the hole. Dirt from the sides rained down on him. He bent and grabbed at the object between his legs. After a few struggling attempts, he straightened, holding a blue plastic lunch box in his hands. She took it and placed it on the ground. Was the journal in there?

She offered him a hand to get out, but he waved her away. His head stuck above the hole by more than a foot. Placing two hands on the ground, he jumped and pushed himself up. The slippery sides stole all his traction. She stifled a laugh as he slid back down.

"Okay, maybe I could use a little help."

She grabbed his hand, dug her boots into the dirt, and pulled with all her might. Once his chest got above the hole, he scooted like an inchworm to wriggle out. When his knees cleared it, he collapsed on the ground beside her.

"What did ..." His breath came in panting gasps. "I tell ... you?"

"You called it." She smiled and shook her head. How did this guy make getting dirty in a graveyard fun?

"Hopefully, it helps."

The sudden wistfulness in his voice made her look at

him. He stared back at her. Clumps of dirt smeared his hair and face. His eyes were too shadowed to give a clue to his mood. Was he thinking about his brother? Did he feel like only half a person without him?

Suddenly, Lucan sat up and grabbed the box, resting it on his lap. She reached over, unfastened the clasp and raised the lid. A set of yellow pages sat in the bottom, protected by a clear plastic zipper bag. He picked the package up with both hands. After ripping open the plastic seal, he flipped on the flashlight and nudged her arm. "Ready to read?"

She nodded and peered at the pages highlighted by the yellow circle of light.

***

February, 1865

A few months after Fred told me of Kuruk's death, the two of us left with the expedition team to search for gold in the Bradshaw Mountains in the Arizona territory. We spent two years staking claims, and losing claims, and trying to avoid the Apache. When attacks from the Apache became unbearable and the gold became scarce, we decided to return to the Superstition Mountains to search for the gold I knew was there.

At the small settlement next to the Salt River in the Arizona territory, we took lodging at a boarding house. The town had grown much since I'd last been there. People crowded the streets, and stores covered many streets in the city. I'd longed to return here, but I hadn't guessed the effect it would have on me.

Every house, every alley, every shop reminded me of my time with Ila. Not that she'd ever been here, but in my countless imaginings I'd convinced her to leave the tribe and settle here with me, a place where I could protect her. In that state of regret, my imaginary memories were just as painful as the real ones.

On our second day in the settlement, I led my burro over to the boarding house to tie the animal to a post, when I heard someone call my name in a German accent. I turned back to face the man. It was Jacob Weiser, my childhood friend from Germany. Besides having the same first name, Weiser and I had almost the same subdued personality. In the thirty years before I left Germany, the two of us had done everything together, from searching for frogs to searching for jobs. We'd enjoyed being around each other more than most siblings. The last time I'd seen him was fifteen years ago, before I'd decided to make my fortune across the ocean.

Weiser hadn't changed much. With skin smoother than my own sun-wrinkled cheeks and a close-cut beard, Weiser appeared younger than me by far. At first I wondered at his arrival, then I realized my greatest humiliation. Fifteen years ago, I had sent Weiser a letter asking him to travel to America. No reply had come before I'd fled to California. During my time there, I had sent him a letter telling him of my move, but had never received a reply. I should have kept writing.

Fortunately, Weiser had only been in the Arizona territory for two weeks. It had taken him all those years to decide to come and to earn the money for passage on a steamship. During that time, he had written letters to me that went unanswered, but he decided to come anyway. I apologized to him and told him I hadn't thought much about the old country, but when I did, I always imagined him as happy and safe in Germany.

He asked me if I believed it was unsafe here. After much thought, I replied that here in town it was safe, but not in the desert. He mistakenly thought I meant the desert animals, like rattlesnakes and coyote. No, I told him, the most dangerous animal in the desert is men.

With that warning, I led him inside to meet Fred. The three of us sat in the parlor together for hours as Weiser recounted stories of his sea voyage. I laughed at the tale of Weiser almost falling overboard during strong winds while trying to save a lady's parasol from the sea.

When Weiser left to return for dinner at the boarding house where he was staying, I spoke to Fred about bringing Weiser along on the expedition. Fred resisted, saying we'd already purchased the supplies. But I would not be dissuaded.

I could not leave Weiser behind when I'd asked him to come to America. Eventually, Fred agreed because he had no choice. He had always believed I could find the mine and didn't want to be left behind. After a day spent purchasing more supplies, we led Weiser into the desert. As we walked, we taught him all we knew about searching for gold.

It wouldn't be long before our search yielded results. If only I would have known then the evil that gold would reveal in the heart of one of my friends.

CHAPTER TWELVE

The sound of deep laughter drifted up from the floor below as Elery got ready for church. Days had passed since she'd heard her father's carefree laugh. Oh, how she'd missed it. Since the mine collapse more than a week ago, he had kept busy at church or with Candace. Although he hadn't asked her about finances, he probably assumed the collapse had hurt the mine. In the last few days, he'd taken to sporadically fasting, a practice that wreaked havoc on his already distressed immune system. Not that he'd admit it to anyone except her, out of fear people at church might find out about his cancer.

Since the mine issues already had him not eating, she still didn't want to tell him about Garrick's disappearance. Hopefully, they'd find him soon, and she wouldn't have to tell her father at all, but every day that passed made it seem less likely. For now, she'd keep up appearances and go to church. Then, she'd meet Lucan afterward to get his next set of journal pages.

She ran a pick through her curls and rushed down the grand staircase. It led her to the front door. She turned right and entered the kitchen.

Her father sat at the table talking to Ron. Engrossed in conversation, they didn't notice her. What were they talking about? Why was Ron here?

She stepped farther into the kitchen, and Ron glanced up, amusement lightening his dark eyes. His hair looked as if he'd styled it, and the bridge of his nose stood out red against his pale skin. Had he gotten too much sun recently? "Hi, Elery. You don't mind if I accompany you both to church, do you? Morty's been asking me for a while, and it finally worked out this weekend." He leaned back in the chair with a grin, as if he guessed how uncomfortable it would make her to mix work with church.

She gave her dad a curious look. He'd never mentioned inviting Ron. And if Ron were so interested in going to church, why hadn't he attended Chad's funeral? She'd have to find a time to ask him. "It's fine with me."

"Great. Then, maybe I could talk to you about some work-related things afterward."

Guilt replaced her irritation. She'd been so focused on finding Garrick she'd let Ron handle almost everything at the mine. Not exactly fair. She nodded and plastered on a smile. Did Ron actually want to go to church or was this his way of cornering her about work?

Her fake smile broke into a yawn, which she covered with her hand.

"Long night?" Ron asked.

"Just didn't sleep much." If he only knew.

She stifled another yawn as they went out to the garage. She drove her dad's car for the short distance to church. He and Ron chatted about baseball, a topic of no interest to her. On the walk in, she let them walk ahead, scrutinizing her father's gait. Since his skin cancer diagnosis a year ago, he'd tried to exercise more to bolster his immune system, and yet his muscle tone hadn't improved. He still walked slow and unsure. But maybe that was the fasting.

They entered the double front doors and joined the usual receiving line where the pastor greeted all the members.

"How are you, Mort?" The pastor's voice sounded artificially gruff, like he'd asked the question too many times this morning.

"Fine, thanks for asking, Pastor Arroyo." He extended his hand and patted Ron's back. "I'd like you to meet a friend and neighbor, Ron Gremming. He works at the mine."

The neighbor part was kind of a stretch. Ron lived in a town twenty minutes away, but her father probably didn't want Ron to feel like a mere employee. Pastor Arroyo reached out and grabbed Ron's hand in both of his. A slight tremor went through Ron's hand. Maybe the pastor made him uncomfortable. She couldn't blame him. Pastor Arroyo had made her squirm on occasion.

"Nice to meet you, Ron. How are you today?"

Ron gave a charming smile, masking any discomfort. "Happy to be alive, pastor. Thanks for asking."

Pastor Arroyo nodded and moved to the next person in line. Elery. He reached for her. "How are you, my dear?"

Awful. Exhausted from grave robbing. Sick with worry about Garrick. She let him take her hand. "I'm hanging in there."

"Oh, my. Sounds like you could use some extra prayer." He patted her hand gently. "I know about Garrick. Come up during the altar call at the end of the service so I can pray for your situation."

Her situation? How had he found out? She opened her mouth to tell him that wasn't necessary, but he'd already moved on to the person behind her. Thankfully, her father had been on his way down the aisle and out of earshot. How long would she be able to keep this from him?

Walking past Ron, she followed her father to a pew a few rows back from the pulpit. As she sat, she felt Ron's eyes studying her. Was he having trouble keeping the secret about Garrick? Or did he have something else he wanted to talk about?

She shifted in her seat to avoid his gaze and focused

on Pastor Arroyo, who strode to the pulpit and flipped on his microphone. "Good morning, congregation." He smiled and his white teeth beamed in contrast with his dark complexion. "I'm so glad to see everyone bright-eyed and feeling great this morning. As well we should. Every day is a great day with Jesus. Amen?"

The crowd gave a hearty "Amen." Elery stayed silent, unable to conjure any gratitude.

The pastor ran a hand over his smooth hair. "I want us to think about sin today." He gave an insincere chuckle. "No, I don't want you to think about how to sin, but instead on how sinning affects your life."

He pulled out a clicker. With the press of a button, the slide projector turned on and a picture of Adam and Eve appeared on the front screen. "Because of sin, life is hard. The Bible makes it clear that rebellion against God literally broke everything in the Garden. Sin changed the world and continues to change the world. Nothing works the way God intended it to." Another click and a picture of flooded New Orleans after Hurricane Katrina filled the screen. "Because of sin, we have natural disasters and deformities in nature. Romans 8:22 says, 'We know that all creation is still groaning and is in pain.'"

Click. The slide changed to a picture of a bald person with sunken cheeks, obviously a cancer patient. She shifted in the pew.

"Because of sin, we have death. Ecclesiastes 8:8 tells us, 'No man has power over the wind to contain it; so no one has power over the day of his death.' But God doesn't leave us there, does He?"

On the screen appeared a movie version of Jesus with His hands on a leper. Puss oozed from red sores on the man's face. "Jesus brings healing." Pastor Arroyo clicked and the man's face cleared like magic. "God heals faithful people, but you must believe that He is capable of healing."

Elery glanced over at her dad. He sat stone-faced staring at the pastor. No one here knew of his skin cancer. Pastor Arroyo liked to gossip more than the gray-haired ladies of the church—all in the name of asking for prayer requests, of course. If her father had told him, the whole town would have known, and he wanted to keep it private. He wouldn't be able to stand the pitying looks, the subtle implications that maybe he'd done something wrong, that God was punishing him for something.

Even so, her father insisted they stay at Christ's Body Church. The congregation had supported him through the tough time of her mother abandoning them, and he felt like he owed them.

Swiveling her head, she glanced around at the church members in the pews. How many secrets did these people hold? Her own secrets felt like raw spots of skin, bringing searing pain every time her thoughts touched them.

Movement from the front had her turning back to focus on the pastor again. He gestured with his arms as he paced.

"If you haven't experienced healing in your life, then your sins are getting in the way." Pastor Arroyo's voice rose an octave. "Isaiah 59:2 says, because of your sins, God has turned away and will not listen anymore."

Elery felt condemnation prick her heart. God had plenty of reason to turn away from her and not answer her prayers for her father or Garrick. But her father had never done anything wrong. *Please, Lord, have mercy on him and heal him.*

"The Bible can be trusted, but our evil hearts cannot. If your life is difficult right now, your sin is to blame." Pastor Arroyo glanced over in her direction. Was that a hint of accusation in his eyes? About the mine accident? Or about Garrick?

She avoided his gaze by bowing her head. The pastor

continued his sermon, but she had stopped listening. Her emotions crinkled her brain into a jumble of randomly firing neurons. She focused on her breath, bringing it in slow and letting it out until the fog in her mind started to clear.

Many minutes later, her attention snapped back to Pastor Arroyo as he invited those who needed prayer to come to the front. She glanced around in panic. No way would she go up there, but if she didn't the pastor would corner her before she could leave, and he might say something about Garrick where her dad could hear. She bent her head, pretending not to have heard.

Soon after, Pastor Arroyo dismissed the congregation. She kept her eyes away from the podium. Ron stared at her for a minute before he leaned over and whispered. "I'll keep the pastor busy while you make your escape. Wait for me at the café so we can talk."

She gave him a grateful smile and nodded. Whatever Ron wanted to talk about had to be better than facing Pastor Arroyo.

***

The café buzzed with the after-church crowd. Elery selected a corner booth big enough for the three of them and settled in to wait.

A few minutes later, Ron came strutting in. He spotted her immediately and headed for the booth.

"That didn't take long," she said.

He sat across from her and grinned. "I know how to make a quick getaway when necessary."

"Where's Dad?"

"Morty decided to stay and chat with a few of his friends. He said he wasn't eating lunch today anyway."

She shook her head. "Yeah, the fasting thing." Her dad could fast until his skin stuck to his bones, and it wouldn't change anything. From what she could see, God preferred to let people muddle around in confusion rather than answer prayer. Then again, it was probably only her prayers He left unanswered.

The waitress came by, and they ordered sandwiches. As she left, Ron scooted closer in the booth. "You've been spending a lot of time with Chad's brother. Something going on between you two?"

How did he even know that? Most of the times they'd met, she hadn't told anyone, but in this small town someone was always watching.

"No, he's just helping me."

Ron twisted his lips. "How is he doing that? I thought his dog was still recovering."

Although Ron's attitude appeared casual, all the questions made him seem overly interested in the time she spent with Lucan. Did Ron want to date her and somehow she'd missed it? If so, she'd have to convince him to keep their relationship professional. He was an attractive guy, but she wouldn't date an employee. "We're going on the theory that if we find the mine, we'll find Garrick."

Ron leaned back and put his hands behind his head, smirking at her. "The Dutchman's Mine? Come on, Elery. You don't really think it's out there, do you?"

She'd said too much. "Not exactly. But Garrick does. So, we're following up some leads, hoping we're on the same trail as Garrick." No need to mention the crazy things she and Lucan had been doing.

"Like what?"

"Nothing that's panned out yet." She brushed a mass of curls behind her ear. Time to change the subject. "Did you want to talk to me about the mine?"

"Yeah. There's no easy way to say this." Ron leaned forward to rest his elbows against the table. "The Mine Safety and Health Administration report came back."

Her blood pressure spiked. They'd completed the investigation in a week? Since when did the government work that fast? "What does it say?"

His Adam's apple bobbed up and down. "It defines the cause of the cave-in as a faulty ceiling stabilizer, model number CA12004, approximately twenty-two years old."

She dropped her forehead to the table. It was truly her fault. If she would have replaced the stabilizer, Chad would still be alive. She couldn't make up for that. Chad was gone because of her and as soon as Lucan found out, he'd never forgive her. She bit her lip, the pastor's words emerging all too quickly. Her sin caused God to turn away. God might never forgive her either.

CHAPTER THIRTEEN

Elery swung open the front door of the boarding kennel and walked past the empty reception desk. Lucan must have had a key to unlock it because the kennel wasn't open for business on Sunday. Why did Lucan want to meet here? Whatever his motives, this would be a private place to tell him about the Mine Safety inspector's report. Her stomach rolled over at the idea.

The sound of barking animals echoed from the rear of the building. On second thought, maybe she'd wait for a quieter place. Elery yelled over the noise, "Lucan?"

"Back here."

She navigated around the desk, then passed through a doorway to the kennels in the back. Several crates sat along a narrow corridor, half of them filled with animals begging for attention. She found him in a separate brick-walled room. The sound of the barking dogs in the other room still echoed in here, but it was much quieter. Lucan crouched in front of a crate with the name "Sienna" affixed to it on a plastic card. "Isn't she still at the vet hospital?"

"She is." He raised the metal pan from the bottom of the crate to reveal a sealed plastic bag. "My next set of journal pages." He tugged them free and stood. "The fourth set. We split it so I had the even, Chad had the odd." A sad smile crossed his face. "He used to say it was fitting because he was the odd one."

She didn't know what to say. Chad was a little odd, but probably only because of his obsession with gold mining. Then again, maybe Lucan had a bit of an obsession himself—a four-legged one. "You hid the pages under your dog?"

He wrinkled his forehead. "Hey, I trust everybody who works here. And no one would think of looking there. Plus, Sienna tends to be protective of her crate when she's here."

"All good points."

"Before we read these, let's work on the clue for the fifth set, so we know where we have to go next."

"Okay. Read the clue again." The words had tumbled around in her mind all day, but it wouldn't hurt to make sure she had them right.

He handed the new plastic bundle to her, then grabbed Chad's other pages from the counter. "When you are bored, you reach for this more. Not the place of work, but the residence door."

Elery rolled her eyes. "That's it?"

Lucan put an arm around her shoulder. "Have patience. Let's think about this."

Her skin tingled under his touch. *Whoa.* She needed to keep her emotions contained.

As if he heard her thoughts, he dropped his arm and began to pace. "My brother liked to play word games with me. Well, he liked to play all kinds of games, actually."

She took several deep breaths to slow her racing heart. "People reach for games when they're bored. Could that be it?"

"Maybe board games?" He ruffled his hair, but it flipped back down into place "No, that doesn't sound right."

"Okay. Other stuff people do when bored. A newspaper? TV?"

Lucan stopped pacing and met her gaze. "He must have meant me specifically. When I'm bored, I reach for sweets."

She opened her mouth in a wide smile. "Julia Thomas Schaffer ran a bakery."

"And I love bakeries. It fits. But the clue says not her place of work. We're looking for her home. Do you know where she lived?"

Elery tapped her chin. "In downtown Phoenix. A few years ago, Garrick convinced me to look at an old map from the late 1800s. I remember we had a tough time trying to figure out what happened to Mohave Street."

"Mohave?"

"Dutchman experts and authors have long believed Julia's house was located on the corner of Jackson and Mohave Streets. Jackson is a pretty major street still, but modern-day Mohave runs parallel to it. They never cross. The only modern cross streets have numbers instead of names. Then, we found a map displaying the original street names from 1885. Sure enough, Mohave Street used to cross Jackson. It was two roads over from Central Avenue."

"Two streets over." Lucan grabbed her arm. This time the tingling spread from there down to her stomach. "You mean Mohave is Second Avenue?"

She lifted her arm to brush her hair over her shoulders, forcing him to let go. "Yep. Once we figured that out, Garrick visited the current location, but he must not have found anything interesting there because he never mentioned it to me again."

Lucan took off out of the room. "Let's look it up."

She followed him to the front desk, the thrill of discovery burning through her, or was that the lingering effects of his touch? With everything happening at once, all of her emotions ran at a new height. Her adrenaline had peaked three days ago with Garrick's email and never come down.

She leaned against the desk as he sat down in the secretary's chair. "Are you sure this is okay?" she asked.

He waved her off. "Sure. Whenever I'm here, they let me use the computers."

After pulling up a search window, he typed in "2nd Ave and Jackson, Phoenix, AZ." A few business pages came up. As he scrolled through them, she sneaked glances at his profile. The curve of his mouth brought out a tiny dimple in his cheek. Why hadn't she noticed it before? Probably because most of the time they'd spent together had been very serious. From the half-smile now on his face, he was enjoying the thrill of the chase, as well.

"A business consulting firm, lawyer's office, a warehouse." He flipped the screen up to the legal listing and clicked on it. "Odd, though. This morning I went over to Chad's apartment to go through some papers and I found a lawyer's card. I don't know if this is the same one or not, but he never mentioned visiting a lawyer. I'll check the card when I get home." He pointed at the screen. "You up for another trip to Phoenix?"

"I suppose. Especially if it doesn't involve digging in a graveyard." She turned her eyes to the ground as disappointment swamped her. Since these were all businesses, they wouldn't get any answers until tomorrow, which meant another day of not knowing what happened to her brother.

Lucan took the plastic-covered papers from her hand and started unwrapping them. "I guess we might as well read these now."

She ran her hands through her loose curls, then leaned against the desk to peer over his shoulder. The journal still seemed like her best shot at finding where Garrick was headed, but it was taking too long. He'd gone out into the mountains almost a week ago. How much longer could he survive?

***

March, 1865

After a week of slow travel, a result of Weiser not being accustomed to the difficult terrain, we finally reached the entrance to the cavern where I had met with Ila so many years ago. Fred and Weiser followed me inside, without asking any questions. Their complete faith gave me courage for the difficult task. I would find the gold and use my portion of it to honor Ila somehow.

I planned to help people in need just as she did when she found me on that unfavorable prospecting journey. That day, I had made the severest of errors born out of exhaustion. In my zeal for gold, I became tired and careless. An errant step on a slab of rock caused it to flip over bringing with it an angry rattlesnake. The animal bit my knee.

The flesh swelled instantly. I limped down the mountain as best I could, finally collapsing near a creek where I intended to wash off the wound. After that, I remember nothing more until I awoke to her lovely face.

She assisted me in climbing to the cavern and nursed me for weeks. I slept through the hot days, but at night we would talk late into the evening, covering topics from food to lizards to church.

Ila had lived alone in that cavern for seven years with no one to talk to. My arrival had brought her companionship, but later it also brought her death.

At the cavern entrance, I squeezed through into the main room. The empty sound of my footsteps echoed the barrenness of my heart. This was the last place I'd seen her alive.

In the center of the floor, a dark brown area caused my breath to quicken. After so many years, I hadn't expected to see the remnant of her blood. Because of the isolated nature of the cavern, the rock itself had guarded the memory of her life. I dropped to my knees and traced the outline of the stain.

Fred and Weiser entered behind me. After a minute of exploring, Fred approached me. He'd searched, but found nothing left in the cavern. I told him to check in the far end where the tunnel turned abruptly.

As he continued the search, I stood and leaned against the nearest wall, needing distance between me and the bloodstains. The dream of Ila had never died. No matter how many times I tried to accept it, my heart couldn't—or wouldn't—believe she was gone.

Fred returned with a piece of cloudy quartz, its rough surface glassy like spilled milk. Buried within the quartz, a tiny fleck gave off a yellow glow.

Gold.

Fred was excited. Weiser looked surprised. But much more gold had been here before. Fred asked me where the Apache might have taken it.

I shook my head. Where they had taken it wasn't our goal. This area had merely been a holding place. We needed to find the source. Ila had told me about a mine hidden nearby. Her tribe called it the "Riches of the Thunder Spirit."

We left the cavern the same way we had come in. Fred and Weiser followed me down to the flat mesa on the west side of the mountain. Here, the tall man and Kuruk had laid Ila's body as a lure for me. But this rock, weathered as it was, held no trace of her blood. Had her killers cared enough to bury her? If so, I'd probably never find her grave. This was the closest to her resting place that I was likely to find.

I shrugged off my pack and pulled out an iron stake. Kneeling down, I hovered over the place where her heart would have rested against the warm basalt. I wish I knew whether it had drummed its last beat here or if it had already given up by the time they laid her down.

As Fred and Weiser looked on, I dug the stake in, chipping away at the dark gray rock and carving the rough shape of a heart. My two friends seemed to understand I needed to accomplish this myself.

The afternoon sun was hot. Sweat dripped from my brow while I worked. When the outline reached the thickness of an iron tack, I rested, but I wasn't done. I pressed into the rock again, this time working in the middle. I scraped and scratched until the letter "I" cut as deep at the heart outline.

When I finished, Weiser brought me a canteen for a drink. I swallowed and examined the work. Ila's grave marker. Certainly not noble enough for her, but I had nothing else to give.

By this time, the sun was low in the sky. We needed to think about shelter for the night. Sleeping out in the open brought the possibility of curious coyotes, unless we set a fire, which then brought the risk of Apache seeing the camp. We weren't far from the cavern, but I didn't have the resolve to go back there again. I searched the surrounding terrain for a suitable shelter.

High up on the next mountain, across a shallow ravine, I saw a small cave. The slope looked moderate. It offered a good vantage point to plan our search of the area, and it was far enough away from the cavern that I could focus on the task at hand. My partners were out here to find gold, not help me make peace with the past.

We decided to sleep in the cave for the night, so I led the way across the ravine. As we started up the slope, the solid rock became more friable the higher we climbed. Halfway up the mountain, what had seemed like a gentle slope from a distance turned into a steep incline. I kept up a steady pace for we were chasing the sun as it slid toward the horizon.

At one moment on the way up, Fred yelled the word Apache.

I spun around, already pulling my gun from my pack. Fred laughed and pointed at a large rock protruding from the mountain and hanging over the desert. The basalt crags stuck out in the shape of a warrior's face: the sloped forehead and nose, small chin, and even the characteristic feather over the ear.

Ignoring him, I returned my pistol to my pack and continued up the hill. As I glanced again at the cave, still quite a distance away, a sheer cliff wall came into view. It wasn't large for these mountains, maybe ten yards or so, but unclimbable without a way to anchor a rope from the top.

When I stopped, Fred came up beside me. He suggested we reach the cave by climbing to the top on the west side and coming down to it. I agreed, and we kept climbing, setting a slower pace for Weiser, who was breathing in loud gasps.

We climbed for an hour, pausing several times to let Weiser rest. Along the way, Weiser asked where we would stake a claim if we found gold. I laughed, then quickly explained. Staking a claim would let everyone in town know we'd found something—an invitation for thieves. Fred and I had already lost one claim to theft in the Bradshaw Mountains. We had no plans to repeat our mistake. Besides, no one in this area enforced claim ownership. Secrecy was our best option.

Near the top of the mountain, I stopped to marvel at the landscape. Four peaks rose up to the north like sentinels guarding a hidden treasure. To the northwest, in the distance, the peak known as Weaver's Needle stretched toward heaven. Along the west, the old Military Trail meandered through the area as if a child had drawn in brown paint across a masterful painting.

Similarly affected, Weiser declared his intention to live in the mountains forever. His eyes were wide with love, and I feared for him. The desert mountains would make a difficult paramour. He suggested we sleep right there for the night, not knowing how cold it would get when the sun fully set.

He accepted sound reasoning, and we shifted our course downslope toward the cave. Somehow the way down proved more difficult than going up. My legs, more than fifty years old, wanted to give out with each step.

A short time later, we found the way down almost completely blocked by a huge boulder the size of a wagon cart. A foot-wide rock ledge lay between the boulder and the cliff wall drop-off. We needed to go around the rock, then along the ledge before we could descend farther. Weiser seemed unsure, but Fred was eager for the challenge—one of qualities I liked most about him.

The slope steepened the closer we came to the massive rock. Near the base of it, I lost my footing and fell with hands spread against the rough exterior. When I looked down between my fingers, shiny crystals of mica shone. Pink feldspar gave the rest of it a rosy hue. This boulder wasn't basalt like the rock under our feet. It was made of granite.

Such a dramatic change in rock composition caused my heart to thump harder, but I tried to stay calm. A bit of granite did not mean gold was near.

Hugging the large sphere, I slid my feet along the narrow space between the boulder and the ledge. Weiser followed my example, while Fred put his back to the boulder, facing away as he went.

As I let go of the boulder and reached for the rock wall behind, my hand slipped, propelling me forward. I stumbled along the narrow ledge, too close to the edge. To compensate, I leaned away from the edge and grabbed for the rock. My hand scraped against the wall, then fell into empty space.

My body dropped into darkness. I landed hard on my back. Sharp rocks cut through my thin shirt.

I knew I hadn't fallen into the cave we had seen, since we hadn't gone down far enough. This was something else. It resembled a shaft dug by men. The opening was barely big enough for a small person. Had I not been hunched over, scrambling away from the ledge, I might never have discovered it.

After reassuring Weiser and Fred that I wasn't injured, I asked them to bring me a lantern. I began to explore, moving forward slowly, letting the darkness surround me except for the lantern's weak bubble of light. The rock walls were the usual dark gray basalt found in this area. Both the floor and the walls had evidence of pick work, long gouges as if the rock had been beaten with an iron whip.

As I walked, I searched for hidden dangers—side shafts, traps or sleeping rattlesnakes. At first, Fred had wanted to come in with me, but at the mention of the possible hazards he agreed to let me go alone. Fred was a man of adventure, but not one to volunteer for danger.

After the first few feet, the shaft narrowed. I crouched to get through, scraping my scalp along the roof. When the walls opened up, I was in a large chamber, approximately ten yards high and twenty yards in diameter. A weak column of light came through a small skylight in the roof, man-made or natural, it was impossible to know.

On the ceiling, in the dim light, a white stripe stood out against the dark basalt. Quartz.

It split the room in a narrow swath like one of the veins on the back of my hand. Often gold could be found clinging to quartz in veins just like this. But I couldn't reach the vein from here.

I circled the room. On the far side, another tunnel stretched deeper into the mountain. I stepped inside and checked the ceiling. No quartz vein.

After walking a short distance more, I came upon a

side tunnel. I explored it for only ten feet before having to turn back because it ended.

I returned to the main tunnel and continued on. Gradually, a small area of white appeared on the ceiling. The white strip grew as I walked until a thick ribbon of milky quartz stretched out overhead.

Reaching up to touch it, I savored the smooth, waxy feel. As I moved my calloused fingers along the vein, I detected several places where they hitched—rough spots in the quartz.

Lifting the lantern, I examined the rock. Light bounced off most of the quartz in conchoidal waves like broken glass, but in many areas the light dulled. I touched one such area and a small part of the rock came off in my hand. The thick quartz fragment contained a tiny yellow spot.

It was too dark in the tunnel for me to see what it was.

I hurried back, rushing through the cavernous room, clasping the sample in my fist. As I came out into the sunlight, I dropped to my knees and leaned over, peering at the rock. I had to make sure before I gave Fred and Weiser hope.

The light of the setting sun illuminated several dull yellow flakes buried in the quartz. In my hand, I held rich gold ore.

I smiled and handed the sample up to Fred, who let out a loud yell. With a thankful heart, I turned my gaze to the heavens. By God's providence, I'd found the richest gold mine in the Superstition Mountains.

CHAPTER FOURTEEN

After leaving the boarding kennels, Elery trudged up the concrete steps to Angela's apartment. This was probably a wasted trip, like the last three times she'd come and knocked on the door, only to be met by silence. But there wasn't any need for her to go to Garrick's apartment. His roommate insisted Garrick hadn't been there in a week and promised to call if he showed up. Since, they couldn't find more of the journal pages until tomorrow, she had nothing better to do than try to find Angela. Again.

Tomorrow morning, she and Lucan would visit the lawyer from the card Lucan found in Chad's apartment. It seemed an eternity to wait. Part of her was tempted to head out immediately to search for the mine, but the journal page didn't give enough details on the location. Most of the clues—the Indian's face, Weaver's Needle to the northwest, the four peaks—were all known from Dutchman lore. She had nothing new to go on.

At Angela's apartment door, Elery knocked several times. No answer.

She knocked harder, causing the door to shudder. A few seconds later, it swung open.

"What in the world?" Angela's brow was drawn into a scowl, until she saw Elery. Then, her eyes went wide, her tanned face went pale. "I wasn't expecting you."

"Obviously." Elery pushed past her and into the apartment, hope soaring in her chest. If Angela was home, could Garrick be here, too?

"Please, come in." Angela's sarcastic tone gave Elery pause.

She had barged into the apartment, but as far as she was concerned Angela had gotten Garrick involved in her pointless search, which made her responsible. Elery scanned the small living room. No one else here. Nothing out of place, just a beat up backpack lying on the floor beside the couch. She faced Angela, taking in the dark circles under Angela's eyes, the sunburn on her nose. "Where's Garrick?"

Angela let the door close until the latch rested against the frame, as if she expected to open it again any second to usher Elery out. "He's not here."

Elery stared at her. If Angela was acting, she had movie-star talent. "He sent me an e-mail saying he was with you."

"He was." Angela stared down at her bare feet. "We got into a fight. It was stupid, really. I said he only wanted to be with me because I could help him find the gold. He said he'd keep looking for the gold with or without me."

That sounded like Garrick. Nothing would keep him from finding the treasure.

"You might not believe this," Angela roped her light hair behind one ear. "But I care about Garrick. I thought he was into me, too. Turns out, he only wants the gold, so he went on without me and told me to go home."

Elery shook her head. That *didn't* sound like Garrick. "No way. He wouldn't have left you in the mountains alone." And from what Elery had seen, Angela wasn't the kind of girl who could have gotten out by herself.

Angela glanced up at the ceiling for a moment. When she looked back, moisture glistened in her eyes making them bright blue. "He didn't leave me. I left him. It took days to hike out by myself and catch a ride. I got back only an hour ago."

Had it happened like she said? Other than the dark

circles and sunburn, Angela didn't look any the worse for wear. And yet, the time line didn't add up. It left several days when Garrick could have called after he knew his distress email had been sent. Then again, maybe he'd been out of cell phone range.

As Elery's emotions waffled between confusion and anger, the cell phone chimed in her pocket. She slipped it out and glanced at the screen. A call from her father. She'd have to call him back.

Angela leaned forward and grabbed Elery's other hand. "You have to believe me. The last time I saw your brother he was alive."

What an odd thing to say. Elery hadn't questioned whether Garrick was alive. And calling him "your brother" seemed strange also. As if not using the name Garrick helped Angela distance herself. She knew something. And yet, her eyes held a glint of truth. Elery pulled her hand away. "Where is he?"

Angela focused her eyes down again. "I don't know. He said he'd go it alone."

Garrick had gone out there alone plenty of times, but he'd never sent her a note telling her to look for him. Elery stared at Angela, trying to get Angela to meet her gaze. Finally, Angela gave in. Her eyes were tinged in desperation. "I'm sorry he's not home yet."

Based on her body language, that was also a nugget of truth. But what about the rest of it? Elery didn't trust Angela, so could she believe this story?

Maybe if she could get Angela talking, something would slip out. "Do you know anything about a heart Jacob Waltz might have etched in the mountains?"

Angela's face went slack, but her eyes lit up. "No. It's not on my map. Who told you about it?"

Elery had no intention of giving out that information. "A friend."

"I don't get it." Angela put a fist on her hip. "Are you looking for the mine now, too?"

"I'm just trying to find Garrick." Elery crossed her arms over her chest. "And I think you know more than you're telling me."

A subtle glance down the hallway to where the bedroom had to be. Did Angela have somebody back there? Had she left Garrick and found another guy already?

Elery took a step toward the hall. "What are you hiding?"

"Nothing." Angela moved in front, blocking Elery's path. "My bedroom is a mess. That's all."

Sweat beaded on Angela's brow. She was too nervous to be worried about a messy bedroom. But what could Elery do? Knock her over and invade her home? "Fine. If you're not hiding anything, then let me have a copy of your map, so I can go after Garrick."

"It's ... it's lost. I took the copy out with us, and it blew away in the wind. Before we left, the original got too close to the stove and caught on fire. It's ruined. I've got nothing."

Elery gaped at her. Ridiculous to expect her to believe both the original and the copy were gone. Angela was lying, but why? To protect her claim to the mine or to keep Elery from finding Garrick? "I don't believe you."

"I don't care what you believe." Angela stomped her foot.

Elery pressed her hands together to ease her tension. Fighting wouldn't get her anywhere. "If you know something that can help find Garrick, you have to tell me."

"I don't know what to say. I can't help you."

Then why all the nerves? Elery would swear Angela was lying, but with no proof to back up her suspicions, she couldn't do anything about it. Maybe the sheriff could get more out of Angela.

Her phone buzzed this time—a text. From her father.

El, I went for an appt in Phoenix. Doc said I'm dehydrated. He's admitting me to hospital for an IV. Come see me when you can.

A knot of fear tied up her stomach. Dehydration in a cancer patient could be serious. Pushing Angela harder would have to wait. Elery threw open the door and ran out to her car.

***

Her father sat propped up in the hospital bed, reading a magazine. His face had more color and vibrancy than she'd seen in days. He looked normal again. "How do you feel?"

"Better."

If she'd have realized he was in the hospital, she would have answered the phone immediately. She hadn't gotten much out of Angela anyway. Hopefully, the sheriff would. On the way to the hospital, Elery had called to let him know Angela was back. He had promised to go visit her.

Sitting down next to her father on the bed, Elery spoke in a gentle voice. "Why did you do this to yourself? Fasting weakens your body. You know you need strength to fight the cancer."

He stared down at his hands. "I didn't realize I was hurting myself. After a few days, being weak and hungry felt normal."

She covered his hands with hers. "But why were you fasting? Was it about the mine?"

"Yes. I thought if I sacrificed long enough, then God would answer my prayers for the mine."

She squeezed one of his hands. She understood the feeling of owing God something, but the mine was her fault, not his. "God doesn't want you to get sicker."

"No, of course not. But fasting can be a good thing. The Bible says to do it during earnest prayer. I thought I was doing it for the right reasons. Then, today, after they admitted me, I felt God telling me that my fasting was really a spiritual drought."

She wrinkled her brow.

"I didn't have faith that God would hear my simple prayers. I thought I could work the system, somehow get Him to pay attention by long periods of fasting."

Why wouldn't her father think God listened to his prayers? He'd never done anything wrong. No sin stood between him and God, at least not anything like what she'd done.

"And I made myself worse in the process." He gave a low chuckle. "In a way, Pastor Arroyo was right. My lack of faith made me sicker."

She frowned, failing to see the humor in him ending up in the hospital. "Does the pastor know you're here?"

"No. I called the mine office looking for you and then, I called your cell phone." He let out a long sigh. It had to wear on him, not feeling comfortable confiding in his pastor.

"Good. We can keep this quiet."

He pressed his lips together, the chapped surface cracking. "I'm sorry I've forced you to keep this secret."

Her thoughts flew to the secret she was keeping *from* him. "You didn't force me. I want to protect you in whatever way I can."

A fire lit behind his eyes. "You can't protect me." He fingered the spot on his upper chest where one of the larger melanomas had left a nasty scar. "We can't even protect ourselves. God's the only one who can do that, sweetheart."

The truth of his words burned a hole through her heart. She couldn't protect Garrick. She didn't even know where he was. "You'll let the doctors take care of you, and you'll eat?"

"Yes. I promise, no fasting today."

She gave him a stern look.

"Or tomorrow."

"That's better. They said you could probably come home tomorrow or maybe Tuesday at the latest." She squeezed his hand one last time and left him to rest.

Across the hall from his room, she found an empty chair and sank into it. The light coming in the windows had dimmed with the setting sun. Was Garrick still out there in the dark somewhere waiting for her? If she didn't get to him in time, she'd never forgive herself.

Hot tears stung her eyes. She let them spill over and run down her cheeks. Was her father right? Would God protect Garrick until she could find him?

A nurse or two walked past, but no one spoke to her. She savored the blessed silence as she poured out all her emotions. Her father's cancer, his fasting, the mine collapse, Garrick's disappearance. It was all too much. She put her elbows on her knees, hung her head and let the tears fall, darkening the fabric of her jeans.

Eventually, her eyes dried up. She straightened in the chair, wrapping her arms around her midsection in a hug. But her arms weren't the ones she wanted to feel wrapped around her, and that realization hollowed out the pit of fear in her stomach. She struggled with the urge to call Lucan. His temporary comfort would soothe her for the moment, but the two of them didn't have a future together. He would never be able to look at her without thinking of his dead brother.

CHAPTER FIFTEEN

Lucan held the door open for Elery as they entered the office of Fitz and Simmons, a reduced fee law firm offering representation to anyone in the greater Phoenix area. The card he'd found in Chad's apartment displayed the name of one of the partners. And the location was perfect—the corner of Jackson and Second Avenue—exactly where Julia Thomas Schaffer's house had stood. Hopefully, it meant his brother came here to hide the next set of pages. But would these pages lead them to Garrick? From what Elery had said about her confrontation with Angela, Garrick was out there alone.

A young secretary looked up with a smile that was way too cheery for a Monday morning. "May I help you?"

He returned the smile, trying not to look like someone on a crazy treasure hunt. He'd opted not to call for an appointment, hoping instead to catch the lawyer first thing when the office opened. "I'd like to see Miriam Simmons if she's available."

"Your name?"

"Milner."

"Just a moment, please."

The young woman spoke into a headset coming down from her ear. "Mr. Milner to see you, Ms. Simmons." When the receptionist turned back to them a moment later, she nodded. "Ms. Simmons is finishing a call and will be with you soon."

Lucan waited for Elery to sit in a chair near the door,

then he took the seat next to her. Elery leaned over to whisper, and her arm brushed against his, the touch distracting him. "What are you going to say to her?"

He glanced at her out of the corner of his eye and winked. "I'll use my Jedi mind tricks to find out whatever she knows." Elery pursed her lips, clearly suppressing a smile. He'd rather make a joke than admit how anxious this made him. Retracing Chad's steps had cut deeper into his grief than he wanted to let on. "In other words, I'll wing it."

Elery leaned forward and put her elbows on her knees. Her light oak-colored hair fell like an ocean of waves between them. He fought the urge to reach over and brush her hair behind her ear. What was drawing him to this woman when she was the last person he should want to touch? Her stubbornness maybe. He'd always had a thing for the strong-willed type. Or maybe it was the vulnerability that came out every time they talked about her brother.

A door opened behind the secretary and a short dark-haired woman stuck her head out. She had an oval face with a large Romanesque nose. "Mr. Milner. Please, come on back."

They followed her through the door into a sparsely furnished office. A worn oak desk sat at the far end of the room, framed by a large bookcase filled with legal volumes and a dusty file cabinet. Miriam sat in a chair behind the desk and gestured for them to sit in the two chairs in front.

"Good to see you again. What can I do for you?"

Lucan took a seat before addressing the obvious mistake. He hadn't told the secretary his first name. "You think I'm Chad, don't you?"

A furrow cut through her eyebrows. "You're not Chad Milner?" Her eyes widened in understanding. "You're the brother." She spun around in her chair, opened a file drawer and pulled out a manila envelope. "In that case, I have something for you."

"How long ago did Chad come here?"

She spun back around, holding the envelope between two fingers. "About three months ago. He's not the kind of guy you forget. Funny, flirtatious, and persistent. I've got a serious boyfriend, but that didn't deter Chad."

It sounded like his brother. Chad went after whoever and whatever he wanted no matter the cost. Lucan took the envelope, opened the seal and tugged out a plastic sleeve with a set of yellowed pages inside.

"He said you might come looking for those." Miriam slid her hands into a desk drawer, searching for something else.

His stomach churned like a cauldron. Chad hadn't trusted him to leave the pages alone? "He thought I'd come?"

"Not to worry. He was fine with you having these, as long as you sign a legally binding document." Miriam flipped a sheet onto the desk and slid it across.

Lucan picked it up, glancing through the typed words: *... entitled to journal pages, if and only if, the signatory provides fifty percent of the proceeds of said mine to the original partner.* This was an agreement to give half the mine to Chad should Lucan find it. He tossed the paper back down and clenched his teeth in frustration. His own brother thought he'd take the mine for himself.

"Don't think of this as a negative thing." Miriam's tone was gentle, although her expression remained stoic. "This is meant to be an insurance policy for both of you to have legal and equal rights to the mine, if it's ever found. Chad didn't intend for you to see this unless you were already trying to find the mine on your own."

Of course not. But then Chad hadn't intended to die either.

"It's not personal." Elery touched his arm gently. He

looked into her face. Her eyes held no pity, just sympathy. "The sure sign of a Dutch Hunter is paranoia. I can't tell you how many times Garrick freaked out about someone getting his gold. *His* gold. As if he had more claim to it than anyone else."

Miriam placed a silver-plated pen on the paper. "She's right. I draw up more of these documents between partners than you'd think. I suggest you talk this over with Chad to smooth out any hard feelings you might have about this."

Lucan picked up the pen and quickly signed his name. "Too late, Ms. Simmons. My brother is dead."

Miriam bit her lip. "I'm sorry to hear that." She actually looked sorry, but so what? She barely knew Chad.

He waited as Miriam also signed the document, made a copy on a nearby printer and handed the copy to him. He placed it on top of the journal pages and left without a backward glance.

As they came out of the office, he turned to Elery. "Let's go somewhere else to read these."

She looked at him with shell-shocked eyes. Had his abrupt statement in the office brought back her guilt about what happened to Chad? If he asked, would she open up about it? And why did he want her to? He shouldn't be trying to get to know her. Instead, he should harbor anger, even thoughts of revenge. But as much as he wanted to blame her, he couldn't. Her guilt, her pain, draped her like a blanket. Maybe when he actually let himself think about the accident, he'd feel differently about Elery, but for now, he didn't have time to process it all.

Gesturing with the papers, he pointed down the street. "There's a shopping district this way. I could really use some coffee."

She nodded. He led her a block over and three blocks up to the open air coffee shop. After ordering coffee, they walked to the center of the courtyard and sat beside each other on stone benches. Water jetted out in fountains from a central water feature, the rhythmic sound easing his frayed nerves.

Elery curved her slender hands around the paper coffee cup resting on her knee. She anxiously tapped the sides of the cup with her fingers. He could reach out and still them, but decided it was better not to. Every time he touched her lately, electricity shot through him.

Her brows were set in a firm line—her determined look. He longed to say something funny to calm her. She took a sip of coffee, then twined a curl around her finger. What would it be like to let his hands get lost in her soft waves? He straightened his back and smoothed the plastic protecting the pages. This physical attraction was getting out of hand. He needed to focus on the job of finding Garrick.

"Before we read, I have to tell you something." Elery placed the cup beside her on the stone bench and folded her hands in her lap. "I should have done this yesterday when I found out, but I didn't know how to say it."

He leaned back, concerned about where this might be going. "Just tell me."

She gathered her curls into a loose pile at the back of her neck before releasing them in a wild mass. "The official investigation report came back. Equipment malfunction caused the cave-in, specifically the ceiling stabilizer. I thought it was in good repair. We hadn't had any problems. But I knew it was twenty-two years old, too old for safe operations. I didn't have the money, so I let it go." Her lips turned down and moisture filled her eyes. She picked up the coffee cup and clasped her hands tightly together on it, bowing in the sides. "I'm really sorry. It's all my fault. I should have replaced it."

The truth pierced him like an arrow, tearing through the fragile scabs on his grief-stricken heart. He sucked in a breath through clenched teeth. Her negligence *had* caused the accident. Chad's death could have been prevented. It changed everything to have it confirmed.

And yet, it didn't change how he felt about her. She wasn't a heartless mine boss. The remorse in her eyes made it clear, she'd trade places with Chad if she could. "Is that why you don't want to go back to the mine?"

She blinked a few times as if that wasn't the reaction she was expecting. "Finding Garrick is my priority. But you're right. I'm not sure I can go back anyway. The mine is better off in my supervisor's hands right now."

Lucan leaned forward to force her to meet his eyes. This woman would forever bear the weight of Chad's death in a way that Lucan wouldn't. He couldn't let the guilt crush her strong spirit. *Lord, give me the strength to forgive and the words to say it.*

He took a deep breath, letting the tension flow out as he exhaled. "It was Chad's time to go."

She shook her head. "No, it wasn't. I caused his death. I took your brother away from you. What I did is unforgivable."

She tried to look away, but he reached up to cup her chin. "Elery, nothing is unforgivable. God forgives us for everything. Surely, your pastor would tell you that."

A dark cloud passed over her face. "God blesses our faith and curses our sin."

Where did she get that? From her church? "God doesn't curse those who believe in him."

"I'm not saying I'm cursed. I just don't have enough faith. God doesn't answer my prayers, and I don't blame Him. My father has skin cancer because of me. I'm the only one he has told about it, so I'm the only one who can pray for him, but my faith hasn't been strong enough to cure him."

"You think you should be able to cure him?"

"Yes ... I mean, no ... I don't know." She pulled away,

and this time he let her go. "The Bible says we can cure diseases with the Holy Spirit. Nothing is beyond us if we have faith. But my faith is clouded by sin. It's like a fog that God can't see me through."

Did she mean Chad's death? "What sin are we talking about here?"

"I hurt someone, when I was younger ..." She clamped her mouth shut. Her gaze darted around like a trapped rabbit. "I can't talk about it. I shouldn't even have told you about my dad. If anyone at my church found out, Dad would be mortified."

He didn't understand. If her father had cancer, why wouldn't he want support from the church?

She gazed out at the splashing fountains and let out a heavy sigh. "Let's just read the pages."

Her mouth was set. She avoided eye contact. She was done sharing. Until she decided to open up, all he could do was pray.

***

April, 1866

The three of us had mined gold for a year with no trouble. I left Fred and Weiser alone every three months to purchase supplies in town. After one such journey, I returned to find the mine chamber empty.

In the main room, I noticed a pattern of black drops trailing in a curve along the gray floor of the cave. If not for their shine, I would have missed them. Bending down, I rubbed a finger in one. It came back cranberry red—blood.

I worried the Apache had attacked, forcing my friends to flee. Clearly, one of them was injured and in need of help.

Hurrying out into the sunshine, I searched the side of

the mountain. No one near. I hadn't passed them on the trail from town, although I knew they could have taken the old canyon trail.

After climbing down the north slope of the mountain, I ran across the valley to the tiny, stone cabin where we stored our supplies. It sat behind the edge of the cliff to keep it hidden.

Inside, I found three empty cots and a table with no one sitting at it.

I ran back outside, then paused to listen. In the valley, my burro stamped its hooves as it fought against the strap tying it to a rock. I walked to the animal and placed a hand on its backside to calm it.

Once the sound of its stamping ceased, I heard something else. A noise I couldn't identify coming from the south, near the base of the other side of the mountain, the side opposite of our mine.

Dropping my bag, I pulled my shotgun from its straps. I didn't know if it was Fred and Weiser, or if it was other prospectors. In those mountains, anyone who thought they had a claim to defend was dangerous.

I climbed through the pass between the two mountains. As I traversed the highest ground, the scene in the valley shocked me so that my feet halted in place. In the shallow river sediments, Fred dug with a shovel, his back to me. On the ground nearby lay Weiser's still form. Crusted blood covered his chest and face.

I ran down the slope to Weiser's side and threw myself on the ground next to him. His pale cheeks were cold, his clothes shredded like dusty rags from being dragged over the rocks.

Looking back at Fred, I demanded to know what happened. He hesitated. From his guilty expression, I knew. There was no outside danger, no Apaches, only Fred. I glared up at him and yelled, asking how he could do this to my oldest friend.

Fred looked down at my hands and backed away. I glanced down, as well. I still clutched the rifle in my right hand, my knuckles white on the stock.

I stood to face him, keeping the rifle at my side.

Fred paced along the edge of the dried-up creek as he gave me his excuses. He told me Weiser went crazy, that he wanted to cut both of us out of the mine and keep the gold for himself.

I knew it couldn't be true. Since the three of us had started mining last year, Weiser had talked more about the places he wanted to explore in the desert mountains than what he'd do with his share of the gold. I'd been gone for barely two weeks, and Weiser wouldn't have changed his mind so quickly.

Fred stopped pacing and gave me a pleading look, but he was trying too hard with his reasons. Weiser wasn't killed in defense.

Fred had murdered my friend for gold.

This was a senseless tragedy, like Ila all over again. Except this time, I could avenge the death. I raised my rifle and leveled it at Fred. He deserved to die. What right did he have to take Weiser's life? My finger grazed the trigger. I'd brought Weiser here to America to give him a better life, but I made a mistake by introducing him to Fred.

Fred threw his arms out to the side, his hands shaking, his voice pleading for his life. He said I'd be a murderer.

Truly odd, the murderer throwing out his own label to save his life.

He was right, though. This wouldn't be in defense either. I would have to live with this decision for the rest of my life.

The rifle weighed down my arm like a burro laden with gold.

Gold. All of this for gold. A cold, precious, inanimate rock.

To me, gold meant freedom. The freedom to come and go, to not answer to anyone. But it seemed gold meant much more to Fred.

I focused on the center of his chest. An easy shot. No chance of missing. The same odds he'd given Weiser.

As I ran my finger along the length of the trigger, I imagined the scene. The blast, the blood, another body to bury.

I couldn't live with that. And Weiser wouldn't want me to. He believed in the same God I did. A God who watched, even now.

Slowly, I lowered the rifle and threw it into a scraggly bush off to the side. Fred sank to his knees with his head in his hands.

Trembling, I turned away and walked over to Weiser. The gunshot had hit him in the chest, sending out splotches of blood that covered him from face to stomach. His eyes were wide and his mouth open. He hadn't expected the blast. It was a complete betrayal. I knew someday Fred would do the same to me.

I turned to him again and told him I was done with gold mining. All I wanted was enough to live on each year. He could have the rest. At my declaration, he refused to give me anything. But he reconsidered when I said I would stake a claim on the land and advertise its location to every prospector in the territory.

I had made a deal with the devil. But this was one devil the Lord would have to take care of personally. More bloodshed wouldn't have brought Weiser back.

Fred returned to the mine, and for the next several hours I dug Weiser's grave. After I pushed his stiff body into the hole, I recited a few prayers I'd heard at funerals. Then, I began to cover him with dirt, a process more grievous than digging the hole. Every shovelful covered a part of my friend whom I wouldn't see again until heaven.

When I finished, a small mound of dirt rose from the valley floor. It wouldn't last long in the flash floods of the desert. Searching around in the creek bed, I found two skinny rocks, one long and one short. I dug through my pack for a portion of thick, flexible metal wire I normally used to reinforce baskets carrying gold. Bending the wire around the rocks, I fashioned a marker and pushed it into the ground.

It was the last grave marker I would make. A desert cross for the man who fell in love with the desert at first sight.

CHAPTER SIXTEEN

On the hour long trip back to Quartz Creek, Jacob Waltz's words from the last set of pages danced through Elery's head.

A desert cross.

Just like on Angela's map. Maybe Elery needed to pay Angela another visit and get her to turn over the map she insisted didn't exist anymore. Then again, maybe they could find the mine without Angela's map once they had the entire set of journal pages.

Lucan pulled over at the bank and parked. She checked her watch. They had made it ten minutes before the six o'clock closing time.

"I won't be long," he said.

"Okay. I'll wait over there." She pointed to a bench at the park across the street.

She grabbed the papers, got out and crossed the road, flopping down on the wooden bench. The cooler air of the early evening should have refreshed her, but every cell in her body felt bone tired.

As she waited for Lucan to retrieve the next set of pages from his safety deposit box, she mused on the clue Chad had left them pointing toward the final set of pages. Over and over again, she read Chad's scrawled handwriting on the bottom of the page.

In a field of gold, the Thunder Spirit runs free, slipping from his feet to bow to Peralta.

What in the world could it mean? She tapped her foot on the grass. Would any of this lead to Garrick?

Lucan exited the bank and crossed the street to the park. "Here they are." He passed a paper-clipped bundle to her, then slid onto the bench. "Any luck on the clue?"

"Not yet." She placed the new bundle underneath and returned her attention to Chad's words. "I think the field of gold can only mean Goldfield, a small town near here. It was built just a year after Jacob Waltz died when the Mammoth mine was discovered. Some people think Mammoth mine could be the Lost Dutchman Mine because it was discovered so soon after his death. But no serious Dutch Hunter believes that."

"Of course not, because then there wouldn't be a mine to chase after."

She looked over at him, but he had raised his eyes to the tree above them, where the branches bounced in the light breeze. His hair also flipped about in the wind. The worried furrow of his brow gave him an intense aura like a soldier on a mission. He looked over and caught her staring. Their eyes locked, and a tiny swarm of butterflies invaded her stomach.

He quickly turned his gaze to the pages in her lap. The butterflies did a spiral roll and crash-landed. Wherever these strong feelings were coming from, she had to crush them. Lucan would never consider being with her. And why would she want to be with him? Staring at his face every day would remind her of what she'd done.

"What is the Thunder Spirit?" he asked.

She scooted a few inches away from him and crossed her legs. "The Apache believed a Thunder Spirit lived in the Superstition Mountains. It was a sacred place to them, which is why many people believe the land is cursed."

"I thought it was because so many people have died out there."

"That, too." Was he thinking of his father?

He laid his arm along the back of the bench, barely touching her, but distracting her all the same. "Okay.

So, the Thunder Spirit doesn't have anything to do with Goldfield."

She uncrossed and re-crossed her legs, angling her body away from him. "No, although Peralta might."

"How?"

"Nobody lives in Goldfield anymore. It's a ghost town tourist attraction with a museum." She pushed a curl out of her face. "And one of their most popular exhibits is the Peralta Stones."

"And those are?"

"A set of stone maps found in the 1950s, said to have been carved by the Mexican Peralta family to show the location of their mines. The Peraltas were in this area before the Dutchman. Many Dutch Hunters believe the Lost Dutchman Mine is a Peralta mine."

"Do the maps lead anywhere?"

She shrugged. "People have followed them all over the place and not found anything. I personally think they're a hoax."

"Even so, it sounds like Chad might have made this museum part of the clue. We need to check it out."

Elery looked at her watch. "It's already 6:00. The museum is probably closing up for the night."

"I guess we'll have to wait until tomorrow then."

A heavy weight settled on her chest. More waiting. If only one of these journal pages would give her something to go on to help find Garrick.

Lucan reached over and tapped the other bundle of papers resting in her lap. "In the meantime, let's read these."

***

March, 1867

Upon my next yearly return to the mine, I found

the entrance silent. No noise from the steam-powered arrastra, grinding up the ore. No sound of an ax striking the rock.

It was too quiet.

I thought perhaps Fred had gone to get supplies, but he wouldn't have left the entrance to the mine open. He would have covered it with the rock screen we had created to conceal it.

In the main cavern, I dropped my pack and looked around. The arrastra was cold and a rock pick lay on the ground nearby.

Nothing seemed ominous, until I moved farther in. The air in the cavern turned metallic and putrid. The smell came from the side tunnel. I hesitated for fear of what I might find, but I decided I had to discover the source of the smell.

Covering my nose and mouth with the sleeve of my coat, I stepped into the tunnel. My eyes quickly became accustomed to the dark. Even then, I could only see a few feet inside. I returned to the main cavern, lit a lantern and entered the tunnel again.

With one hand over my mouth and the other holding the lantern, I moved into the side tunnel. The circle of light shone before me, revealing a large mass lying on the floor several feet away.

Fred.

The smell of blood overwhelmed my nose. I dropped to my knees, vomiting onto the wall. When I had nothing left in my stomach, I leaned back in Fred's direction. I had to know what happened to him.

Blood covered every wall of the tunnel, along with bits of hair and flesh. It was easy to surmise who had done this. The Apaches had nearly scalped him in their fervor to protect the Thunder Spirit's gold.

A barely audible shuffling noise came from the main cavern. I wiped my mouth and stood. If the Apaches had returned, they had me cornered. There was nothing more to do, except meet my fate.

I walked into the main cavern where three dark-skinned men stood in a semicircle with their legs wide. They were dressed in warriors' tunics.

The two men on the ends held long daggers, the tips pressed into the floor. The man in the middle looked at me for a long time. In the deep brown of his eyes, I saw both ruthlessness and pride. People in town called them savage, and certainly they had done savage things, but this man believed himself to be honorable. I wondered how many men like me this Apache had killed to uphold his honor.

The center man stepped forward. For the first time, I looked at his hands. He held a thick blanket made of horsehide. As he approached, he presented the blanket out in front, as if inviting me to take it.

In a low voice, not threatening and yet full of authority, he asked if I was Jacob Waltz.

When I nodded, he took a step closer, pushing the blanket in my direction. I took the offering. He said it was for my dead.

I was confused. They'd killed Fred, then came back to give me a blanket for his body? I didn't know what else to do so I thanked him.

He told me his name was Pravar, and that he had come because of Ila. As Kuruk lay dying, he confessed to killing Ila for the gold in the cavern. Pravar shook his head as if this was a shame he, himself, bore. He pointed at my chest and said I was there when it happened.

I nodded again, the memories already close at hand. It was a scene similar to this one. But I'd thought Ila was killed because of my presence.

Pravar told me he was sad.

I didn't understand what he meant. Was he saddened

by what Kuruk had done? Or by what they had done to Fred?

Pravar pointed to the quartz vein running above our heads, then turned his finger to me. In short sentences, he said I could take the gold, but only here and only me. Then, he stepped back until he stood in line with his companions.

With his arm, he gestured toward the tunnel where Fred lay and told me all others would die.

I turned and glanced back at the tunnel. Fred hadn't just died. He'd been tortured. For decades, the Apache had done all they could to keep the white men out of their sacred areas. I had difficulty believing they would actually spare me and let me profit from their land.

Turning back to the main chamber, I found it empty. The men had left without a sound.

I let out a full breath. They'd spared me because of Ila. Somehow, she was still protecting me from the grave.

Returning to the tunnel, I placed the blanket over Fred and began to drag his body out of the mine. As I labored, the Apache leader's words repeated in my mind.

Only you.

CHAPTER SEVENTEEN

Elery drove back from Lucan's apartment and parked her car at the curb in front of her house. She shut off the engine, then leaned her head against the steering wheel. The journal pages were a rare peek into the life of the famous Dutchman, but they weren't leading anywhere. She'd never find her brother this way. Lucan had told her to have hope that Chad's last set of pages would hold a clue, but what if it was more of the same?

This was crazy. By now, the sheriff should have found another canine unit to help search. She grabbed her cell phone and dialed the Sheriff's Office.

"Pinal County Sheriff's Department. Can I help you?"

It wasn't the sheriff's voice or his receptionist. "Yes, this is Elery Hearst. Who's this?"

"Deputy Hellerman. What do you need, Elery?"

The familiar way he said her name put her on edge. She barely knew the guy and hadn't found much reason to talk to him since the sheriff had hired him about a year ago. "I need to talk to the sheriff."

"Sorry, he drove into Phoenix today to assist with the presidential visit. If you ask me, he's following some Secret Service guy around drooling after the job."

"While my brother is missing?" Anger flared in her chest. The sheriff wasn't taking this seriously. But maybe it wasn't surprising, given the number of times Garrick had disappeared before. "Is he at least trying to find another search dog while he's there?"

"I don't know." A long pause came over the line. When Hellerman spoke again, his voice sounded unnaturally cheerful. "Have you considered the possibility that your brother found what he was looking for and is too busy mining to come back home?"

She longed for that to be true, but Garrick would have contacted her. "Just have the sheriff call me when he gets back."

"Sure thing."

Elery ended the call, got out of the car, and climbed the stairs to the front porch. At the top, she stopped, frozen in midstep. Pastor Arroyo sat in the porch swing, not swinging, with his hands folded in front of him. He didn't visit regularly. What could he want?

"Pastor?"

"Hello, Elery. I came to talk to your father. Will he be home soon?"

"No. I think he's ..." She hesitated. He'd gotten home from the hospital that afternoon, and then gone out again. Did the pastor know of her dad's relationship with Candace? Was that the problem? "He's at a friend's house." Great. She'd made her father sound like a five-year-old with a play date.

Pastor Arroyo lifted his dark eyebrows. "In that case, may I come in and speak with you?"

"Sure." She unlocked the door and held it open for him.

After he entered, she followed, closed the door and led him to the formal sitting area. He sat on the love seat. She chose to sit in a velvet chair across from him. He leaned back into the cushions as if he came here every day, and yet he hadn't been here in ten years—not since her mom had left.

She dropped her purse on the floor and waited for him to tell her why he had come.

"Thought I'd check in with your father. How's he been feeling lately?"

Her heart rate picked up. An innocent question? Or did he know something? "He's fine."

"Just fine?" The pastor leaned forward, putting his elbows on his knees. "Any problems I can pray about?"

Elery tugged on her lower lip. He'd definitely heard something, but he seemed to be fishing for information. Lying to her pastor was not an option. What could she say to skirt around the issue? She glanced across the room, her eyes falling on the ornate lamp on the side table. A decorative antique that no longer worked. Rather than throw it out, her dad preserved it, claiming its age made it more valuable. Why wasn't that the case with people? She took a deep breath. "You know how it is. Dad's getting older, but he's still active."

Pastor Arroyo pursed his lips and lowered his head. Waves of salt and pepper hair covered his face. When he spoke his voice was muffled by the hair. "I'll be honest with you." He drew out the word "honest," and she squirmed in her seat. "I've heard a rumor." He raised his head and stared hard at her. "I've heard a rumor about your father having skin cancer."

She held her breath. Denying it would be lying, but affirming it would betray her father's wishes.

"I can see in your face that it's true." He pushed off the love seat and turned his back to her. "Why didn't both of you come to me?"

Another question she shouldn't answer. How could she tell her pastor it was a personal matter? That her dad didn't trust him to keep it private?

He paced a few steps, apparently disturbed by her silence. "This is hard for me to say, Elery. We're asking you and your father to leave the church."

"What?" This would crush her dad. She jumped up,

suppressing a sudden urge to spin the pastor around and smack him in the face. "How could you?"

He advanced on her until he stood less than a foot away. Anger pulsed from his eyes for a millisecond before he gained control of himself. "You lied to us." His voice was soft, but with an abrasive edge, like fine sandpaper.

"We didn't lie. We just didn't tell anyone."

"It's deception either way. You can't be trusted. And it's obvious you and Morty aren't faithful to God. Otherwise, you would have asked the church to pray over him." For a moment, heartbreak passed through the pastor's dark eyes, then they turned rock hard. "Now, it's too late. We can't help you."

"Who's 'we'?" Surely, all the elders hadn't agreed to this.

Pastor Arroyo puffed out his chest. "Rather than involve other church members and have word of your deception spread, I made this decision with the assistance of the church counselor. This way, you'll be able to leave quietly, and it will keep the rumor mill to a minimum."

Sure it would. She dropped down into the chair and slumped back, defeated. How would her dad handle this? He was dedicated to Christ's Body Church. What would his new girlfriend do? She worked at the church.

All reasons why they had kept his condition a secret. So, how did Pastor Arroyo find out?

She'd told no one else, besides Lucan. Although, Lucan hadn't mentioned knowing Pastor Arroyo, he must have told someone who told the pastor.

Or maybe he had gone directly to the pastor as some sort of revenge against her. She clenched her jaw. If his vengeance only involved her, she'd let it go because she deserved it. But she wouldn't let Lucan mess with her dad's life.

***

Lucan ran a hand along the wire of Sienna's empty crate. Although she stayed at his apartment most of the time, the boarding facility was her official police-sanctioned home. The vet wanted to keep her at the office for a few more days, so why had he come here? An undefined restlessness had forced him out of his apartment. He couldn't sit still, and it had nothing to do with his dog.

Every time he closed his eyes, Elery's face appeared. If he sat on the couch, he imagined her next to him, distractedly nibbling on her bottom lip. As he ate dinner, he imagined her eating at the table across from him. Thoughts of her engulfed his mind.

Maybe his subconscious had focused on her to avoid dealing with his grief. Chad's death had left a black hole inside him big enough to swallow the Milky Way. Was that it? Was he replacing Chad with her?

The bells on the front door of the kennel jangled. The soft pad of footsteps on the tile floor. He turned to stare out at the dark hallway.

Elery appeared in the doorway, blinking against the light in the room. Her hair draped over one shoulder, a tempting cascade of curls. Instead of the jeans he normally saw her in, she wore shorts and a salmon-colored T-shirt. His eyes traveled to her long, tan legs. Impure thoughts rocketed through his mind. He quickly focused back on her face. "Hi. What are you doing here?"

She stepped into the room, but barely. "Looking for you."

Her voice had an edge to it. Was she angry? "Well, I'm here. What's up?"

She folded her arms over her chest. "My pastor came over and confronted me about my dad's skin cancer."

"Whoa. How did he find out?"

Her eyes burned a hole right through him.

He took a step toward her. "Wait. You think I told him?"

"It had to be you."

The anguished look of betrayal on her face turned his insides into spaghetti. She couldn't truly believe he'd do something like that. He moved toward her until he was well inside her personal space. Lowering his voice to a whisper, he leaned in close. "It wasn't me."

A flash of doubt bolted across her face. Deep down she had to know him better than that. Then again, they'd only known each other for a few days. It just seemed much longer.

She blinked, and her resolve hardened her face again. "*No one* else knew."

Strange to have her anger directed at him when he'd been fighting through his own anger about what happened to Chad. Somehow his fury dissipated every time he looked into her eyes. The accusation should offend him, but he only felt a desire to comfort her. He inched closer. "What happens now?"

She turned her head away. "He's kicked us out of the church."

"Seriously?"

"Yes. My dad will be devastated."

He touched the side of her arm. "All I can tell you is, I didn't do it."

She turned her head to face him and a stray curl brushed his chin. "No one else knew."

So logical. So stubborn. What if he did something to break her out of that? Before he took time to think through the impulse, he cupped her chin in his hand. Leaning down, he brought his lips to hers.

For a moment, she didn't move, and his lips lingered. The smell of lilac fabric softener drifted up from her shirt. He had to be certifiably insane for acting on these feelings. This woman had contributed to his brother's death and accused him of spilling her father's secret. And yet, he wanted to pull her closer, kiss her harder. Instead, he forced himself to pull away.

She stared at him, her lips parted, surprised. Another rush of heat flamed in his cheeks as he waited for her response. Did she want to slap him or did she want him to kiss her again?

Seconds ticked by, and she didn't hit him. It was worth the risk.

Slower this time, he brought his lips gently to hers. She responded, leaning into him and wrapping her arms around his neck. Pulling her against his chest, he kissed her until his body was on fire. Until he couldn't breathe. Until ... a little bit more!

From deep within, he managed to draw up a reluctant measure of self-control. Pulling away again, he stood staring at her, breathing heavily. Her lips looked swollen, and he smoothed his thumb over her bottom lip. She sucked in a sharp breath and leaned back.

"I have to go." Spinning on the balls of her feet, she ran toward the door.

He turned to follow, but she slammed it behind her. The wall shook, causing a picture of a playful puppy to crash to the floor.

He pressed his forehead against the back of the door and blew out a breath. "That went well."

CHAPTER EIGHTEEN

Elery stood in front of the island countertop and pressed two pieces of bread together, squishing the peanut butter and jelly. She brought the sandwich to her mouth, biting into the soft, gooey center—comfort food to ease the nervous energy buzzing through her. When Lucan had brought his lips to hers, she couldn't have pulled away even if she wanted to. His stare was hypnotic, his touch magnetic. She had to stop this. Lucan would eventually realize he couldn't be with her, not after what she'd done. If she didn't guard her heart, it would splinter unpredictably when he left.

The front door slammed shut.

She set the sandwich on her plate. "Dad?"

"Yeah, it's me." His voice sounded strained. Hopefully, he hadn't talked to Pastor Arroyo yet. She had to find a way to change the pastor's mind before her father discovered they'd been ejected from church. If only Lucan had kept his mouth shut.

A worm of doubt wiggled its way through her mind. After she'd accused him, Lucan had kissed her. A long, spine-tingling torrent of a kiss. Not the normal reaction of a guilty man. Unless, he was trying to distract her.

The setting sun draped the kitchen in shadows. She flipped on the overhead light, then reached for a knife to cut the sandwich in half. Her appetite had suddenly fled. "Do you want half of my sandwich?"

"No." His footsteps paraded through the hall and into the kitchen. "What I would like is some answers."

She put the knife down and looked up. Her father's hands were behind his back, his face as hard as stone. Pastor Arroyo must have already gotten to him. Turning her eyes away, she spoke in a soft voice. "What do you mean?"

He took a step closer. "You've been running around with Lucan Milner quite a lot lately. Why?"

This was about Lucan? Did everybody know she'd been with him? She fumbled for an answer. "I'm helping him with something." The lie tasted sour on her lips. The truth was the exact opposite. Despite what she'd done to Chad, Lucan was helping her. And that was what didn't make sense. Why do that if he was going to betray her?

She risked a peek at her father. He still had his hands behind his back. His eyes were focused on her, probing her in that human-lie-detector way every father could.

"Please, tell me the truth, Elery."

"Come on, Dad. Why all the questions?"

He ground his teeth together before answering. "I know Garrick's in trouble. No more lies."

Her eyes went wide. But how could he know? Had Lucan also told someone about Garrick? Or had her father found out from the sheriff? A defeated sigh escaped from her lips. "Lucan has been helping me search for Garrick. I didn't tell you because I have nothing to tell. I don't know where he is. I don't know if he's hurt or if he's still hunting for the mine and isn't ready to come back."

Her father frowned and whipped his hand from behind his back, thrusting a paper at her. "Well, now we know. This was stuck to the front door."

The front door? There wasn't anything there when she'd come home. She took the paper, quickly reading the typed words.

Your brother is safe—for now. Find the mine and leave a map of its location in the Hearst Stone mailbox

by Wednesday evening or you can search for pieces of
your brother spread all across the desert. I will know if
you contact the police.

Elery sucked in several deep breaths as adrenaline flooded her system. She stumbled back, leaning hard against the counter. Garrick wasn't just missing. Someone had taken him.

Her father shook his head, slamming the note down on the counter in front of her. "How could you keep this from me?"

"I thought Garrick was still searching for the mine. I didn't want to worry you. You couldn't do anything to help look for him." Her excuses sounded feeble even to her own ears.

He crossed his arms over his chest. "But I could have done something very important, Elery. I could have prayed."

Shame coursed through her. She should have told him. Just because God didn't listen to her, didn't mean He wouldn't listen to someone like her father. At this point, Garrick needed all the prayers he could get.

She looked down at the paper and swallowed hard.

Pieces of your brother.

Wednesday.

Prayers wouldn't be enough. If she couldn't find the mine in time, they'd kill Garrick.

***

A light shower of pebbles rained down on Garrick's head. He glanced up, longing to see someone up there, but the shadows of night obscured everything.

"Hello?" His voice barely rose above a rasp.

No answer.

No one was up there. The mountain's weathering had fooled him many times already.

He'd been stuck down here almost five days. What was taking Angela so long? Something bad must have happened to her. He tried to keep his mind from following logic down to the inevitable conclusion, but it went there on its own. Angela was the only one who knew where he was. If she didn't bring help, he wouldn't make it.

The days ran together in a scorching haze, while the nights stretched out in shivering solitude. His stomach constantly cramped from hunger. His throat burned from thirst. At least, the rain from a couple of days ago had provided something to drink. But it wasn't enough. If it didn't rain again soon, he'd dry out into a sack of bones.

He twisted his torso around in the cramped crevice. Searing pain burned through his leg. Trapped from the mid-thigh down, only a few positions brought relief from the excruciating pain. No doubt his leg had broken near the ankle since it seemed to shift back and forth even as the rest of his leg was held tight by the huge rock that had smashed next to his knee.

The mountain had him wedged in like a cork in a champagne bottle. Taking a steadying breath, he sat up and reached down into the crevice to pull on his foot. He'd tried moving it several times, and it hadn't freed him yet, but he couldn't sit here and do nothing. When he grew dizzy with pain, he let go of the foot.

An image flashed through his mind—the man who cut his own arm off to save himself after a rockslide fell on him. Not that Garrick could try it. He'd left his backpack at the base of the mountain. Other than the water bottle and his jacket, he didn't have a thing with him. And he certainly couldn't gnaw off his own leg.

Turning his head, he looked out at the dark horizon. Several hours before, the light had shifted and scattered between the peaks, a kaleidoscope of fading colors. Now, moonlight bounced among the same spires, turning them into shadowed impenetrable walls.

A morbid thought crept in, slithering through his mind. If nobody came, this would be his last view—day or night, he would slowly turn as lifeless as the rocks surrounding him.

He turned his eyes to the sky and the half-full moon. Was God up there watching him die?

Pastor Arroyo said God blessed those who believe. It wasn't true. Garrick had believed with complete faith that he would find the Dutchman's mine, that God wanted to bless him with the discovery. And yet, here he was.

Of course, he'd always understood the flaw in the pastor's logic. In a finite world, not everyone could be blessed with what they wanted. But even so, Garrick thought he'd beat the odds.

The shadow of a large winged bat swooped over him. He wrapped his arms around his shoulders as the temperature dropped, and he began to shiver. The skin on his forearms, cracked with blisters, protested, but he had no choice. He needed to conserve heat.

He tucked his head against his chest, preparing for a long night. The shivering would reach its apex in the next few hours. Sleep came easier in the scalding heat of the day, but then waking up was brutal. It would be better not to wake up at all. He coiled further into his body. If God planned on taking him, He should just do it tonight.

CHAPTER NINETEEN

A loud pounding vibrated Lucan's apartment door. Who would be visiting him at night? He approached the door cautiously, then swung it open to catch the other person off guard.

Elery pushed past him, rushing into the living room. A morose frown pulled on her lips. Her eyes were dry, but crusted streaks from earlier tears ran in lines down her cheeks. The strong desire to wrap her in a hug sucker-punched him. Something was wrong with him. This woman had walked out without a word after their kiss, but as soon as she showed up on his doorstep, none of it mattered. His heart was a fool.

Pacing in front of the couch, she blurted out, "Garrick isn't missing. Someone has taken him."

He grabbed her by the shoulders and looked into her eyes. "What happened?"

She shook him off and pressed a note into his hand. He smoothed it, scanning the brief sentences. Garrick had been kidnapped? If the kidnappers had him this whole time, why just contact Elery now? It didn't make sense. Unless the kidnappers were watching them and thought they were close to finding the mine.

He looked up at her, and his heart flipped upside down. She paced with her hands over her mouth, her tawny curls bobbing as she shook her head. "I don't know what to do. I don't know what to do."

He grabbed her shoulders again, forcing her to stop. "We'll find him."

"How?" She raised moist eyes to meet his. "We don't even know who took him."

Leave it to Elery to make a good point in the middle of a crisis. He placed a hand on her cheek. "I don't know how, but we will find him." Hopefully, his voice carried more certainty than he felt. Her anger toward him had seemed to evaporate in the face of this new threat, but this wasn't the way he would have liked them to make up. At least she wasn't accusing him of being the kidnapper. "Who else knew about Garrick's disappearance?"

"I didn't want my dad to find out, so I didn't tell anyone besides the sheriff." She huffed out a breath. "Angela would know, of course. Could she have helped kidnap him?"

"Maybe. But if her story is true, he could have been kidnapped after she left him."

"I suppose."

"Maybe the sheriff asked around about Garrick. More people might know than we think."

She nodded. "The sheriff told Jayna Rowan."

"Who's she?"

"A geologist from a different state. Wisconsin, I think. She's up here to map for some guy with the name Peralta. She thought he might be an illegal miner."

He directed Elery to sit on the couch. "Okay, we should find her and ask more questions about her employer. Has anyone else mentioned Garrick's disappearance that you hadn't told?"

"Just Pastor Arroyo. I figured he heard it from the sheriff also." She drummed her fingers on her knee. "Although, I guess there was one other person I did tell. I was gone so much from the mine that I thought he had a right to know why, so I told Ron."

Ron? Lucan sucked in a sharp breath. The name brought a chill to his spine. It couldn't be a coincidence.

He pushed off the couch, ran his hand through his hair, then turned back to Elery.

Her face had paled. "What's wrong?"

"Your mine supervisor. His name is Ron?"

"Yes, Ron Gremming. Why does it matter?"

"Where does he live?"

"In the next town over. In Superior." Elery crossed her arms. "What's going on?"

He slapped a hand against his forehead. "Ugh! I knew he lived in this area. Why didn't Chad tell me?"

She stood and took a few steps away from him. "You're not making sense."

Lucan placed both hands on top of his head, intertwining his fingers. "Do you remember why Chad and I hid the journal pages?"

A small divot marred her brow. "You said your cousin thought the pages belonged to him."

"My cousin has searched for the mine in this area for years. When we moved to town, he broke in and tried to steal Chad's pages. We came back from dinner one night and caught him in the act. To get away, he punched Chad in the jaw and then tackled me in the hallway. He's a violent guy."

"Okay. Why are you telling me this now?"

Lucan turned his eyes to the ceiling. "Because my cousin is Ron Gremming."

***

An hour later, Elery glanced out her window at the darkness as Lucan steered the truck toward Apache Junction. She had no options, except to go after the mine now. According to the note, they only had two days to find it or Ron would hurt Garrick. Given the deadline, they couldn't wait until tomorrow to get into the Superstition

Mountains Museum to search for the last set of pages. It had to be tonight.

Even as they sped down the highway, the contradictions piled up into a massive roadblock in her mind. Could Ron really have kidnapped Garrick? If he had, then why did it look like Garrick had gone off on his own with Angela? Were Angela and Ron working together?

In the last hour, she'd called Ron's cell phone several times. No answer. They'd driven by his house in Superior. No answer at the door either.

More questions swirled through her head. She understood why Chad hadn't told her he was related to Ron because she probably wouldn't have let Ron supervise a family member, but why hadn't Ron told her, especially after Chad's death? Was he keeping even more from her?

Looking back on the past year since she'd taken over the mine, Ron had missed several days of work and come in late other days, but he always made up for it by working longer hours on the days he came in. She'd only recently begun to suspect he might be a closet alcoholic, but what if he were doing something else? What if he was a closet Dutch Hunter?

Outside Apache Junction, Lucan turned onto Highway 88, the start of the loop that circled around the Superstition Mountains. A few minutes later, she touched his arm. "The museum should be just ahead." She let her hand linger a moment longer than necessary. Somehow, touching him stabilized her.

He slowed the vehicle and turned into the museum parking lot. Bypassing the Old West movie set buildings, he drove to the back of the museum and parked far away from the lone streetlight. He turned off the motor.

The sudden quiet grated on her frayed nerves. "Now what?"

"We wait a few minutes. I want to see if they have a security guard." He folded his hands in his lap. "Do you mind if I pray?"

She let out a long sigh. Hopefully, God listened to Lucan's prayers more than hers. "Please, do."

"Dear Father, we need Your help tonight. We have to find the pages, and we need wisdom to recognize any clues to the mine. Neither I nor Elery care about the gold. We care about Garrick. Protect us and him from those who would kill for it. In Jesus's name we pray. Amen."

As he finished, he dropped his hands to the seat. She let her hand fall over his, savoring the warmth of his skin. "Thank you. For the prayer. And for everything else."

They sat in silence for a while, neither of them moving their hands apart. Ripples of electricity coursed up her arm and through her chest. What had stabilized her moments ago now distracted her. She couldn't afford to be distracted right now. She needed to focus on Garrick. Reluctantly, she pulled her hand away from his. "So, what's the plan?"

"Don't worry. I've got it covered."

They fell into silence again. Anxiety twisted her stomach into knots. Breaking into the museum would be the first illegal thing she'd done. But what other choice did she have? To help Garrick, she'd have to trust Lucan and his plan.

The slow tick of time had just about driven her nuts when Lucan grabbed a bundle of cloth and reached for the door latch. His gaze met hers, lighting with determination. "Ready?"

She nodded, nerves pulsing through her body.

"Let's go." He slipped out of the truck and eased the door shut. His figure darted across the parking lot toward a shed attached to the back of the building.

She jumped out of the vehicle and chased after him,

bending at the waist. The museum didn't appear to have security cameras, but just in case, she kept her head low.

He went to the edge of the shed, then paused, giving her time to catch up. "This would have been a little easier with a security guard. My badge might have gotten us in."

"You have a badge?"

He shot her a shadowed glance. "I work with the police department."

"Yeah, but as a rescue worker, not a cop."

He turned his back on her and approached the rear entrance. "Surprisingly, a lot of business owners put more security on the front door than the back. They tend to think of the back as an employee entrance."

That information had to be from his police training, and now he was using it to help her break the law. Crouching in front of the door, he unrolled the cloth and laid a set of skinny metal tools beside him. No doubt preparing to pick the lock. Lucan was full of surprises. She opened her mouth to protest, but nothing came out. They didn't have time to wait until tomorrow when the museum opened, and this was the least violent means of getting in.

He selected a thin screwdriver and a tool with a hook on the top. He slid the screwdriver into the lock, then twisted the hook tool beside it. Technically, this was breaking and entering, but they weren't going to steal anything, except what belonged to Chad. Her justification turned her stomach rock hard. But if they found Garrick, it was worth becoming a criminal.

"Where did you learn to do this," she whispered.

"My dad taught me. He was a locksmith. It seems I'm a little rusty, but I should have it soon."

Several minutes went by as he fumbled with the mechanism. She glanced around the parking lot. All was quiet, and yet her nerves buzzed in her ears. If Lucan didn't break into the lock soon, someone might stumble upon them.

With a click, the lock caught. Lucan spun the hook tool, then stood and tried the door. It swung open.

Elery breathed a sigh of relief. Maybe they would get through this undetected.

He stepped inside first. A glow from a security light played over his hair and shoulders, giving him a yellowish cast. She hesitated, briefly glancing up to the sky. Once she stepped over the threshold, she could add burglar to her list of wrongdoings. But this was the fastest way to get to Garrick.

As she stepped in, she paused to let her eyes adjust to the semidarkness.

A loud bark broke the silence. Fast movement came from the front of the museum.

She recoiled as a massive dark shape ran at them. Lucan moved to shield her, his stance widening.

Peering from underneath his arm, she saw a large Rottweiler stop a few feet from Lucan. Its lips curled into a snarl. A low growl rumbled from its throat.

Lucan reached behind and gave her arm a squeeze. "Don't run. I've got this."

She froze, torn between listening to him and sprinting for the truck. He was a dog person, but could he tame a well-trained guard dog?

"Relax your breathing." It took her a second to realize he was talking to her and not the dog. "We don't want this little guy to be afraid of us, do we?"

Little guy? This thing had to weigh at least hundred pounds and not a single pound looked afraid of them. Angry, yes. Afraid, no.

Taking a slow step, Lucan put a hand out toward the dog's head. It snapped its teeth, but didn't actually get close to biting him. "See that? That was a warning. He doesn't want to bite me. He's just afraid because we aren't supposed to be here. We have to convince him that it's fine for us to be here."

Lucan slowly put one knee on the ground, then the other, until he was at the same level as the dog. The animal shuffled on its feet, its nails tapping the hardwood floor. It continued to growl, but didn't advance.

"You just need someone to tell you it's okay, right?" Lucan's voice was so soft and smooth she now wished he was talking to her instead of the dog. What would it feel like to have him hold her and whisper those words?

The dog wrinkled its face and tilted its head. The growl morphed into a high-pitched whine. Lucan put an open hand out, palm down. The dog dropped to its stomach. Maybe it wasn't such a well-trained guard dog.

"That's right. Come here, boy." The dog scooted forward, using its paws to slide closer. Lucan rubbed the top of its head and checked the collar. "Ozzie. A great name."

He scratched behind Ozzie's ears while glancing back at her.

A side smile crinkled his cheek. "Elery, would you like to come pet Ozzie?"

She lifted her brows and stayed put. "Not so much."

He chuckled, a low, carefree rumble she hadn't heard often. "That's fine. Just stay behind me." He rose to his feet. Ozzie got up also, frenetically wagging his tail.

As Lucan moved down the hall, Ozzie turned his dark eyes on her. She took a step forward. Ozzie wrinkled his face and let out a low growl. She stopped. "Uh, Lucan, can you call off your new pet?"

He looked over his shoulder and made a sharp noise that sounded like the warning alarm in a nuclear power plant. The noise made even her snap to attention. Where had he learned that? Police training or dog obedience class? Ozzie glanced at Lucan, then walked away, heading for a dog bed in the corner. He lay down with a thump and glared at her.

She slipped past the animal on tiptoe. "How did you do that?"

"I established benevolent dominance. He knew I wouldn't hurt him, but I let him know I was in charge."

"What are you? The Dog Whisperer?"

He shrugged. "It's all about attitude."

"I've never heard of such a thing."

Winking, a sly grin stretched across his face. "It works on people, too."

Benevolent dominance? That might be what she found so attractive about Lucan. But was his benevolence real or did he try to "work" her like he had the dog?

She looked around, scanning the room with her flashlight. They had entered the main exhibit area packed full of display cases. Nearest the door, one contained a set of woven reeds shaped like a pair of feet. Across the aisle another case held vases and bowls of old pottery. In front of her, was a miniature diorama of a Western town. A glance at the rest of the room revealed at least twenty display cases and several exhibits. "What was the clue again?"

Lucan quoted from memory. "In a field of gold, the Thunder Spirit runs free, slipping from his feet to bow to Peralta."

"Okay, we're in Goldfield, so that leaves the Thunder Spirit bowing to Peralta." Elery walked slowly through the museum until she found the display containing a large, square, rose-colored stone with a heart inset. Engraved symbols covered the flat faces of the rocks. "These are the Peralta stones." She pointed over her shoulder at a full length case filled with old copies of maps, the original newspaper obituary for Jacob Waltz, and other articles detailing the search for the lost mine. "And that's the Dutchman exhibit."

"But I don't see a Thunder Spirit exhibit." He moved in a slow circle, scanning the large room. "So, what could the Thunder Spirit represent?"

"The mountain, I suppose, since that's its home." She tugged her hair up into a haphazard bun, holding it for a few seconds, then releasing it. "If it represents the mountain, maybe it represents the gold also."

"What does that mean, then? The gold is bowing down to Peralta?"

"Maybe." He gave her a skeptical look, but she ignored him. Could it be simpler than that? Putting one hand on the display case, she pretended to bow and peeked beneath the case. Nothing.

"We're missing something."

She ran the clue back through her mind again. One word stuck out as odd. Slipping. Why wouldn't Chad just say the Thunder Spirit bowed to Peralta? Then it clicked. Those woven reeds she'd seen when they first came in. They looked like slippers.

She raced back through the room, stopping at the display case right next to the back door. Her heart pounded as she read the placard inside with the heading "Look what a cowboy found in a cave." It was a pair of Mexican slippers found among hundreds inside a cave in the Superstition Mountains area. *Slipping from his feet to bow to Peralta.*

With one hand on the display case, she bent at the waist. Something was stuck to the base underneath. A plastic package hanging flush with the lip of the case. "Aha!" She grabbed it, ripping off the tape.

As she swung back to standing, Lucan moved to her side. "You're brilliant."

She smiled, grateful that in the dark he couldn't see the flush climbing up her neck. Giving him the package, she took the lead. "Okay, let's get out of here."

As she turned toward the door, her gaze fell on the

dog. Ozzie's ears were perked, his lips curled, a low growl emanating from his throat. But he wasn't looking at her. His eyes were focused on the closed door beyond her.

The door swung open and slammed against the outside wall. A bright light flashed in her eyes, blinding her.

"Don't move. Both of you." The light shifted from her to Lucan. She blinked to clear the stars from her vision. Two police officers stood in the back doorway, their guns drawn, twin barrels pointing at her and Lucan.

CHAPTER TWENTY

Elery sat on the worn bench of the jail cell next to Lucan, trying to ignore the lingering smell of vomit. She stared at the charcoal metal bars. Bars that divided up her view of the hallway in the same way certain events had divided up her life. Her mother's abandonment, Garrick's injury, her father's cancer, Chad's death, Garrick's disappearance—all segments of her life that carved her apart like mine shafts cutting through her soul. If only she could delete a segment or two. Like tonight.

Breaking and entering. Her father would be ashamed of her. How would she explain this to him? He'd gone to bed before she'd left, trusting her to do something to help Garrick. After his stay in the hospital, she wouldn't call and wake him. With any luck, they would be released tomorrow and her dad would never know. Her heart stuttered a bit. He'd find out if her case went to trial.

Lucan had decided not to call his mother, who had returned to Kansas yesterday. At least Elery wasn't the only one who wanted to hide her mistakes. She glanced at his profile, strong and resigned. This situation could be even worse for him since he worked with the police.

He turned and bumped his shoulder into hers. "Nice of them to put us in here together."

She frowned. "There's only one jail cell."

"And only one person I'd like to be locked up with."

She bit back a smile. Now was not the time to savor his comment. Sitting here wasn't helping her find the mine to rescue Garrick. "What if they don't give us the papers back?" Without the pages, they had no chance to find it.

He bent forward and rested his head in his hands. A sliver of shame pricked her heart. She needed to stop asking questions that had no answers. It put Lucan on the spot, and he seemed to care as much about finding Garrick as she did. But then again, rescuing people was part of his job.

Lucan lifted his head and turned to face her. "Hey, I need to ask you a question. I don't have a right to ask, but I want to know something."

She shrugged. He probably had a right to ask anything he wanted.

"Why do you believe God doesn't listen to you?"

The question hit her square in the heart. She drew in a breath and blew it out. Could she tell him? She'd never told anyone. Not even her father. She didn't want to talk about it, but Lucan had given her so much—access to the journal pages and the chance to help Garrick. And now Lucan faced the same legal consequences she did. He deserved an answer. But would he understand there are some things you can't make up for?

She pushed matted curls from her forehead. "I was eleven and having a rough time. A group of kids bullied me every day on the way to school, and at recess, and on the way home, because of my mom. Mostly, they were kids from church."

"Why would church kids bully you?"

"My mom was depressed. When the church leaders found out, they prayed over her, laid hands on her, but it didn't work. She needed medicine. My dad made the mistake of getting the pills at the local pharmacy, so everyone in town knew. The church kids called me what their parents called my mom—crazy, lazy, faithless." She shifted on the hard wood bench. "I told my mom. I think it was part of the reason she left us. She believed what they said. She convinced herself she was a terrible mom, and we'd be better off without her."

Lucan wrinkled his brow. "All because she needed medicine?"

"I think they just didn't understand. Our pastor used to say, 'If you're not letting the Holy Spirit renew your mind, you will slip into darkness.' People assumed her faith wasn't real if God hadn't renewed her mind."

"That completely negates the idea of mental illness."

She put up a hand, asking him to hit pause on the argument. If she didn't get the rest out, she might lose her courage and clam up. "My mom called her medicine 'happy pills,' so I thought that's what they were. All I wanted was to be happy again, so I started stealing them. At first, it worked. I didn't care as much what the other kids said. But after a few weeks, I felt different."

She gripped the bench until her knuckles turned white. Lucan scooted closer, his fingers brushing against hers. "Different, how?"

"Angry. I was so angry." She focused on the gray cement between her feet. "A week after my mom left, Garrick came into my room and asked to use my roller blades. I told him no because he was too little and they were mine." Her blood pressure spiked, making her a little lightheaded. What she'd done to Garrick couldn't be undone and telling Lucan couldn't be undone either. He'd never look at her the same. Moisture burned her eyes. She blinked and pushed through, suddenly desperate to get it all out. "Garrick wasn't happy with my decision. He started to scream that I pushed mom away. I tried to ignore him, but after a few minutes his scream felt like metal spikes piercing my skull. I had to make it stop." Swallowing hard, she forced the final words to come. "I screamed back at him and knocked everything off the top of my dresser, including the TV. It landed on his leg."

Lucan sucked in a sharp breath. She couldn't blame him. What she'd done still shocked her.

"Garrick tried to jump out of the way, but he slipped and fell just as the TV came crashing down. The heavy base crushed the lower part of his leg." Elery swiped at a tear. "I can't explain why I did it. I knew I could hurt him, but in that moment, I didn't care." She rubbed her eyes, then turned toward Lucan. "Garrick told Dad it was an accident, that he was jumping around too much. No one else knows what I've done. Except for God."

Lucan moved closer, slipping an arm around her shoulder. She wanted to lean into him, but instead held herself stiff. "Elery, you know it was the medicine."

She shook her head. "Yes, but no, not completely. Some of it was me."

"That's the guilt talking."

"You don't understand. When I'm pushed to the breaking point, I don't cry out to God, I don't curl into a ball, I lash out at the people I care about most."

She kept her gaze locked on the floor, refusing to see the disappointment in his eyes. She wasn't the woman he imagined her to be, and it was better he discovered it now. Once they found Garrick, Lucan needed to stay away from her. For his own safety.

***

"Wake up, you two." The gruff voice intruded into Elery's sleep.

Her eyes shot open. Where was she? Her head lay sideways against a rough wall, the edge of her forehead touched Lucan's. The jail cell. They had slept here the entire night. She sat straight up, wiping a few drops of drool from the corner of her mouth. As she moved, Lucan jerked awake.

Officer Montgomery, a young officer with expressive

eyes, dangled his keys in front of the door. "I talked to Sheriff Turner bright and early this morning. He filled me in on your issues." He held the keys on his hip. "The museum swears nothing is missing, and you didn't break anything. Plus, we caught you leaving and the only thing you had were some papers the museum says aren't theirs. Frankly, I'm surprised because those papers looked ancient." He cocked his head. "So, I can't understand why you were there ..."

He paused as if giving them one more chance to confess their reasons. Neither she nor Lucan spoke.

"Okay. In deference to the sheriff, and because there really wasn't any harm, I'm going to let you go without sending charges to the DA. But you must agree not to enter the museum, even as a paying customer, for the next full year or else."

Elery expelled a breath of relief. They wouldn't have criminal records. "Thank you."

Lucan stood and walked to the bars. "Will we get the pages back?"

Officer Montgomery waved off his question and unlocked the cell door. He led them to the front desk where they signed a paper stating they would stay away from the museum, and then collected their things: truck keys, cell phones and plastic covered journal pages.

Officer Montgomery pointed to the northeast. "Your truck is in a lot half a mile up the road. An easy walk."

"Yes, sir." Lucan tugged her out into the sunshine.

She breathed deep, letting the fresh air chase away the vomit smell still stuck in her nose.

Lucan handed the pages to her. "You can read out loud while we walk. I'll guide you."

What was this? Hadn't they had enough exercises in trust? She slipped her cell phone in her back pocket and held the pages in one hand, allowing him to pull her along with the other. "This won't be easy. The writing is chicken scratch compared to the others." She glanced at the date at the top. October 1891. All of the journal entries read like they were written later in life, but this one had to have been written very near to the time of Waltz's death.

She focused on reading the words aloud and found deciphering them got easier the longer she read. As the words jumped off the page, she analyzed them for any detail that might prove useful. This was the last set, and if they didn't get any clues from this, they were out of leads.

***

October, 1891

I took gold from the mine occasionally. Enough to purchase a house with land for a farm and wood for my carvings. I lived in my house by the Salt River alone for almost thirty years, but it's gone now—drowned by a flood.

A friend rescued me from the tree where I had escaped the floodwaters and brought me to Julia Thomas, a woman that I supplied with produce from my farm and carved wood furniture for her boarding house. Julia took me to her home and has nursed me for several weeks.

Despite her efforts, my pneumonia is worsening. In bed, I can scarcely find a position where air will come freely into my lungs. There's nothing more Julia or Rhinehart, her adopted son, can do for me.

They have taken good care of me, checking on me in the night, making creams to open my lungs, and massaging my weak muscles. They deserve the fee they asked for and soon they will have more—the gold hidden under my bed. But I cannot give them what they want most.

Day and night they ask about the mine, saying it would be unfortunate for the gold to be lost in the desert mountains. Like the others who have asked over the years, they don't know what they are asking. Gold comes with a price.

I am convinced the Apache still watch the mine. If I told Julia and Rhinehart how to find it, the price would be their lives. So, I have taken to giving them clues, some real and some false, the best way to confuse them. Rhinehart has grown suspicious, though. Every time I give a new clue, he wrinkles his face, trying to work out the conflicting information.

Although Julia and Rhinehart take care of me, I spend much of my time alone. I cannot help but think of Ila more now than ever. Both in wakefulness and dreams, I am touching her face and kissing her lips. Ours will be a sweet reunion in heaven for I know she loved the one, true God as much as I still do.

I believe she will not have to wait much longer for me to arrive. Pain fills my chest with every breath. I escaped the intense flooding of my house, only to be killed by moisture in my own lungs.

After I am gone, Julia has promised me she will send my lizard carving to my dear sister. It is my most realistic carving and the only thing I have left of Ila. It is my greatest treasure.

For a moment, I had to pause in penning these words because Julia and Rhinehart came in, asking for clues. I described a conical pit mine that they would walk over and not see unless they knew its location. They left with expectant smiles on their faces.

I pray God will understand and forgive the lies told with my last breaths. Protecting them is for the greater good. For now, the Apache roam the mountains, but it will not always be so. The more prospectors they kill, the more soldiers come to hunt them. Their eradication will be an opportunity for your descendants, my dear sister.

Fatigue pulls, drowning me. I am too tired to fight it. I may not survive until tomorrow, but I will seal what I have penned. A trusted friend will send this document to Kansas in the morning. May God guard these pages and the legacy contained within them.

CHAPTER TWENTY-ONE

Elery stared at the fragments of mountain and desert whizzing by the window as Lucan steered the truck back toward Quartz Creek. Somewhere out there, the mine waited. Jacob called it a legacy. But how did these pages lead to it?

A knot of panic twisted inside her chest. She looked over at Lucan. "Jacob didn't want Julia to find the mine. We don't know if there's any truth in his words at all. This is useless."

"Chad believed the journal held a clue. Now that we have all the pages, we can sit down and comb through it." He glanced at her out of the corner of his eye. "Together, we'll find something."

The panic traveled up into her throat, choking off her air supply. She'd pinned all her hopes on this last journal entry. What if it didn't lead anywhere? All this time was wasted when she should have been searching for whoever held Garrick.

"Jacob sealed the letter so Julia and Rhinehart wouldn't see it because he wanted his sister's grandchildren to discover the mine one day, when it was safer to look for it." Lucan touched her arm briefly, then put his hand back on the wheel. "Jacob would have left a clue for them. We just need to think like him. Let's start with the last set, since it's closest to the time he died."

His confidence loosened the knot in her throat a little. What choice did she have? Either she admitted defeat and called the police—a risky move the note warned her against—or they continued to hunt for clues.

She sucked in a breath and held it, letting the air permeate deep in her chest. Her fears for Garrick had to be put in a box. She needed to focus on the journal. What clues did Jacob leave?

She blew out the trapped air and turned to Lucan. "I think you're right. In these pages, Jacob says he deliberately misled them, which means Julia and Rhinehart couldn't have read them. All the local documentation suggests they went looking for a pit mine as Jacob described. They had no idea he was lying."

"My dad said Jacob's sister, my great-great-great-grandmother, received a package wrapped in brown paper with the pages facing inward. Two unbroken wax seals secured the pages along the sides. If we can assume Jacob sealed the journal pages himself, then no one else read them."

Compassion filled her for Julia. She nursed Jacob as he died, maybe hoping to profit, then sold her bakery business to hunt for the treasure. Eventually, she ended up poor, trying to sell altered copies of the map to survive. She never knew Jacob had protected her.

Lucan turned right, bringing the truck onto Main Street. "You know everything I know. Chad thought Jacob had left some sort of clue, but ..."

His voice lowered as his words trailed off. She knew what he was thinking. Chad hadn't been able to discern any clues from the journal. It was up to them.

Grabbing the final journal entry, she thumbed through it. "This last set is short. The only other thing he discusses with Julia is the lizard carving he made after Ila's death."

"As far as I know, my family never received a carving, just the journal pages."

"Okay. So Julia promised to send the lizard to Jacob's sister, but she didn't do it."

Wait, a lizard. She'd seen one recently, but where? The stray memory bounced around the edges of her mind, wiggling away every time she tried to grab it. Fragments of the image came—bleached wood, exaggerated limbs, bulging eyes.

A lizard resting on a bookshelf.

Elery pointed at an angle out the windshield. "Turn left here. I know where we need to go."

***

Wham, wham, wham. Elery slammed her fist into the apartment door. What would she do if Angela wasn't home? Lucan put a pacifying hand on her shoulder. He was right. She had to keep calm. Angela already didn't like her. If Elery came on too strong, Angela wouldn't help them.

Long minutes passed with no sound from inside. If Angela looked out the peephole and saw Elery, she probably wouldn't answer the door.

"Here," Elery whispered as she moved to the side of the door. "You knock, maybe if she sees you, she'll open the door. I know she doesn't want to talk to me."

Lucan stepped up and gave the door three long raps. No answer, not even a hint of movement inside. Could Angela be that stealthy?

He reached for the door handle and twisted. The door swung open easily, giving them a view of the kitchen. No sign of Angela.

"Hello?" Lucan pushed the door, and it opened wider, revealing the small living room. Light poured in from the open window blinds. It was also empty.

Had Angela left and forgotten to lock the door? It was the best-case scenario for them. No one to stop them from searching. Technically, they would be entering without permission, but they hadn't broken in. Hopefully, that would make a difference if they got caught.

Elery took a tentative step inside. Lucan followed, but stopped a few feet into the entryway.

Her gaze jumped to the two sets of bookshelves on the far wall. Sure enough, on one of them the bleached lizard rested exactly where she'd remembered. She moved toward the bookcase, passing the desk on the way. A piece of paper with several wavy lines sat on top. The lines looked familiar. She stopped and traced one with her finger. In the lower right quadrant, a cross was drawn. It wasn't complete, but Angela had tried to recreate the map. Maybe she had actually lost it.

Leaving the unfinished map in its place, Elery went to the bookcase and grabbed the lizard carving off the top. As she turned around, something by the sofa caught her eye. A single blue sandal lay in the narrow opening between the chair and the other side of the couch. Odd for Angela's spotless apartment, but maybe she'd kicked them off earlier and forgot about them.

Elery passed by the sofa, then came to a halt. A small irregular red stain darkened the carpet. It looked like runny ketchup. Or blood.

"Lucan, is that ..." She pointed at the spot.

He squatted down to look at it. "If it's blood, Angela might be in trouble." He stood and turned toward the only hidden part of the apartment, the bathroom and bedroom. "Angela! Are you here?"

His shout echoed down the hall. When no answer came, he walked carefully to the bathroom doorway. Elery followed, peering around him. The counters were free from clutter and the room smelled like cleaning solution. No sign of anything wrong.

"Angela?" She skirted around Lucan and took slow steps down the hall. For Angela's privacy, it was better to have her check out the bedroom. The door stood open halfway. At the threshold, Elery tapped the door to push it open.

A bed sat on the opposite wall with a nightstand next to it. Nothing looked amiss, but the smell told her something wasn't right—coppery and acidic together, it coated the back of her throat. Her gaze swept down the line of the comforter and to the floor. A clump of straw marred the beige carpet. Again, odd for such a pristine apartment.

She circled around the bed.

Her feet froze in place. Her breath caught in her throat.

The straw wasn't straw. It was hair. Angela's light hair, splayed around her pale face.

A dark red stain covered the front of her pink blouse.

The image of Angela's body wobbled with Elery's escalating adrenaline. Her blood pumped loudly in her ears. She pressed a hand to her mouth to keep from vomiting. The smell of blood overwhelmed her nose. If she didn't breathe, she'd pass out. She forced herself to take a deep breath.

Lucan came from behind and threw his arms around her shoulders. His touch was comforting, but her eyes stayed locked on Angela, whose eyes stared at the ceiling.

Angela was clearly dead. Her death after Garrick's disappearance couldn't be a coincidence. Was she killed for the map? Elery tightened her grip on the lizard. Or did somebody else know about the journal and the carving?

She broke out of Lucan's grasp, spun around and fled the apartment, still clutching the lizard to her chest.

CHAPTER TWENTY-TWO

The afternoon sun burned down on Jayna's head as she climbed the tall mountain. Despite the heat, she pushed her legs to keep climbing. Halfway up, the slope had dramatically increased. Her calves burned, but her soul soared. She much preferred the challenge of a mountain to the peaceful valley she'd slept in last night. Although the meandering river had lulled her to sleep, the view from the top of this mountain would be awe-inspiring, once she got there.

Besides, her employer wasn't looking for a placer deposit in the gravel at the bottom of a river. Peralta wanted a mine. And not just any mine. One found in the side of a mountain and full of chunky gold ore—the Lost Dutchman Mine.

Could she find it? Possible, although not likely, when so many others had tried and failed.

Reaching around with one hand, she tugged her marked-up map out of the side pocket of her pack. She noted a sharp change from basalt to granite on the map, then entered a rock description into her field notebook. Gold ore could be found both in granite and in separate veins of quartz that cut through the dark basalt, but she hadn't found any of the precious metal in these rocks so far.

She stopped and shrugged off her backpack. The afternoon sun burned down on this side of the mountain. After pulling her sticky T-shirt out in back, she extracted her rock pick. With the flat end, she whacked at the granite to expose a fresh surface, then turned the pick around, stabbing at the rock to break off a chunk. She picked up the small piece and examined it under her magnifying loop. No gold. She dropped it back to the ground.

It felt good to get back to where she belonged, among the dirt. She was made for this—walking alone on a mountain immersed in the evidence of God's creation. His hands were all over these rocks. The same hands that guided her every step.

After last year, she'd thought her career as a geologist was over. The U.S. Geological Survey had fired her for questioning the science behind their age-dating methods, effectively ending her chances at getting another geological position. If it weren't for her fiancé's financial help to start her own firm, she would have been done with geology permanently.

Now, she just needed to successfully complete this job, her first job. Hopefully, Peralta would be impressed with her mapping, even if she didn't find the lost mine.

She walked a few paces to the edge of the mountain and looked around. About two-thirds up now, but even so the view took her breath away. Half of the sun had dipped below the horizon, casting long shadows that striped the desert floor in varied shades of rust and gold. A breeze blew wispy clouds overhead, their shadows changing the patterned landscape as they passed. Everything was a reflection of magnificent earth tones, except for something directly below her.

She dropped to her knees and peered over, careful to keep her balance. A flash of blue.

What is that? She leaned farther over the edge.

Next to a deep crevice, a nylon windbreaker was draped over a boulder.

Her breath caught in her throat. Next to the jacket, a man lay with his eyes closed, seemingly unaware of her presence. She'd almost missed him, his dark skin closely matched the surrounding rocks.

The man resembled Elery's brother, Garrick. She'd found him. But was he alive?

"Hello? Can you hear me?"

No answer. No movement.

She tried again. "Garrick? Is that you?"

His head rolled to the side. He was alive!

"I'm going to get you out of there." She leaned back on her heels and grabbed her pack before remembering she hadn't brought any rope. This mapping assignment wasn't supposed to require any rock climbing. "Oh, man."

She leaned forward again. Garrick had opened his eyes and now stared up at her with a quizzical expression, as if he couldn't decide if she was real. Not that it mattered since she couldn't do anything for him right now anyway. Her cell phone had no signal out here, and she hadn't wanted to spend the money for a satellite phone until she received her first paycheck. "I don't have a rope. I'll have to go for help. You're Garrick, right?"

He blinked a few times and gave a slight nod. At least, it looked like a nod. With two fingers, he tapped on his left thigh. The leg below the knee disappeared into the rocks surrounding the large crevice next to him. He tapped on his thigh again. He must be trying to tell her it was injured. No wonder he seemed so weak.

"In the meantime, I'll throw down some food and water." She couldn't very well drop the can of pork and beans she had brought for dinner. Instead, she dug out her last granola bar, balanced it on the edge for a second, then let it drop. It fell straight, but hit a rock near his waist and bounced, plunging down into the crevice. She pressed her hand to her forehead. "Sorry, let's try the water."

Water was more important anyway. She grabbed the

plastic bottle, lay on her stomach and curled her arm around the lip of the cliff. She had to release the water as far from him as she could. If the bottle hit him after falling thirty feet, it could injure him further. She let it go and held her breath. The bottle hit the side of the cliff and bounced, but instead of bouncing over him, it thudded into Garrick's arm. No harm done.

He grabbed it with a weak, trembling hand. The cap had stayed on. At least, he would get some hydration.

She jumped to her feet and yelled down for the last time. "I'll be back with help. Hang tight."

Leaving him alone again in this condition stirred up the acid in her stomach, but what else could she do? She forced her feet down the mountain. He'd endured the punishing sun for days and the drop in temperatures at night, all with an injured leg. How much more could he take?

She picked up the pace, sliding down as much as she could. The sun rode low in the sky and she had a long ten-mile trek to her car.

At the bottom of the mountain, she turned south, heading for the river. The incessant splash of the water now sounded like heaven after her hike down with nothing to drink. She bent down to fill up her reserve water bottle, screwed the filter on the top, then drank half the bottle. Still kneeling, she dipped her hand in the cool water and splashed some on her face.

A loud blast echoed through the mountainous canyons.

It sounded like a faraway shotgun blast, only louder. The noise had come from behind her. She tilted her head to angle her ear in that direction. All was quiet.

She walked partway up the next mountain and scanned the surrounding area. Above a nearby ridge, a gray curl of smoke rose into the air.

People.

There weren't supposed to be any settlements out here. But some people liked to live off the beaten path. And the others were usually involved in something illegal, like smuggling or mining.

But what would cause an explosion with so much smoke? A couple of shotguns wouldn't do it. Something bigger had blown up. A stove or maybe a smelter?

She narrowed her eyes to judge the distance—about two miles from here, but in the direction away from her car. Whoever lived there would probably have a rope, or even a satellite phone. Garrick could get help hours sooner.

But what if they didn't like her showing up unannounced? Most people who lived in isolation didn't appreciate visitors. Then again, she could hike most of the way before it got dark, sneak up to the settlement at night and check it out before making her presence known. It was risky because if these people couldn't, or wouldn't, help, she'd have wasted hours.

For several seconds, she stood frozen in indecision. Garrick's life hung between these two possibilities. *I need guidance, Lord. What should I do?*

No compelling certainty came. Still, she had to decide. Turning toward the smoke, she began to walk.

***

Elery sat on the curb outside Angela's apartment as Lucan gently rubbed her neck. The grating sound of sirens blared behind them. She twisted around to look. Two police cars made a U-turn in the street, parking along the curb next to them. Sheriff Turner pushed his rotund body out of the front vehicle and approached them, followed by Deputy Hellerman.

The sheriff hitched his thumb at the building. "There's a dead woman in there?"

"Yes." Elery shot a pleading look at Lucan. He stood and took over, giving the sheriff more details of what they'd discovered.

"Well, that's seriously crazy." The sheriff pulled his gun out of the holster. "Okay, wait here."

Both men entered the building, the sheriff in the lead. Elery got up, trudged to the truck and climbed in, leaving her legs hanging out so she could face Lucan. But instead of Lucan's face, she saw Angela's—her pale skin, her staring eyes, and the small circle of blood on her chest.

Elery dropped the carving to her lap and pressed her hands over her eyes. Angela wouldn't be giving them any leads on Garrick. Whatever she'd known had gone to the grave with her. Why would someone do this to her?

Did it have anything to do with the lizard? Probably not, since it hadn't been taken. She grabbed the carving again and rotated it in her hands. Up close, the lizard was intricate, its toes individually carved, the tail whip-like with tiny cuts meant to represent scales. Jacob Waltz had skills. She poked and prodded at the wood surface. Everything felt solid, except for the right eye which pushed in slightly, but that didn't seem to do anything. Why was this thing special enough for Jacob to mention it in his journal, even calling it his real treasure?

"Let me see." Lucan held his hand out, and she passed it to him. "Sometimes, it takes a combination of things to get results." He pushed the right eye in and held it while working with the rest of the base.

She looked over his shoulder at the entrance to the apartment building. Complete silence, no noises at all.

When she glanced back, Lucan had removed the entire top of the lizard from the base. "How did you do that?"

He flashed a brilliant smile. She fought the urge to smooth her palm over his face, to somehow join into this small bit of victory. "It rotated off. My dad was a locksmith, remember? This is a key of sorts."

Inside the carving lay a folded piece of light brown paper. Another journal page?

Lucan extracted the paper, carefully unfolded it and held it out to Elery. She took it, examining the series of contour lines, hash marks and double circles. It was a map!

This one was similar to the one Angela had shown her, but with some additions. In the center, a heart was drawn. Could it be the one Jacob etched for Ila? A short distance from the heart was the cross, in the same position as she'd seen it on Angela's map. Beyond it to the west was an ornate letter O. Near that another heart with the letter O inside it. A variety of other symbols dotted the area around those.

Angela had never known her map was incomplete. Even so, Angela and Garrick might have gotten close to the mine, assuming one of these other symbols represented it. But if so, which one? Did the O stand for "oro," the Spanish word for gold?

Sheriff Turner came out of the building and headed their way. Behind him, Deputy Hellerman strode to his car while talking into a walkie-talkie affixed to his shoulder. Elery jumped down from the truck.

The sheriff placed a hand on her shoulder and shook his head. "You were right. The girl is gone. You said her name is Angela?"

"Yes. Angela Harmon." Elery bit her lip. "She went with Garrick to look for the mine."

Sheriff Turner frowned. "Oh, that Angela. I hadn't been able to find her to talk with her. Now, I know why. Deputy Hellerman is calling the county coroner right now. Do you know anything more about her?"

"Garrick said she was a student at the college in Phoenix. She lived here and drove every day for classes."

The sheriff flipped open a notebook and wrote down her response. "Any ideas on next of kin?"

"Garrick said she had family in Texas, I think."

Deputy Hellerman came up behind the sheriff. "The coroner is on his way."

The sheriff nodded to him, then glanced down at the map in Elery's hand. "What have you got there?"

"Believe it or not, I think it's a treasure map." Elery tugged on her lip. Angela had been the last one with Garrick. Now she was dead. It couldn't be a coincidence. This had something to do with Garrick's kidnapping. The note had warned her not to talk to the police, but would the kidnapper, especially if it was Ron, keep his end of the deal if they found the mine? Or would Garrick end up like Angela?

She looked the sheriff up and down. He had always dealt fairly with the people in town. She trusted him, and somebody should know where they were going, in case anything happened. She spent several minutes explaining the note and the journal pages. As he listened, the sheriff folded his arms, his bushy eyebrows raised. Deputy Hellerman stood off to the side, listening with no expression at all.

When she finished, Lucan took over. "I believe Ron's behind this, but he won't hurt Garrick until he's sure he doesn't need him anymore. If we can find the mine, I'm sure Ron can be bought with gold."

Sheriff Turner rubbed his chin. "So, you plan on going out into the mountains again?"

They both responded by nodding. Lucan met her gaze and gave her a half smile of encouragement. Her heart swelled with gratitude. She had no way to repay him for all he'd done.

"All right." The sheriff leaned against the rear tire of the truck. "Then, I'm going with you."

"Oh." Elery shifted her eyes away from him. "We appreciate your help, but ..."

"Hey, this isn't a game. Angela was shot. Somebody wanted to stop her from searching for the mine."

Elery focused back on his large frame. That wasn't her point. No doubt they needed more help, but the sheriff wasn't the man to protect them in the mountains.

Sheriff Turner turned his eyes to Lucan. "This is a more dangerous rescue mission than you're used to. I'm not letting you two go out there alone."

"No offense, sir." Deputy Hellerman scratched at his goatee. "But you're not exactly in mountain-rescue shape." He pounded a fist on his trim midsection. "I'll go with them."

Sheriff Turner rested an arm across his belly. "Probably a better idea. I'd slow you down. I'll stay here to work on Angela's case. You three go and find the mine."

CHAPTER TWENTY-THREE

The setting sun drew broad brushstrokes of umber and rust across the desert plains, broken only by the dark blue shadows of the mountains. Lucan wiped a sheen of sweat off his forehead. The temperature had yet to drop far enough to cool him off.

He alternated between watching the ground to keep from tripping on scrub brush and staring at the scrub brush patches of hair growing on the back of Hellerman's shaved head. The officer led them along a barely existent trail that had some connection with an old military trail. Apparently, Hellerman thought the mountainous contours on the map looked like an unnamed mountain near Millsite Canyon.

"How do you know this area?" Lucan asked.

Hellerman turned his head a few degrees. "I've done some recreational hiking around here recently."

This area was pretty remote, but it made sense. All of Hellerman's answers made sense. Still, something seemed odd about the man. It wasn't that he had volunteered to come. Lots of cops would do that. It wasn't that he took the lead on what area to search. Maybe he *had* done hiking here recently. No, it was the way he made eye contact, like he was sizing up the competition. Was Hellerman merely the competitive type or did he have interest in something else? Elery? The lost mine?

As Hellerman turned to face front, he spoke louder out of the corner of his mouth so Lucan could hear. "Don't you think you need a weapon out here?"

Lucan shifted the heavy pack on his back, trying to get some air in between his shoulder blades. "Haven't needed it yet." He only carried pepper spray. Although he'd completed firearm training, he wasn't required to carry a gun on rescue missions, and he preferred not to.

Hellerman patted the holster on his hip. "Funny thing about a gun. If you don't have it, the one time you need it will be the last."

Elery spoke up from the back of the group. "Let's check up there." Using the corner of the map, she pointed to a rough, high peak.

The hope in her voice twisted his gut into knots. They were running out of time. They had come this far, but what if they couldn't find the mine? Would Ron really kill Garrick? Maybe they could offer him a trade—the map for Garrick.

Hellerman adjusted his heading and led the way up the mountain. Lucan dropped back to allow Elery go in between them. He felt better being behind in case she fell backward. With her nose buried in the map, she could trip over anything.

She shifted the heavy pack and sleeping bag higher on her shoulders. He would help her with the load, but he didn't dare offer. It would only offend her.

Halfway up, the mountain flattened into a small mesa, an island oasis for their burning legs. He sucked in several deep breaths and rubbed his hands over his thighs. In front of him, Elery tucked the map between her legs, took a hair tie off her wrist and twisted her curls up into a messy bun, exposing her graceful neck. He imagined running a hand along her neck, then cupping the base of her head and drawing her lips in close. The memory of their passionate kiss hit him full force. His heart rate picked up, and his gut tied in knots. He tore his eyes away from her in time to catch Hellerman staring at Elery as well.

Lucan narrowed his gaze, but Hellerman glanced over at him and winked. Lucan couldn't blame him for finding Elery attractive, but Hellerman didn't even know her. Not that Elery was interested in either of them with Garrick's life on the line. She paced the length of the mesa, still focused on the map.

Lucan touched her elbow. "You should rest."

She pulled away and kept walking. "No, we need to keep ..." She fell forward onto her hands and knees. The map crumpled beneath one of her palms.

Lucan grabbed her under the armpits and brought her back to a standing position. "Are you okay?"

"I'm fine." She opened her hands and examined her palms. Minor scratches, but no cuts. The map, however, was a wrinkled, dusty mass.

While she brushed dirt off the map, he backtracked her steps to find out what she tripped over. Using his toes, he discovered a flat edge of rock sticking up from the surrounding matrix. He bent down and ran his hands along the rock. The tips of his fingers dipped down into a depression about an inch deep. He moved his fingers back and forth, following the depression. It was too uniform.

"I think there's something here." He dropped to his knees to inspect it, blowing dust off the smooth rock. A groove ran through the basalt, coming to a point, and then curving around the other side. Running his fingers over the whole of it, he traced a heart.

Elery's mouth dropped open. She'd recognized it, too. "The heart on the map." She spread out the paper and touched the area. "The one Jacob carved for Ila."

"What?" Hellerman's question threw him. Lucan had almost forgotten he was there.

"It means we're close." Elery refolded the map to a square showing the heart, the letter O and the O with the heart inside.

Lucan waved a hand at the setting sun. "We're close, but we aren't going to make it there tonight. Let's start thinking about a place to camp." The mesa was flat, but full of large rocks. Not much fun to sleep on in a sleeping bag.

An hour later, they had climbed back down and selected a sandy area close to the nearby creek. No rain was expected for several days, so they didn't have to worry about flash floods.

Lucan laid out his sleeping bag, complete with built-in pillow, then helped Elery with hers. Hellerman headed out into the dark with a compact flashlight to relieve himself.

Lucan and Elery sat on their separate sleeping bags, staring at each other in silence. Moonlight played off her features, making her skin glow. If only, he could tell what she was thinking. She had to feel the ticking clock as much as he did. Despite the pressure, she seemed to be holding together okay. But would he know if it was an act?

She reached over and grabbed a jacket from her pack.

"Are you cold?" He moved closer, putting his arms around her, enjoying the excuse to hold her close. "What do you think of Hellerman?" he whispered in her ear.

"I don't know. He's kind of a Jesse James type, but the sheriff trusts him."

"I'm not sure I do."

The crunch of footsteps signaled Hellerman's return. Lucan dropped his arms. Not that he'd done anything wrong, but it was awkward to hold her in front of someone else. She slipped on the jacket.

"No fire, and we should sleep apart from each other at least fifteen feet," Hellerman said. "Less chance of all of us getting attacked."

Did he mean attacked by wolves or people? For Elery's sake, Lucan wouldn't ask. No fire was certainly to keep other people from knowing their location. That he could understand, but he wouldn't keep his distance from Elery. "I'm sleeping right next to her."

"Suit yourself, lover boy. I'm just trying to tell you what's safest." Hellerman carried his backpack twenty feet away. "You might want to throw your packs next to mine over by the river. Better safe than sorry if predators come looking for food."

Lucan grabbed Elery's pack and walked them both over, then he left to relieve himself as well. When he returned, Elery went to do the same. Hellerman carried his sleeping bag to a spot fifteen feet away. As he walked, the moonlight caused a faint shadow to trail along behind him, long and thin, like a walking stick. He unrolled his bag, then walked back for his water bottle. Holding the bottle in one hand, he gave Lucan a shove with the other. "I get why you're hot for her. Curves in all the best places, wild hair, pretty face. But be careful, man."

Lucan couldn't believe this guy. "What do you mean?"

"That one, she knows how to push." Hellerman tossed the bottle into his other hand. "She's a hard one to control."

More like, hard to resist. Lucan stared in the direction she'd gone. He could get used to being the one who could get past her defenses. The one she bent her strong will for. Only he didn't know if she wanted him to be that person. He ignored Hellerman and climbed into his sleeping bag. Elery's strong personality didn't threaten him. It drew him in like a honeybee to a hive.

***

Darkness completely surrounded Jayna as she climbed over the last ridge. Finally, she had a clear view of the location where she'd seen the smoke. About fifty feet away, a gentle slope led up to a large gaping hole in the rock. The sharp smell of burning gasoline floated on the breeze, although the smoke itself had dissipated. A mangled plastic box sat abandoned on the ground.

The area was deserted except for one man standing with a rifle, his silhouette illuminated by a soft haze of light coming from the opening behind. She crouched down in the scraggly bushes. A guard wasn't a good sign. Her pistol rested in the front pocket of her backpack, but she hesitated to get it. The man hadn't seen her, and the noise from the zipper would alert him to her presence. She should just leave.

After flicking a cigarette onto the ground, the man moved off to her left side, fiddling with his pants as he walked. This was her chance to leave, but curiosity tugged at her. Why was he here? What was this place?

Loud, animated voices poured out from inside the cavern. All male voices. The sound waves bounced around her, making it seem like a dozen people were in there. Outside the entrance, a pile of ashes lay mixed with cigarette butts and used paper plates. No way was this a settlement. It had to be a mine, probably an illegal one. She needed to get away from here fast.

She moved a step backward, sinking deeper into the tangled foliage. Rustling noises came from behind. She froze. The guard with the gun passed twenty yards behind her, blocking off her escape route. He was doing a perimeter sweep, scanning the desert night for intruders. She crouched in between him and the cavern entrance. Not a good place to be whenever he decided to return to his post. But if she tried to leave and he glanced back, she'd be silhouetted against the light from the cavern. She either had to move fast or stay put and hope he didn't stumble over her.

She kept her eyes on him. The man continued to move parallel to her position, much too close for comfort.

Carefully placing her feet, she silently moved to the left, approaching the west side of the mountain.

A beam of light swept the area to her left ahead of her. She dropped to the ground.

Prickly scrub brush scratched at her face. She peered up between the dry plants. The circle of light grew until another man stepped out into the night, holding a lantern. He'd come from an opening in the western side of the mountain. It was a different entrance to the cavern, only ten yards away from her.

The new man had his head bent over an electronic device that he held in one hand. The device emitted a quiet beeping sound.

The man took a few more steps, then placed the lantern on the ground. With his eyes still locked on the device in his hand, he reached behind his back and pulled out a pistol.

She ducked her head and held her breath. Now, she couldn't see him at all. Hopefully, that meant he couldn't see her either.

The beeping sound traveled off to her right. The frequency of the beeps slowed. She risked a peek. He was moving away.

She let out a shaky breath. As soon as he moved out of earshot, she'd quietly sneak away.

The man turned and the intensity of the beeps sped up. He was coming back. She lowered her head again. What was he looking for with that thing?

A stomping in the bushes ahead gave away his position. She was still partially hidden, but if he kept advancing toward her, he'd trip over her soon. She had to move again.

Scooting backward, she kept her head low. All she could see was the device sweeping in a wide circle. The beeps diminished every time it moved away from a direct line pointing to her.

Suddenly, the device was pulled away, replaced by the black barrel of a gun. She lifted her head a fraction. The man scanning the area had piercing dark eyes. Her stomach lurched. It was Peralta. He was involved in more than she had imagined. She needed to get out of here so she could turn in his illegal mine.

But he was too close. She had nowhere to go where he wouldn't see her. Tensing her legs, she prepared to flee. Then, realization settled in, thick and bitter in her throat. It didn't matter if she ran. The device was a GPS locator. Somehow, he'd tagged her.

Peralta took two giant steps until he hovered over her, his lips curling. He raised the pistol, pointing it at her head. "Funny, this isn't the area I asked you to map, Jayna."

CHAPTER TWENTY-FOUR

Elery woke as the first rays of sunlight threw themselves across the jagged peaks. Rolling over, she came face to face with Lucan. The depth of his brown eyes, dark on the outer ring and amber stained glass on the inner, lulled her into thinking she was dreaming. Until he spoke.

"Good morning." He smiled, but it didn't reach his eyes. "I've got bad news."

She shot up, dragging half of the sleeping bag with her, and scanned the area. Two sleeping bags on the ground. Not three.

Hellerman was gone.

She sucked in a quick breath, and the crisp air shocked her lungs. "Where did he go?"

Lucan stood and began rolling his sleeping bag. "Probably after the mine."

She kicked off the rest of her sleeping bag, shoved her feet in her boots, and raced over to her backpack. Dropping to her knees, she dug into it.

But Lucan confirmed her fear before she got too deep into the pack. "That's the bad news. He took the map."

She shoved the backpack away. Now what? How would they find the mine or get Garrick back without the map? Today was Wednesday. According to the note, they had to find the mine today. She fisted her hands on her thighs. "I guess your instincts about him were right."

Lucan's footsteps crunched on the rocks as he walked over to her. He squatted down so close their lips were inches apart. "I must have heard you wrong. Did you just say I was right?" His teasing tone might have made her smile if not for the situation. He grabbed one of her hands and uncurled her fist, then he pulled something from his back pocket and pressed it into her hand. Rising, he went back to packing up their stuff.

She looked down at her hand and sighed. "Your cell won't work out here."

"Look at it."

She glanced down. The screen was dark, but he obviously meant for her to turn it on. She pressed the center button. When the screen blinked to life, a picture came up. Her mouth fell open. It was a picture of the map.

Jumping up, she locked eyes with him. "You took a picture of it before we left. Oh, I could kiss you for this." As soon as the words left her mouth, she regretted them. It was the truth, but she didn't want to toy with him. Lucan deserved better than her.

He dropped her sleeping bag and took a step forward, his mouth set in a lopsided grin. "Is that a promise?"

The memory of their previous kiss brought heat to her face once again. Better not to go there. They had enough actual problems without throwing their feelings into the mix. Like having to go up against an armed deputy to get to the mine. How would she live with herself if Lucan got hurt? "On second thought, you should give me the map and leave. Get away from this whole situation while you can." Elery turned her back on him.

Lucan left the gear and walked over to her. She felt his presence, but he didn't try to touch her. "I'm not letting you do this anymore. What's happening isn't your fault and it has nothing to do with Chad's death or Garrick's injury from fifteen years ago."

"It's not that simple. I'll probably die trying to find Garrick. I don't want you dying with me." Even though God was set against her, she had to follow this path, but

Lucan didn't. "Pastor Arroyo was right. My faith is too small."

Lucan grabbed her shoulders. She tried to pull away, but he held tight. He firmly spun her around. "About that, he *was* right. You're making your faith all about you and not at all about God."

What did he mean? Of course, this was about God.

"God is so much bigger than your guilt. Don't they teach the Bible at that church of yours? The Bible says God forgives us for anything." Lucan shook his head. His eyes bored into hers. "God has already forgiven you for everything, but instead of gratefully accepting it, you turn your back on Him."

No, he had it backward. "God doesn't want to help me. How else can you explain all this?" She gestured around to indicate their present situation. "And my dad, and Garrick spending his whole life crippled and ..." She was going to say Chad, but his name stuck in her throat.

Lucan let go to press both hands to his chest. "What about me? It was my brother who died. Should I think God is mad at me?"

"Of course not. You're the good guy, the rescuer. You probably bring home stray dogs and push spiders out the door rather than flush them."

He stared at her with wide eyes. "Is that what you think of me? That I've never done anything wrong?"

She stared back, sure that her eyes gave away her thoughts. Lucan was the most forgiving, most generous person she'd ever known. No matter how many times she'd thought about being with him, she'd never be worthy.

He backpedaled until he hit a rock outcrop where he sat heavily. "I'm not deserving of a pedestal, Elery." He ran a hand through his hair, but it stubbornly flipped back down again, refusing to stay a mess. "When my dad died, Chad and I were sixteen. Both of us were angry. Angry at

God, angry at our mom for moving on, even angry with everyone else for not understanding how angry we were. So, we started acting out. I told myself I was following Chad around to make sure he didn't get into trouble, but it was a lie. I made my own decision to be a part of it." He wiped his hands down his jeans. "It started with a simple dare. Pick the lock on a nearby toy store. I did it just to see if I could. We only meant to skateboard around the store in the dark, but the cash register was right there. Fifty bucks seemed like a fortune back then."

Seriously? Lucan had been a thief as a kid? That didn't fit with her image of him. What had happened? He couldn't have a record or they wouldn't let him work with the Sheriff's Office. She opened her mouth, but couldn't seem to figure out what to say. Instead, she sucked in a huge breath of the cool air.

"When my mom found out, she turned us in."

Elery stifled a gasp.

"It was the best thing she could have done. The two of us spent thirty days in juvenile hall. We met a pastor there who led us back to the Lord. He told me God forgave me, but at first that didn't change my life. I couldn't accept it. It didn't make sense. Why would God freely offer such a gift?"

Her mind spun. She understood the feeling. Forgiveness shouldn't be free. Everything had a cost. No way would she let herself off the hook while others paid the price for her mistakes.

"My life didn't change until I understood why." Lucan pushed off the rock and approached her. He stopped mere inches away, looking down with his dark eyes locked on hers. "Do you know *why* God offers forgiveness, Elery?"

The way he said her name was intimate. She shook her head, not trusting herself to speak.

"He forgives because He loves. Do you believe in love?"

Did she? The idea of love was wrapped in fear. She was supposed to strive for God's love, for God's blessing, and try to outrun the curse of her sins. Only she could never get away from them.

When she didn't answer, Lucan continued. "Losing my brother was like losing a part of me, like an arm or a leg. I'll never be the same."

She hung her head as the pain she'd caused him clawed at her heart.

He lifted his hand, put two fingers under her chin and tipped her head back up. "But my pain is not yours to carry."

"Of course it is. It was my fault."

"We've all done bad things."

"Some more than others." Elery spoke between clenched teeth. He didn't get it. The things she'd done weren't little white lies or petty crime and he knew it. He might have stolen some money, but he'd never hurt anyone.

"Do you think it matters to God how much you've sinned?"

"How could it not matter?"

"People put labels on sin, even calling some acceptable or understandable, but God doesn't do that. Sin is sin."

Elery backed away and dropped her chin to her chest, expecting him to stay put. Instead, he inched closer.

"God doesn't care how much sin you have. One sin or fifty, cheating on your taxes or killing someone, He wants to forgive them all. Don't walk away from Him because you're too proud to accept it."

Was Lucan right? Had she been the one to push God away every time something bad happened? She stared down at the laces on her boots. The left one had come undone and was twisted up into a knotted mess. Her heart was no less tangled, entwined by the constricting strings of guilt, strangled by ropes of fear.

"Remember Job from the Bible. He lost his wealth, his family, even his health. Job probably felt the same way you do. Persecuted."

She lifted her head and met his gaze. "I know the passages. Job hadn't done anything wrong to be persecuted. I have."

"That doesn't mean God is persecuting you."

Pastor Arroyo would completely disagree. He'd believe she was getting what she deserved, and he'd have Bible verses to back it up. Why didn't Lucan see it that way? God's persecution was her penance. "I have to somehow pay for what I've done. I took Chad's life."

Lucan pinched his lips together, closed his eyes, and took a slow breath. She wanted to take the words back, erase the pain on his face, but she couldn't. She was the cause of his pain.

When he opened his eyes, sadness and peace shone in them. "I miss my brother, but I know God is in charge of it all." Lucan reached up and held her chin between two fingers. "I forgive you as He forgave me."

She stared into his warm eyes, wanting nothing more than to melt into them. His mouth, his lips were so close. A hot breeze blew up, setting her skin on fire. "Why are we talking about this now?"

His jaw tensed for a second, then relaxed. "I need you to believe in love." He ran his knuckles down her cheek. "God's love and mine. I'm falling in love with you, Elery."

Her heart skipped several beats, then raced off at a marathoner's pace. The memory of the brief kiss they'd shared at the kennel filled her with a warmth the sun couldn't match. She shifted her eyes to study him, perfect hair draped across his forehead, the subtle shadow of day-old stubble, the hint of a dimple in his hopeful smile.

This amazing man was falling for her. Her heart soared at the idea, but the rest of her acknowledged the sad truth. She couldn't look him in the face every day, knowing she'd killed his brother.

Turning away, she slipped out of his grasp. If only this could be a normal romance, but it wasn't. In a gentle voice, she whispered, "Can we please get going? We don't have much more time."

His shoulders dropped. She'd disappointed him, again. "You're right. We can put this on hold. For now."

She gave him back the phone and reached for her pack, intent on pretending this conversation never happened. If she didn't respond to his declaration, maybe he'd reconsider his feelings.

They walked for half an hour, following the wandering path of the stream. Elery trailed behind Lucan, who unknowingly made it difficult for her to concentrate. The muscles in his lithe body were in constant motion, capturing her gaze like a baited hook.

Her foot caught on something, pitching her forward. With a startled gasp, she flew into Lucan. He swung his arms around and managed to catch her on his back before she fell to the ground.

For several heartbeats, they stayed that way. His arms encircling her backward. Her chest pressed against the muscles of his back. As he relaxed his grip, she righted herself. "Sorry, I tripped."

He glanced over his shoulder. The gleam in his eyes said he didn't mind her falling all over him. How could he be so open about his feelings when she'd all but stomped on them earlier? He was beyond resilient.

She retraced her steps to find what she'd tripped over this time. Feeling along the ground with the toes of her boot, she hit the lip of something solid buried in the ground. Kneeling down, she brushed dirt off the area, revealing an object constructed of two pieces of granite.

The rocks were held together by a rusted wire. She slipped her fingers along the sides and pulled it upright. A stone cross. This had to be the cross marked on Angela's original map and also on the map from the lizard.

They had found Weiser's grave.

What were the chances of her tripping over both the heart rock marking Ila's grave and this one? She glanced up at the clear, blue sky. Maybe somebody up there was looking out for them, after all.

She turned her attention back to the map. Now that they had two points of reference, finding the other symbols should be easier. Lucan held the cell phone in front of her. "If this is the cross here, then we have to look up there for either the O or the heart with the O inside. Those are the largest symbols on the map." He pointed to the mountain behind them.

She peered at the magnified image. He was right. At least they didn't have to traverse the river, although the cool water would feel incredible right now. She stood, letting the carved cross fall back into its dusty resting place.

As they headed up the mountainside and the slope increased, she concentrated on keeping upright on the slippery slope. They hadn't gone more than twenty yards when Lucan stopped abruptly. She ran into his back. "Hey."

He held himself stiff and didn't answer. Something was wrong.

She peered around his arm. Next to a large boulder, Hellerman stood with his legs wide. In his hands, he held a rifle pointed at Lucan's chest.

"You should have just gone home." Hellerman walked slowly to within a few paces of them. He gestured with the rifle to the valley between the mountains, heading northwest. "Now, you're coming to see the boss."

CHAPTER TWENTY-FIVE

Two hours into the hike, Hellerman hadn't said a word except, "Keep moving."

Not that she was in the mood for conversation, but she had to get him talking. They needed to know what they were up against. "This boss of yours, does he go around kidnapping people too?"

Hellerman glared at her, but maintained his stony silence.

She pushed her legs faster to walk even with him. "Of course not. He would leave that kind of thing to you. Predictable."

Hellerman let out a nervous laugh. "You'll be surprised by how unpredictable he is." He turned to glare at Lucan. "Both of you will be."

"Well, I don't know why you work for a guy who forces you to do all the dirty work. What does he pay you for this?"

A nervous tremor ran through Hellerman's lower lip. "Out here, you take what you can get. It's better than working for a sap like the sheriff."

Beneath the bravado, Hellerman seemed afraid of his boss. And that scared her more than anything else.

They hiked for an hour more before Hellerman directed them to climb a mountain she recognized as La Barge Mountain. During her hikes with Garrick, they had circled around La Barge, but never gone to the top. Hellerman led them to the southwest side and up a steep slope to a rounded opening in the side of the mountain.

Near the opening, a tailings pile mixed with trash told Elery exactly what this was—an illegal mine. But whose?

Hellerman grabbed her arm and forced her to move in front of Lucan into the shadowed tunnel. Weak light came from lanterns hung at odd intervals on the walls. Hellerman yanked her along for about fifty feet to where the tunnel curved. As they came around the curve, she caught a glimpse ahead. The tunnel ended in a cell with metal bars. It wasn't empty.

Sitting on the floor, leaning against the rock wall, was Jayna. Her eyes were closed, dirt streaked down her face. Why was she here? And then it clicked. Jayna had suspected her boss was involved in illegal mining. This had to be Peralta's mine.

Hellerman pushed Elery against the bars, then dug something out of his pocket. He twisted a black key in the padlock and flipped the lock onto the ground. The cell door squeaked as he pulled it open. He shoved her inside, shut it and secured it with the padlock. "Stay here and make friends. Your boyfriend has someone to see."

Elery grabbed the bars as she watched Lucan's back disappear down the tunnel. Why would Peralta want to see him?

Despair seeped into her chest like caustic acid. None of this would have happened if Lucan hadn't been helping her find the mine. Even knowing Hellerman was out there with a gun looking for the same mine, hadn't convinced her to give up. This was all her fault. She dropped to the ground, leaning her forehead against the metal bars.

"What do they want with Lucan?" Tears blurred her vision. "And where in the world is Garrick?"

"Not here." A note of confidence filled Jayna's voice as she scooted closer.

Elery slowly turned around to face her, wiping the tears with the back of her hand. For all she knew, Peralta had him in a cell somewhere nearby. "Why do you say that?"

"I've seen Garrick." Jayna chewed on the side of her thumbnail.

"Where?"

"He fell into a crevice a few miles away. I found him, went to get help, and ended up here."

It didn't make sense. If Garrick was stuck in a crevice, what about the note? Could Jayna be mistaken? "You're sure it was him?"

"As sure as I can be. Blue windbreaker, dark hair, dark eyes, just like the picture you showed me." A pained expression crossed Jayna's face. "Except he's pretty emaciated."

Elery's emotions bounced around like a yo-yo. Jayna had found Garrick. He was alone and stuck in a crevice. Had he fallen because of his crippled leg? What if he died out there while she sat in here? Her hands trembled. She pressed them into her chest. "I can't seem to make anything right. Chad, Garrick, Lucan ..." She waved a hand at Jayna. "... and now you."

Jayna crawled to the bars and sat with her arms around her knees next to Elery. "What do you mean?"

Elery hesitated to open up. But what difference did it make if Jayna knew? "Because of what I've done, everyone I come in contact with ends up suffering."

Jayna shook her head, sending her sleek ponytail flipping over her shoulder. "I'm pretty sure we're in this cage because of Peralta, not because of you."

"You're here because you took my advice and spied on your employer. All of this is punishment for what I've done."

"Actually, you're wrong. I'm here because one of Peralta's men exploded a gas container with dynamite. I heard it and came to investigate. But what do you think you're being punished for?"

Elery dropped her head into her hands. Jayna knew about the mine accident, but if Elery told Jayna about her past, there was no telling how Jayna would react. They barely knew each other.

Jayna placed a gentle hand on Elery's shoulder. "You don't have to tell me, but whatever you did, God has already forgiven you for it."

"Forgiveness." The word came out in a whisper. Lucan had told her to accept God's forgiveness, but how could she? She didn't deserve it. The words spilled out then, a long torrent of guilt and sorrow. As she told her darkest secret about what she'd done to Garrick, Jayna listened and nodded as if none of it surprised her.

When Elery finished, Jayna looked her directly in the eyes. "We're all flawed, Elery. Forgiveness isn't just about faith. It's about understanding yourself and the nature of God. I have some pretty intimate experience with forgiveness myself."

"How so?"

Jayna drew her knees up again, resting her palms on her kneecaps. "When I was young, my father abused me. My mother did what she could to get me away from him, but he came back. After I graduated from college, he found me and killed some people to get to me."

Elery blinked. This peaceful, kind woman was related to a murderer. It didn't seem possible. "Where is he now?"

"In prison, where he should be. I don't have a relationship with him, although God has helped me to forgive him."

"How do you accept what he did?"

Her smile lit up her bright blue eyes. "That's the crazy thing about forgiveness. It's not saying something is okay. It's actually identifying that something really bad happened, but not holding a claim of judgment against the person who did it. I'm not going to hold my father's sin against him, even though I know he hasn't changed. God is the perfect judge, not me. If I refuse to forgive and hold onto my anger, I'm using it to keep control, instead of giving everything up to God. Releasing judgment to Him is how you find peace."

"So, you're not angry with your father?"

"Of course, I still get angry, and I work through it with God's help. But forgiveness isn't a feeling, it's a choice. I choose to leave my father's judgment in God's hands." She tilted her head and smiled again. "You can choose forgiveness, too—for yourself. As a child of God, you can claim forgiveness."

Logically, it didn't make sense for God's forgiveness to be available to everyone, except her. But knowing that in her head didn't make it travel to her heart. "If only it were that easy."

"You're right. It's not easy." Jayna bumped Elery's arm with her elbow. "Especially when you refuse to try."

***

Lucan slowed his pace as the tunnel took a hard left turn. Hellerman shoved him forward, digging the rifle into the flesh between his shoulder blades. "Don't worry, I'm sure you'll get back to the ladies soon."

"Who is this boss of yours?"

Hellerman snickered. "I call him Peralta."

"Like the Mexican Peraltas?" The ones Elery said were the first gold miners in the area. Was this guy related to them? And what was so amusing about the name? He had to be missing something, but Hellerman didn't seem inclined to fill him in.

A few minutes later, music echoed down the tunnel in a low, thrumming beat. More light played along the walls. The tunnel opened into a large room with the same rough-cut walls lit by a dozen lanterns.

Hellerman hung back, motioning for Lucan to enter first. "You might know him by a different name."

As Lucan passed through the opening, he came to a halt. His stomach hardened into stone. Two men sat behind a makeshift desk. One of them—the one with his arms crossed over his chest—was his cousin.

Peralta is Ron?

Puzzle pieces dropped into place. Ron wrote the note. This mine was his, but he wanted the Lost Dutchman. He'd kidnapped Garrick, knowing Lucan would use the journal pages to help Elery. And now Ron had the map, which meant he'd leverage them against each other until he found the mine, then he'd have no use for any of them.

Ron waved away the man next to him. "Looks like it's family time."

The man got up and left out a back opening. Ron stood and strode over to face Lucan. Ron's messy dark hair and almost-black eyes barely resembled the kid Lucan remembered seeing once every couple of years while growing up. But Ron looked every bit as devious as the day Lucan had last seen him—the night Ron had attacked him in the hallway of Chad's apartment building. The same night Chad and Lucan had decided to hide the pages.

Ron squared his shoulders and turned to Hellerman. "Did you find it?"

Hellerman straightened to his full height, several inches taller than Ron. "My search was interrupted by him and his girlfriend."

Turning back to Lucan, Ron worked his jaw back and forth. "You should have gone home, Luc."

Funny, Hellerman had said the same thing. These two really deserved each other. Lucan relaxed his shoulders. If he stayed calm, maybe he could find out where Ron was holding Garrick. "Good idea. Let me and the ladies leave, and I'll do just that. I'll go home."

Ron threw his arms up and laughed. "You always were the reasonable one. Sure, I'll let you go."

The sarcasm didn't bode well for any of them. Change of plan. If he ended up back in the cell with the women, he'd need something to pick the lock. Feigning submission, he dipped his head and scanned the ground. Empty containers, loose rock and plastic zip ties littered the floor. None of it usable.

Wait. A metallic object lay a few feet to his right. A nail?

"If I let you go, then what? You call the sheriff and report my little operation here?"

He didn't bother to deny it. Instead, he raised his head and tried to think of what he could say to anger Ron.

"It's a shame, really." Ron took a few steps closer. "I know you don't care about the mine one way or another. That was all Chad. And yet, here you are. A living testimony to Elery's powers of persuasion."

Ron said her name with respect and lust all at once. It made Lucan cringe, but maybe she was the chink in Ron's armor. Lucan flipped a hand through his hair. "Elery." He rolled the middle vowel slowly over his tongue to draw out her name. "You're right. She's definitely hard to resist. She wants the mine as much as you do." It wasn't really a lie. She wanted to find the mine to save Garrick.

Ron narrowed his eyes and came closer until only a foot of empty space separated them. Was he buying it?

Lucan kept his gaze riveted on Ron's eyes, refusing to back down. "Her father's retirement and his medical bills are all wrapped up in the Hearst Mine and ..." He shrugged. "Well, you know how that's going. I guess she needs the money."

A muscle in Ron's jaw twitched. If nothing else, creating sympathy for Elery might ensure Ron kept her alive for a while. But it wasn't getting the reaction he wanted. Lucan had to keep pushing.

"I suppose that's why she worked so hard to convince me to help. She said she'd make it worth the trouble." Lucan touched two fingers to his lips. "I must say she's kept up her end of the bargain. She's a great kisser."

Ron threw a punch at Lucan's stomach. All the air rushed out of his lungs. He doubled over, leaned to the side and fell to the ground. The blow was harder than expected, but just the cover he needed. His hand closed around the broken nail.

As he crawled back to his feet, he slipped the nail into his shoe.

"Probably doesn't feel worth it now, does it?" Ron stepped back, folded his arms across his chest and nodded at Hellerman. "Take the fight out of him, then stick him in the cell until we have time to deal with him."

CHAPTER TWENTY-SIX

Elery rested her head against the rock wall in the far corner of the cell. Fatigue dragged at her eyelids. They had hiked for hours before being kidnapped by Hellerman, who forced them to hike several more hours. And Lucan had been gone almost an hour. Was it still late afternoon outside or had night already fallen? She couldn't tell in this prison. The only light came from the series of lanterns lit by candles on the walls outside the cell.

Jayna leaned next to Elery and rubbed her arm periodically. Strange, and yet comforting, to have another woman mother her, especially one who couldn't be more than a few years older.

A rustling in the tunnel drew her attention. She got up and moved to the bars with Jayna following behind. Had Hellerman come back with Lucan?

Two shadowed figures approached. Even before they came into the soft glow of the candles, she recognized Lucan by his easy stride, but his body tilted a little to the side. Was he limping? Her heart picked up its pace.

The stocky man with Lucan unlocked the padlock, opened the door, and pushed him inside. As the man slammed the door closed, Elery wrapped her arms around Lucan, hugging tight to his chest. "I'm so glad you're okay."

He winced.

She pulled away. "Are you hurt?"

He gingerly circled his arms around her, resting his

hands between her shoulder blades. "Just a little sore. Ron punched me, and then Hellerman had to get a few in before telling someone else to bring me back."

She pulled out of his embrace again. "Wait, did you say Ron?"

"Yeah. This mine is run by Ron."

"Ron is Peralta?" Bile rose up in her throat. Ron had betrayed her. He'd written the note and used Garrick as bait to manipulate her into finding the mine.

"Who's Ron?" Jayna asked.

"It's a long story." Lucan turned from Jayna back to Elery, lowering his voice. "Who is she?"

"This is Jayna."

"Oh, the other geologist. Okay." Lucan nodded at Jayna, then swiveled his head in all directions. "We have to go."

Before Elery could ask how, he bent down and pulled something from his shoe. Then, he leaned in close again, motioning for Jayna to come near. "We have to get out and find where they're holding Garrick." He focused on Jayna. "You've been here longer. Any ideas on where he might be?"

"Garrick isn't here." Jayna pointed to the southeast. "He's stuck in a crevice a few miles away."

Lucan ran a hand through his hair as realization dawned on his face. "Then we really must leave now. Ron has no other options. He'll either try to hurt one of us to find the mine or if he finds it on his own, he'll just get rid of us."

Elery didn't need any convincing to leave, but there was a problem. She smacked one of the bars, causing it to vibrate in the ground. "How do we get out of here?"

Lucan's smile warmed her from the inside out. He lifted his hand and held up a rusty nail. "Locksmith, remember?"

She shook her head and grinned. "Right, I keep forgetting about your alter ego."

"I'm going to need your help." He cupped her chin to make her look at him. "I know it's not your strong suit, but you'll have to be patient."

A half-laugh escaped from her lips. How had he gotten to know her so well in such a short time?

He led her over to the cell door. Taking both her hands, he pulled them through the bars and placed them on the sides of the padlock. His touch sent her stomach into flutter-mode. Really? Butterflies at a time like this?

He tugged on the padlock until it stuck straight out. "I need you to hold it flat, parallel to the ground, so I can pick it with the nail. This won't be quick."

"Okay." She held it as he instructed.

He slipped the nail into the lock, twisting and turning. "Hold it steady."

She tightened her grip as he continued working with the nail. Several minutes ticked by. What would Hellerman or Ron do if they caught the three of them trying to escape?

More long minutes passed agonizingly slow. Her arms ached from keeping the muscles taut. Finally, a soft click accompanied the release of the locking mechanism. Lucan slipped the padlock off the door, swung it open and gestured for Elery to go first.

Jayna stepped out behind her. On the way by, Jayna patted Lucan on the back. "You're a pretty handy guy to have around."

He gave her a wide smile. "Thanks."

Elery ignored the sharp stab of jealousy. Despite what Lucan had said about his feelings, he wasn't hers to claim. He'd be better off with a sweet woman like Jayna.

"Let me lead." Jayna circled around Elery. "They brought me in a side tunnel that cuts across the other tunnels. I think it will be quicker and less traveled."

Jayna tiptoed down the main tunnel. Lucan took up the middle position, keeping one arm angled back toward Elery in a protective gesture. They crept along for about thirty feet, where Jayna turned into a pitch-black opening—the side tunnel. Elery would have never noticed it.

As blackness enveloped her, she put a hand on Lucan's shoulder blade to keep from running into him. Was he also touching Jayna to keep his bearings? Again, she squashed the jealous thoughts. If this was her falling for him, it didn't show promise for rational thinking.

They walked at least another thirty feet without coming to an end. In the dark, time moved as slowly as a broken treadmill. Her anxiety grew along with the pounding of her heart. Someone was bound to notice their escape eventually. She wished Jayna would hurry, but it would be counter-productive. Stealth was their best weapon.

Twenty feet farther and a sliver of light broke through ahead. A cross tunnel.

She peeked around Lucan. Jayna pointed to a dark, round spot in the opposite tunnel wall. It was a little smaller than their current passageway. Using hand gestures, she mimicked walking across the lighted tunnel to the dark one on the other side.

Jayna stuck her head into the lighted tunnel, looked both ways, then darted across into the darkness beyond. Elery had her eyes still fixed on the spot where Jayna disappeared, when Lucan leaned into her, pushing her back into the tunnel. She clamped her mouth down to keep from grunting as he covered her body with his. Twisting her neck, she peered out from beneath his arm.

The sliver of light emanating from the tunnel ahead swelled into a bright stream. Someone was coming.

CHAPTER TWENTY-SEVEN

Elery flattened her body against the rough wall of the tunnel and held her breath. Under Lucan's shoulder, the reflected light bobbed and flickered, sending shadows dancing along the black walls. Her heart spasmed in her chest. Hopefully, whoever it was would pass by without seeing them.

Lucan released the pressure on her, then gently pushed her back the way they had come, shifting her deeper into the shadows. It was the light that would get them caught.

When he stopped moving to listen, he reached for her hand, intertwining his fingers with hers. His touch kick-started her heart into a fast rhythm.

Brighter and brighter the light grew, thinning the shadows into gray streaks. She could make out Lucan's hair, his eyes, the twitching muscle in his jaw.

Footsteps echoed along the rock. The tunnels bounced the sound around, making it impossible to tell how many were there. But they were close.

The light shone even brighter. Lucan tensed the muscles in his back. Would he fight if they were discovered?

A man she didn't recognize stepped into their tunnel. Lucan lunged, throwing the man into the opposite wall. A flashlight clattered down and rolled, spinning light around in uneven spheres. Two water bottles the man had been carrying thudded to the ground.

The man reached for his hip. The barrel of a gun registered as a dark mass in the spiraling light.

Lucan brought his arm back and punched the man in the stomach. The weapon dropped onto the flashlight. Both items flew in opposite directions.

Elery chased after the gun. As the two men struggled, she picked it up and pointed it at the fighting men.

Lucan slammed the man's head against the rock wall. The man punched Lucan in the chest. No way could she shoot. She'd hit both of them. And missing would be worse. She couldn't guess where a stray bullet might bounce in a rock-lined tunnel.

She gasped as strong fingers encircled her throat from behind, squeezing off her air and stemming the blood supply to her head. She clawed at the hand, but the man only pressed harder as he pulled her around to face him. It was Hellerman. He reached down with his other hand, ripping the gun away. Leaning close, he peered into her eyes, then squeezed tighter. White dots danced at the edge of her vision.

The muscles in her neck screamed under the tension. Pain shot up into her head and down to her shoulders. Her eyes watered. She tried to swallow, but couldn't.

He squeezed even tighter, making a fist around her throat. Her airway closed up. Her lungs burned, like being underwater for too long, only she couldn't come up for a breath. She couldn't even cry out to Lucan. Darkness closed in.

Hellerman glanced over at the two men. His words barely audible over the pounding blood in her ears. "You might want to stop before your girlfriend here runs out of air."

Lucan swung around, ready to lunge at Hellerman, but he froze when he saw the gun pointed at his chest.

"Wise choice. I hate it when the mine smells like

blood." Hellerman wrinkled his nose. "You know, coppery, like sucking on a penny."

With an exaggerated splaying of the fingers, Hellerman opened his fist. Elery fell to the ground, sputtering for air. Lucan knelt next to her and put his hands on her cheeks, brushing away a tear with his thumb.

"Are you okay?"

She nodded, still not able to talk. Her throat muscles were on fire.

"All right, you two. It's late. Let's get you back to bed." To make his point, he shoved the gun into Lucan's side.

Elery put one leg up and pushed, trying to stand, but she swayed. Lucan grabbed her around the shoulders and helped her. They moved slowly through the tunnel with Hellerman at their backs, tossing the gun between his hands. At least, the escape plan hadn't gotten them killed. And it hadn't failed completely. Jayna made it through.

"I'm guessing your friend escaped farther than you two, but don't count on her bringing rescue. She won't get far in the dark, and come first light, I'll find her."

Elery's stomach flipped over. *Run, Jayna. Get away from here.*

The trip back to their cell seemed to take a much shorter time than their trip out. As she passed through the open door, hopelessness seeped deep into her bones. They might die here. Two more people lost to the mountains. Two more disappearances to add to the Dutchman lore. Would her dad ever know what happened to her?

Before Lucan could enter the cell, Hellerman grabbed the back of his shirt. "You're coming with me."

"What?" Elery rushed for the door, but Hellerman slammed it shut.

He fastened the padlock, staring straight into her

eyes. "See you in the morning, sweetheart." Hellerman shoved Lucan forward, down the tunnel.

Lucan glanced back at her, but never said a word. His silence unnerved her. Did he know where they were going?

After Hellerman and Lucan disappeared around the bend in the tunnel, the place went quiet, except for the constant drip of wax from the candles. The flames flickered, creating the same level of dark creepiness as before, only then she'd had Jayna with her.

Now, she was truly alone.

***

Lucan trudged up another small hill, scraping past low cacti and stomping on scrub brush he couldn't see in the dark. At first, he'd assumed they were going to talk to Ron again, but then Hellerman had led him outside and told him to walk. At least a mile later, Hellerman had said nothing more. Fear settled in Lucan's stomach like a parasitic worm.

"Where are we going?" Lucan had already asked twice with no response.

Silence met the question, again. Fine, Hellerman didn't want to talk about the location. Time to try something else.

"Can you at least hold the flashlight under my feet, so I don't face plant?"

The light didn't move.

"Why are we walking this far out?"

Hellerman snorted. "Can't dump you in our front yard. How would that look? Besides, we have a special place for you."

"You're going to kill me tonight?"

The flashlight beam bounced as Hellerman gave a fake Miss America clap. "Congratulations, genius. It seems Peralta has harbored a particular dislike for you." Hellerman laughed. "I guess he's not much of a family man. If I were you, I'd make peace with whatever thing you believe in."

Finally, some good advice from Hellerman. *Dear Lord, I may be coming to see You soon. Hope You've got my place prepared like You said. You know I'd love to see Chad again, but I'm not ready to go, yet. I need to save Elery. We have to find Garrick. Please, Lord, not now.*

The terrain leveled out as they came to the valley floor. Rippling water flowed through a nearby riverbed. The water wasn't deep, but maybe he could try pushing Hellerman in. With any luck, he'd hit his head on a rock.

"Keep going." Hellerman shoved him from behind.

Lucan glanced behind as often as he dared, but Hellerman never let his guard down. They walked at least another half-mile before Hellerman said to stop. Lucan turned around to face him. Shadows bounced across the man's angular face. The shotgun he carried extended from his arm like an extra-long appendage, pointing at the ground.

"This is the place." Hellerman rubbed the hair on his narrow chin, then twisted his mouth into a grin. "I was wrong. Peralta does have a soft spot for family. He wanted you to be buried next to your father."

Lucan's heart skipped a beat. Had Hellerman just said his dad was buried here? He couldn't even know his dad was dead, unless ...

A rush of white hot anger swept through Lucan's body. His hands balled into fists. Either Hellerman or Ron had killed his father.

Hellerman lifted the shotgun and aimed it at Lucan's head. This was it. If he didn't do something now, this would be his final resting place, as well. The muscles in his legs quivered, ready to jump.

A shuffling sound to the left made him shift his eyes.

Hellerman heard it, too. He turned his head while still keeping a strong grip on the gun.

Out of the darkness, a blow hit Hellerman's temple and knocked him back a step. Was that a foot?

Lucan took advantage of the surprise blow by throwing his elbow into Hellerman's face. Hellerman staggered back another step. The flashlight fell and blinked out.

Now night blind, Lucan lashed out and connected with another punch. As his eyes adjusted to the dark, he saw the outline of Hellerman doubled over, the gun still in his grip.

No time to think of strategy. Lucan had to get the gun before Hellerman could recover. He raised his leg and directed a kick at Hellerman's hand.

Hellerman howled in pain. The gun clattered to the ground.

Behind them both, a hand reached out to grab the weapon. The flashlight flicked on and feminine features came into focus. Jayna.

Lucan bent at the waist, put both hands on his knees, and expelled several quick breaths. *Thank you, Lord, for sending her to help me.*

Hellerman stared at her, fury contorting his face. She held the gun steady, pointing at his chest. Lucan shook his hands out to ease the adrenaline rush. "Where did you learn that high kick?"

She lifted one shoulder and chuckled. "Dance class when I was eight. But I wasn't much of a dancer."

"Maybe not, but it was a great distraction." He circled around and stripped off Hellerman's backpack. Nodding at the rifle Jayna held, he asked, "Are you okay with that thing?"

"A geologist should always know how to handle a weapon."

Lucan crouched down and dug through the pack

again. "Let's see what he's got in here." He reached inside and pulled out two loops of rope, one thick for climbing and another thinner one, perfect for tying up a murderous deputy.

He took the rifle and handed the rope to Jayna. She tugged Hellerman's arms behind his back, tying the thin rope around his wrists. Pushing on Hellerman's shoulder, Lucan forced him to sit on the ground. Then, Jayna crossed the man's feet and tied them together.

When she was done, Lucan crouched next to Hellerman. "Why did Ron keep Elery?"

Hellerman licked his lips. "Maybe he just likes your girlfriend."

Even if Ron had eyes for Elery, he wouldn't let it stand in the way of business. That just wasn't Ron. "He has to be using her to go after the mine."

Hellerman looked at the ground, confirming Lucan's hunch. He slipped the backpack over his shoulders and motioned for Jayna to follow him a hundred yards away where they wouldn't be overheard.

"We have to get her out of there." Jayna's tone was insistent. Amazing how Jayna would risk her life for Elery, a woman she'd just met. Of course, the same was true for him. Maybe Elery had that effect on people.

"We can't. Ron has all the advantages in his cocoon of a mine." He rubbed a hand along the rifle. "As Hellerman said, they won't kill her in there. So, we just have to wait for them to bring her out."

"Then what?"

"We find a place to stage an ambush."

Jayna wrinkled her brow. "How can we do that when we don't know where they're going?"

She was right. He didn't know where the lost mine was located, although he had a general idea where they might look.

Jayna's hand fluttered up to her forehead. "I know

where. Garrick was on the trail of the mine, so they will have to head back that way." She turned her back and headed uphill, away from the illegal mine. When he didn't move, she rushed back and whispered to him. "Come on. I found this place on my way here. Trust me, it's the perfect place for an ambush."

Casting one final glance at where Hellerman struggled against the ropes, Lucan started up the hill. Hopefully, the knots would hold him until they rescued Elery. Every footstep away from her tugged at him as if they were connected by an invisible wire. He squashed the desire to run back to the mine and shoot anyone who tried to stop him from freeing her. They didn't know how many armed men Ron had. For now, he'd follow the plan. Getting Elery back meant being smarter than Ron.

CHAPTER TWENTY-EIGHT

"I'm really not such a bad guy, Elery." Ron faced her with his shoulders leaning against the bars of the cell. The door was open, but she'd have to run past him to get there, and he'd never allow her to escape. "I worked in your mine for years. Even when you took over, I coached you and helped you." A fly buzzed near his face. He swatted at it. "And despite what you might think, I never actually kidnapped your brother. The note was meant to inspire you to find the mine faster."

Elery sat cross-legged on the floor on the opposite side of the cell, glaring at him. If there was a way for her to get farther away from him, she would, but her back was already pinned against the rock wall. What was the point of this? Maybe he hadn't kidnapped Garrick, but he had kidnapped her. He was evil, and he wouldn't convince her otherwise. Why did he care what she thought about him anyway? Did he feel guilty for bringing her here? If so, she might be able to exploit that.

Softening her expression, she looked directly at him. "You don't have to keep me locked up. Where am I going to go? There are men with guns all over this place."

He slid his hand down the length of one of the bars. "I suppose you could stay in my private room."

Whoa. Better to try a different path for this conversation. "Why didn't you tell me about this mine? I wouldn't have cared if I'd known. I wasn't looking to expand."

An amused glint lightened his eyes. "This is National

Forest land, my dear. This mine is illegal. You wouldn't have overlooked that."

He was right. She would have turned him in. So much for trying to exploit his weaknesses. He didn't have any, except for wanting her in his bed. She wasn't going there. "Where have you taken Lucan?"

A slow smile spread across his face. "You don't have to worry about him anymore."

What did he mean? Did he kill Lucan? No, he wouldn't get his hands dirty. He'd have Hellerman do it. Tears welled up in her eyes, but she choked back the emotions. If Lucan was gone, she wouldn't give Ron the satisfaction of watching her cry.

"You know, I heard from one of my men what you and Jayna talked about last night." Her stomach turned at the thought of him knowing what she'd done to Garrick. He ran a finger in circles along the rock floor. "I agree with her. You're too hard on yourself. All you've tried to do is help people to make up for something tragic."

A warning bell rang in her head. His smooth voice, the open expression, his sudden change in subject. This was a game. Ron was toying with her, trying to get her to open up. Did he enjoy the game or was there a reason behind this banter? Either way, she'd stay silent and wait for him to reveal his purpose.

He leaned his head back against the bars. "It's not you the god is punishing. It's your brother."

The god? He obviously hadn't understood their conversation last night. Did he mean the Thunder Spirit? Why would the Thunder Spirit or any god want to punish Garrick? It didn't make any sense. "I caused his leg to be deformed. How is that his fault?" She clamped her mouth shut, already she'd betrayed her vow of silence by letting Ron bait her.

He lifted his head and waved a hand in the air. "Not back then. I mean, now. The Thunder Spirit is not happy with Garrick. He drew a curse upon himself when he decided to go after the Lost Dutchman Mine."

She rolled her eyes. A curse laid on all people who looked for a mine? It sounded far-fetched, even to her.

He shot her a warning glare. "How many people have gone missing while looking for the mine?"

She switched her expression into neutral and stared at him, keeping silent. Over 200 people had gone missing, and Ron had to know it.

"Garrick shouldn't have tried to find the mine. It's not rightfully his. He's not a descendant."

And, of course, Ron was a descendant, like Lucan. Narrowing her eyes, she examined Ron. His eyebrows lifted earnestly, his mouth was slightly open, his face sober. He meant every word, as if breaking a curse was his birthright.

In a flash, Jayna's words came back to her. *You can claim forgiveness as a child of God.*

Was breaking the curse of sin and guilt *her* birthright? She gazed up at the roof of the cavern. *Could it be true, Lord?*

Ron cleared his throat. She focused on him, again. He looked sideways at her, but continued his speech. "The only way to lift the curse off your brother is to help me find the mine." He slid a paper map toward her—the one from the lizard, the one Hellerman had stolen. "You don't know how happy I was to see a real map, not the useless one Angela gave us."

Her stomach flipped over. Ron had killed Angela because she failed to find the mine for him. It was always about the mine. Guilt or no guilt, if she didn't help him, he'd kill her, too. And then what? After what she'd done, how would God receive her? Would He shrink away from the guilt she held tightly clutched in her hand?

"But this map has lots of symbols. Hellerman already checked the most obvious, the letter O, for 'oro,' but he found nothing. So, we're not sure which one of these others is indicating the mine."

She wanted to spit in his face, but she had to play along, convince him she could help. Crawling forward, she took the map and placed it on her lap, fingering the tattered edges.

"Since you've read the journals, I figure there's got to be something in there to help interpret these symbols."

She stared at the map, again. The markings blended into one another. No ideas came. She didn't care about the map. She cared about Lucan and finding Garrick.

Ron pulled a gun from between his legs.

She swallowed hard. Maybe he was more willing to do his dirty work than she'd thought. "If you can't come up with anything, then I guess I don't need you anymore."

Despite the cool, clammy air, sweat slipped down her brow.

Ron tapped the trigger with his finger. A fierce determination hardened his eyes into black onyx. He would hang onto his dream of gold even if he had to kill her to preserve it. Deep down, a part of her recognized that determination. And responded to it.

You can claim forgiveness as a child of God.

The truth of Jayna's words reverberated inside Elery. She could have claimed forgiveness long ago, except she'd been determined to earn it her own way. She'd used her fierce resolve to even out the balance sheet, but she'd failed. Her balance sheet was still in the red. And now she'd meet God just as she was—imperfect, broken, in debt.

She bowed her head and closed her eyes.

Dear Jesus, I've held onto my guilt tighter than Ron has held onto his gold. I can't do anything to change the past. I can't redeem myself with the future. All I can do is give my guilt to You now. Please take it and forgive me for what I've done.

As she finished the prayer, relief flooded through her, as sweet and pure as a mountain spring. She opened her eyes and looked at Ron. He sat with his arm out, the gun pointing at her head.

The map still rested in her lap. She glanced down at it and instantly, the answer emerged. Yesterday, they'd found a heart Waltz had carved into a rock for his beloved Ila. On the map, in a different location was a circle with a heart inside it. The circle could stand for "oro," and the heart could represent Waltz's love for Ila. Although Ila hadn't died at the mine, it made sense that Jacob would mark the mine with a memory of her, just like the lizard.

Ron blew out a breath. "I'm sorry about this, Elery."

"Wait." She watched Ron's gaze slowly turn hopeful. He lowered the gun a fraction. This could be her one chance to get out of here. "I think I can help. But you'll have to take me out there with you."

***

The next morning, Elery awkwardly climbed up a hill with her hands tied in front. Already several layers of flesh had worn off her wrists, leaving the skin burning and raw. Her mouth felt like she'd swallowed a scratchy cotton ball. But Hellerman wouldn't give her any water. Instead, he tapped his handgun against one leg and threatened to shoot her every few minutes if she didn't move faster.

Every time she glanced at him over her shoulder, he grinned at her discomfort. She'd love to smash that grin off his face for more reasons than her wrists. Hours ago, Hellerman had returned to her cell without Lucan. He'd refused to answer her questions about what happened, but the stony look on his face said it all. He'd killed Lucan. "How did you do it?"

"Do what?" But Hellerman's smile widened. He knew what she meant.

"How did he die?"

Hellerman dropped the smile and gave her a blank expression. Of course, he wouldn't tell her. Withholding the information, gave him control. He grabbed her arm and thrust the map at her. "Do you really think the circle with the heart inside it stands for the mine or are you just messing with us?"

Her eyebrows dipped in anger before she caught herself, returning a disinterested look to her face. She wouldn't let him know he was getting to her. "Since we're out here, Ron must have confidence in what I told him."

"If he had such confidence in you, then he'd be out here." With a shove, Hellerman propelled her down the other side of the hill. "Instead, I'm stuck fact-checking your little idea. So, if you're making this up, you'll regret it."

She already regretted it. This plan had gotten her out of the cave, but how was she supposed to get away from a man who was almost twice her size while she was tied up?

At the bottom of the hill, the terrain flattened into a valley between the nearby mountains. As she rounded a cliff wall, an overgrown patch of vegetation came into view, unusual in this land of sparse scrub brush and cactus. She might have passed right by it except for the square shape of the outline. It didn't look natural. "What's that?"

Hellerman had already noticed it and angled his path toward the anomaly. She followed behind as he walked closer. He kicked at the vegetation. Underneath, she saw a wall about five feet high made of square stones. The granite stones had been rough cut with a heavy pickax. An empty wood-framed doorway hid the rounded curve of another wall leading back into the cliff. Definitely an old prospector's cabin. Her pulse quickened. One of the clues left by Waltz claimed the remains of a cabin sat near the mine.

"Let me see the map," she said.

Hellerman handed it back to her, his attention still on the stone structure. She checked their location. A small letter S was drawn into the curve of the mountain so expertly she would never have seen it as a clue. Did it stand for the stone cabin?

If so, then they were close to the mine, assuming her hunch about the circle with the heart was correct. But as soon as they actually found the mine, she would have outlived her usefulness.

Hellerman approached the doorway. While he was intent on looking for clues in the cabin, she might be able to escape. He bent to duck under the wooden frame.

She took a step back and scanned the terrain. The valley hemmed her in. If she ran, the cliff walls would herd her up the mountainside. She'd be an easy target. Maybe she could quietly sneak back over the hill they had just traversed.

She glanced at Hellerman again. Half his body was in the cabin. Would he hear her if she bolted? She looked at the hill. It was probably her best chance.

Whoosh.

Her gaze switched back to Hellerman and locked in place. What was that?

"Aahhh!" He backpedaled, swiping at his eyes. The gun fell to the ground. He ran in tight circles, trampling on the weapon. Tears ran down his face. "Water!"

He reached around, grabbing at the pack on his back. His fingers closed around the lid of the bottle. When he tugged it free, the bottle popped from the side pocket and flew out in front of him.

"No!" He chased after it, one hand groping on the ground, the other fisted in his left eye.

Whatever was going on, she'd take advantage of it. Rushing over, she reached down to snag the gun in both hands, letting the map flutter to the ground. She raised her arms in front to point the gun at him.

The water bottle rolled to the bottom of the inside wall. He lunged for it on his knees and struggled with the cap.

A tall figure came from behind the exterior wall and stood over Hellerman.

Her heart jumped up and lodged itself in her throat. Could it be?

As he turned to face her, his amber eyes lit up like the sun. It was Lucan. He was alive!

Her mouth dropped open, and the gun fell to the ground again.

Lucan smiled. "I knew you'd notice this place."

Hellerman had dumped half the water bottle over his eyes. He put one leg up to stand.

She pointed at him. Lucan turned around and shoved him head first into the wall.

Thump.

Hellerman collapsed in a heap against the stones.

As Lucan turned back to her, the full impact of his presence hit. She thought she'd lost him. "You're alive." Moisture burned her eyes. Her legs felt weak.

"Hey, El." He closed the distance between them in two strides and helped support her.

Her face flushed with embarrassment. It wasn't like her to faint. She swallowed and tried to regain her composure. "What was that stuff?"

"Turns out, Hellerman kept my pepper spray. We

took it off him last night." He placed a palm on her cheek. "Are you okay?"

"Yeah, I'm fine now." She smiled at him as she held up her bound hands. "But could you do something about this?"

He untied the rope, his fingers brushing against her raw skin. She winced.

"Sorry." He placed a whisper of a kiss on her forehead.

When he pulled back, she glanced up, her gaze stopping at his lips. So warm. So gentle. So perfect. They tilted into a sideways grin. He knew what she was thinking. Heat flared into her face again.

"I found a rope in his backpack." Jayna's voice broke through her inappropriate thoughts. "We'll have to tie him up better this time to keep him from coming after us."

Lucan grabbed her arms and drew her a little closer. Bending down until his lips touched her earlobe, he whispered, "Later." Then, he released her to finish the job of securing Hellerman.

After Hellerman was tied from head to toe with rope, Lucan grabbed the gun and shoved it in the front of his jeans. "We might need this." He bent over to pick up the map. "We don't need this to find Garrick, but I'm not going to leave it for Ron."

CHAPTER TWENTY-NINE

Dust and rocks tumbled down onto Garrick's head. He didn't have the energy to face the weathered missiles landing on his head, his face, his arms. He sucked in a shallow breath, inhaling dust, but no longer bothering to cough it out. Reality had settled in like a boulder on his chest. No one would ever find him. Like all the others who'd gone before him, he would disappear without a trace. Just another crazy Dutch Hunter killed by his own obsession.

Vaguely, he noticed the sun had passed its apex and was going down, again. The fickle sun that overheated him during the day and left his burnt skin to freeze all night in its absence. How long had he been out here? He'd lost count of the days.

The water the unknown lady had thrown down was gone. He'd chugged it yesterday, then promptly threw it all up. A big mistake to overload his dried-up stomach. And an even bigger mistake to waste all the water, especially since she hadn't come back yet. The empty water bottle was his only proof the mysterious woman wasn't just another hallucination. Not that it mattered. If a real person didn't come for him soon, he wouldn't last much longer.

At least in death he'd be free of the pain of his thirst. His leg had given up protesting days ago. But the thirst was constant, relentless. A raging beast continuously gnawing at his mouth, his throat, his stomach.

When his body finally gave up and shut down, would it hurt? Or would he slip into death like falling asleep?

More rocks and dirt pounded his head. What was the deal? Birds? The vultures had started their death watch days ago, never coming close, but always circling, landing, watching.

He pried his eyes open, ripping apart the lids which had stuck together from the salt in his sweat. Turning his head took a massive effort. He shifted and stretched his neck, inching it along the jagged rocks, until finally, he gazed up at the cliff side. The patchy blue sky silhouetted the outline of two forms. People? Or had his shriveled brain mistaken vultures for humans?

"Hello." Too weak. If it was people, they'd never hear him.

He lifted a hand, trying to wave, but it flopped down with barely a movement.

"Garrick!"

Had he really heard his name? No, it had to be his imagination.

"Garrick!"

The sound came louder. His imagination didn't have a volume control. Someone was up there. The voice sounded like Elery. Hope ignited in his chest.

"Elery." Still, too quiet, but she'd seen him. She'd get him out.

He lifted his head and pushed with his arms, trying to sit up. The effort was too much. He slipped and fell back cracking his head on a rock. Darkness closed in, even as his mind screamed his sister's name.

***

Elery lay on her stomach next to Lucan and Jayna, peering over the edge of the cliff. When she'd called his name, it looked like Garrick had moved, but now his body lay still, his head drooped all the way back. Had she really seen movement or was it wishful thinking?

"Garrick!" she yelled again.

No answer and no movement.

She rotated her head to look at Lucan. "What's the plan?"

He rolled over and sat up. She did the same, sitting back on her heels. Tentative joy flitted like a rabid hummingbird through her chest. They'd finally found her brother, now they just needed to get him out. Simple.

Lucan shrugged off Hellerman's backpack and dug through it to pull out a large section of thick rope. "It looks like his leg is stuck. I'll need to go down, free him, and get this around him. Then, you ladies will haul him out."

Jayna crouched next to Lucan and gave an encouraging nod. "We can do it together."

They both looked at Elery as if asking her permission. She nodded. This plan put Lucan at risk, but they had to do something or Garrick would die down there. Maybe he already had.

Please, Lord, don't let him be dead.

Lucan walked to a nearby rock the size of an elephant and looped the rope around it. Then, he made several loops out of the other end and stepped into them. Pulling the front of the rope into a tight knot, he finished the makeshift harness.

Elery puckered her brow. "Are you sure you've done this before?"

"Nope." He gave her a wide grin. "Never."

"This is serious."

His expression turned sober. "You're right. Every rescue is dangerous. I always keep that in the back of my mind."

"How do you deal with it?"

"I don't just deal with it. I thrive on it."

She gaped at him.

"Don't give me that look. I'm not an adrenaline junkie." He flipped the pack onto his back. "Knowing I'm the only thing standing between Garrick and death makes all the other cares of the world fade away. Life becomes simple. I help him or one of us dies."

At his last words, she turned her eyes to the ground and fought to keep moisture from welling up. When she'd thought Lucan was dead, her heart had nearly collapsed in on itself. Now, what if she lost them both? "Please, be careful."

He nodded and gave her a slightly more subdued grin as he walked backward to the edge of the cliff.

The distant sound of a gunshot reverberated off the surrounding rocks. They all turned to look back the way they had come, understanding what it meant. "Ron doesn't tolerate mistakes," she whispered. She turned back to Lucan. "You'd better hurry. Angela might have told Ron where Garrick is, which means he'd know exactly where to find us."

Lucan grabbed her and pulled her into a tight hug. As much as she wanted to savor it, they didn't have time. When he let her go a few seconds later, he pointed at the ground where he'd laid the rifle next to the rope. "Keep it close. Just in case."

She nodded, then she picked up the other end of the rope. Together, she and Jayna brought it taut.

Shifting deeper into the harness, Lucan leaned backward over the side. "Let me down slowly until you can't feel any more weight on the rope. Once I get Garrick tied in, it will take both of you to haul him up. He probably won't be able to help much."

Lucan stepped carefully over the edge, his arm muscles straining from his hold on the rope. Those strong arms had wrapped around her so many times in the last couple of days. For comfort, for help, for support. He was always there. Her rescuer and now Garrick's.

***

Lucan rappelled slowly down the crumbly rock surface toward Garrick, who lay unmoving, covered with a blue jacket. He assessed the situation on the way. This would be a tricky rescue. Garrick lay almost behind the overhanging rock, and there wasn't much room on the ledge near him for Lucan to stand.

Lord, please let this go well. Don't let Elery have one more reason to think You're against her.

As he neared the ledge, he saw it wasn't a ledge at all, but the buttress rocks of a deep crevice. The lower half of Garrick's body had stuck into the crevice like a cork. The top half leaned against the flatter rocks at the mouth.

Lucan landed on the rocks closest to the mountain. "Garrick?"

Garrick twisted his head a fraction, but didn't open his eyes. "Elery?"

"No. My name is Lucan. I'm here to help." He stripped off the rope, then the backpack and tugged out a water bottle. "Can you open your mouth a bit?"

Garrick parted his lips a tiny bit. Lucan dribbled a teaspoonful of water in. Garrick swallowed slowly, then opened his mouth for more. Lucan poured out another teaspoon. Garrick moaned and opened his mouth again.

"Not yet. You've got to take it slow." Lucan removed a salt pill from a packet and dropped it onto Garrick's tongue. Good thing Hellerman had carried the basic desert survival stuff. "This will help you retain whatever fluids I give you."

After giving Garrick a few more drops of water, Lucan leaned back and reviewed their options. Not only was Garrick stuck in the crevice, but his left leg had lodged between two boulders that had previously fallen in. The leg didn't look like it could have gotten much circulation since the fall. If the leg had necrotic tissue, mixing it into his bloodstream could kill him.

Lucan ripped open the pack and extracted a handkerchief. "I'm going to tie this on your thigh so we can worry about your leg later."

Garrick didn't respond.

Lucan crawled over, shimmied the handkerchief under Garrick's thigh, and tied it tight. Garrick grunted and opened his eyes. At least the nerve endings in the upper part of his leg were still active. His eyes fell closed again.

"Is he ..." Elery yelled from above.

"He's alive, but stuck pretty good." And his general lack of response was concerning, as well. "You'll have to pull hard to get him out."

"Okay."

He looped the rope below Garrick's armpits, tied a figure-eight knot, and then straddled the crevice behind Garrick. "Pull!" he yelled to the top of the cliff.

The rope went taut, bunching under Garrick's shoulders and lifting him off the ground. His head lolled back.

"Keep pulling! He's still stuck."

Garrick's torso rose up, but the boulders wouldn't release their captive. Lucan hovered over him, ready to stop any swinging motion when Garrick's body broke free of the rocks.

Slowly, the rope inched upward. Garrick's leg straightened, held tight by the greedy boulders. Lucan crouched down and kicked at the rocks. A few tumbled down into the dark crevice. One large rock refused to move, but the other rocks had cleared out a little room. Lucan twisted Garrick's thigh and tugged on his jeans.

His calf broke free of confinement, but the ankle, bent at an odd angle, was still stuck.

One last hard yank wrenched the leg out of the rock. Lucan held Garrick's body still as it moved slowly upward until he had to let go when Garrick reached the halfway point. Now, it was up to the women. From down below, Lucan could only watch and pray.

CHAPTER THIRTY

Elery pushed her arm muscles as far as they would go. In front of her, Jayna leaned backward, also pulling with all her might. Who knew pulling up Garrick's dead weight would be so difficult? *Dead weight.* No, he wasn't going to die. He couldn't.

Leaning back farther, Elery widened her stance to get more leverage. When she'd started pulling, the rifle had been a few feet behind her, but now she was almost stepping on it. If she did, would it go off? It was a risk she couldn't take. She kicked it to the side out of the way.

Fifteen minutes of torturous straining later, Elery asked Jayna to stop. "Can you hold the rope while I check how high up he is?"

Jayna grunted her assent and froze in position.

Elery scrambled to the edge to peer over. Garrick hung limp in the supporting ropes, close to the top. Just a few feet to go.

"We have to go slow." Elery resumed her place at the rope. "The cliff juts out, and he'll be coming up from underneath. We have to make sure he doesn't hit his head."

Jayna glanced over her shoulder and nodded. Elery gave her a grateful smile. They had found him. He was almost out. But what kind of condition was he in?

A few minutes later, Jayna held the rope taut again while Elery reached down to grab Garrick's shirt. She rotated him until his back hit the cliff first, then she put her hands under his armpits and pulled him up. A shower of weathered rock rained down. As she tugged Garrick onto solid ground, she caught a glimpse of Lucan ducking out of the way.

Elery hovered over Garrick. He looked like he was sleeping, but he didn't open his eyes. "Garrick."

No answer. Not even an eye flutter.

Jayna secured her end of the rope with a large rock and knelt next to Elery. Together, they unwound the rope from Garrick's body. "He's in shock from the injury and lack of food and water. We need to get him out of here."

"Okay. Let's get Lucan up. Then we'll make a plan." Elery leaned forward and threw the end of the rope over the side. She jumped up and spun around, heading for the rope wrapped around the boulder.

Oooff. She smacked into something hard.

She backed up. It was Ron.

The blood drained from her head, making her dizzy.

"Nice to see you again, Elery." He grabbed her arm in a vise-like grip. His other hand held a gun pointed at the ground.

But where was *her* gun? She frantically looked down. Ron held the rifle trapped under his foot. When he noticed her looking, he shifted his hips, pulled his foot back, and kicked the weapon at an angle over the side of the cliff. Her heart dropped like a stone.

Ron circled his gun in the air. "One, two, three people up here, but where's your boyfriend?"

She raised her chin. "Where's yours?"

An awkward smile passed over his face. "You don't have to worry about him. Hellerman was an asset to me in the Sheriff's Department, but out here, he was useless."

Dread swept through her. Ron had killed Hellerman and Angela, and left Garrick to die. How had she worked beside this man for a year, never seeing a hint of his evil?

"Lucan has already left. He's getting help."

A shadow of doubt passed over Ron's face. Elery

stared him down. Ron wasn't stupid. Too smart, in fact. Would her half-truth be enough to protect Lucan?

Ron narrowed his eyes and sneered. "So, you climbed down, attached the rope to Garrick, then climbed back up to haul him out?"

Eying the rope, Ron walked toward the cliff. He reached down and tugged on it. As he released the tension, another tug tightened the rope. Lucan.

Ron turned and raised his eyebrow, in a look that said I told you so. Keeping his eyes on Elery and his back to the cliff, he pulled a knife out of his back pocket and flipped it open. With two quick slices, he cut the rope. It snaked down over the drop off.

He leaned back and stuck his gun over the edge. Her muscles tensed. Could she push him over the edge without falling herself? It was worth the risk. She jumped at him.

Bending sideways, he lowered his shoulder and drove her backward. She fell, landing on her back. The air rushed out of her lungs. She lay stunned, gasping for breath.

Briefly, he pointed the gun at her. Then, he leaned back again and fired two shots into the crevice. "That should take care of any rodents left down there." He turned his gaze to Jayna. "All right, then. It's time for me and Elery to get going."

"What?" Elery pulled her feet under her to scramble away, but Ron grabbed her arm and dragged her up next to him.

"You're coming with me. You promised to help find the mine. I'm holding you to it."

Jayna pushed her way in between them. "You don't need her to find it."

"Actually, I do. The person I don't need is you." Ron swung Elery around by her arm, shoving her behind him.

He raised the gun and pointed it in the middle of Jayna's forehead.

"No!" Elery couldn't get around Ron to reach the weapon. She did the only thing she could. She kneed him in the groin from behind. Ron crumpled in on himself, bending at the waist. The gun pointed at the ground for a second. He growled and raised the weapon again. Elery rushed around and kicked at his gun hand.

A shot went off. The loud blast echoed in her ears.

The gun slipped from his hand, bounced once, and clattered over the edge.

Jayna staggered backward a step. A dark stain seeped onto her shirt near her right shoulder. She put a hand over it and collapsed onto the ground next to Garrick. A groan escaped her lips.

"What did you do?" Elery tried to run to Jayna, but Ron gripped her bicep.

"That's unfortunate." He leaned over the edge, watching the gun fall. If only she could push him over, too, but this time she'd go over with him for sure.

He glanced at Jayna once more. When he turned back to Elery, he raised his dark eyebrows and smiled. "Now that we've tied up the loose ends, we can get back to business."

He motioned for her to head down the mountain. With one last lingering look at Jayna and Garrick, she complied. At this point, it was best to get Ron out of here before he hurt them further.

At the bottom of the mountain, Ron directed her steps across a valley and up the neighboring mountain. Her stomach burned with acid that crept up her throat, setting her insides on fire. Ron was still searching for the mine. What would he do when he found it?

Her legs burned under the strain of fighting gravity. And her heart felt like it would explode, but not from exertion. Jayna and Garrick lay dying on the rocks. She had no idea what had happened to Lucan. Was he dead already? She shoved the thought away. If she fell apart now, she'd lose any chance to escape and get help.

At Ron's direction, she climbed almost straight up for more than an hour. Sweat dripped off her brow. She wiped at it and slowed her pace. She'd give anything for water right now, but if Ron had any, he probably wouldn't share.

"Keep going." He pushed her, but more of a gentle shove. He seemed to have mellowed a little now that it was just the two of them. She was still no match for his size, but the odds had swayed a little in her favor, especially since he no longer had the gun. She shot him a glare and picked up the pace again.

Up ahead, the rocks narrowed into a tight ravine as if a small waterfall had once cascaded down the mountain. Ron stopped to check the map, then urged her on with another push. So nice of him to send her up the waterfall first. Bracing herself by putting both hands out, she lifted up and dug the toes of her boots into the rocky sides of the ravine. She alternated her feet with her hands to climb up. "Why are you taking me with you?"

He let out an exaggerated sigh. "The day your father gave you the mine. Do you remember it?"

Her first day at the mine was a blur of meeting new people and trying to get her bearings. She couldn't fathom what he meant.

"I asked if you wanted me to take over for a while until you felt ready for leadership. And you said ..."

She remembered it now. "I said, 'I may not know how to run a mine, but now that I have one, I won't let anyone take it from me.'" She kept climbing, refusing to look at him.

"Exactly. You're beautiful, Elery. Not in the soft, frilly way most women are. You have hard edges. I don't know any woman who could run a mine like you did.

And when it comes to making tough decisions, you've got a core as solid as granite. You do what needs to be done. We're more alike than you think."

She was like Ron? The words dug deep into her psyche. He admired her strong will, the part of her buried deep within like a land mine waiting to be triggered. The part that exploded out whenever she was confronted by injustice. But it was also the part of her that had refused to let go of her past mistakes. And the part of her that allowed the men to work at the mine under an old ceiling stabilizer. Her tough decisions could kill.

"And of course, you're here because I still haven't found the mine yet," Ron continued. "You read the journal pages and found the map. If anyone can help me find this crazy treasure, it's you."

She anchored her feet, glanced down, and realized from this angle he would be staring at her backside the whole way up the ancient waterfall. Just great. She focused on going up again. "Until we found the map, I didn't think the mine actually existed."

"I know, but even though you didn't believe, the truth still came out."

He probably thought he was destined to find the truth. She pushed with her arms and released with her feet, continuing to climb. "What about your unbelief? I know you aren't exactly a Christian, but you came to church with us. How can you think it's okay to come out here and kill people?"

"It might seem like I enjoy killing people, but I don't. It's worked out that I've had to." He gave a short laugh. "I know enough of the Bible to know even God kills people mercilessly. Remember the poor guy who accidentally touched the Ark and dropped dead?"

She shook her head. He wasn't the first to use the Bible to justify his evil deeds. "So, because you don't *want* to kill, that makes the times you do it okay?"

"Well, it's not like I'm some serial killer who does it for fun. It's necessary, like survival of the fittest."

Lock the emotions in a box and throw away the key. That was how he did it, just like he'd told her. Show one face to the world, keep the evil one locked away.

She pushed herself to the top of the ravine and spun around. If she timed it right, she could kick him as his head came even with the ground and send him tumbling back down.

"Everything I did had to be done, especially the recent events."

"Do you mean Angela?"

"No, Angela had to be dealt with when she didn't give me any useful information. What I mean is, things couldn't go on at Hearst mine as they had been. I needed more time to hunt for the mine." He paused to get another foothold. "Plus, I had to get rid of the only other Dutch Hunter who might actually find the mine before me."

Did he mean Garrick? Had Ron arranged the accident?

"It put you out of business, too—a side benefit."

She furrowed her brow. Where was he going with this? His head rose above ground level in perfect position. She pulled her leg back to kick.

He smiled, apparently amused by her confusion and unconcerned about her intent to kick him. "The night of the accident, I moved the ceiling stabilizer down."

Her leg froze in midair. What did he say? The information filtered through her brain, causing a tsunami wave of awareness. "That's why you came out of the tunnel and sent Chad back in."

"Yep." In a quick move, Ron hauled himself onto the flat ground next to her. She'd missed her chance. "I pulled the stabilizer down two feet from the ceiling before I left."

Her leg dropped to the ground. Chad's death wasn't

caused by the machine failure. Her heart soared on wings of relief for a second before stalling out in a cloud of suspicion. Why was he telling her this? What did he gain from easing her conscience? Or was he trying to purge his own?

"Let's go." Ron pushed her to keep climbing.

She silently headed in the direction he indicated. What could she say to reason with a man who'd destroyed her family's mine, murdered his own cousin, plus Angela and Hellerman, and possibly Jayna, Garrick, and Lucan? Anger grew in the pit of her stomach, a burning fireball of rage. Jayna, whose only crime was working for a monster. Lucan and Chad, who happened to be related to the devil. And she and Garrick, caught in the crossfire. She pushed the savage emotion deep inside. For once, Ron was right. She had to keep it all in a box because she needed every ounce of focus to get out of this situation.

Thirty feet up the slope, a heart carved sideways appeared on a large rock. Except it didn't have a circle around it. Had she been wrong?

Ron followed her gaze. His mouth dropped open as he strode on in front of her. "This is the place. Sometimes the ancient maps marked water with a circle. The heart near the dried up waterfall has to be it."

She hung back, debating how difficult it would be to climb down the steep ravine. He looked back and noticed her hesitation. In two strides, he reached her side and grabbed her arm. "No, no. You want to see this, too. I know you do."

Did she? She'd listened to legends about the Lost Dutchman Mine her entire life. Finding it piqued her curiosity, but the mine was the reason for the devastating peril that Garrick, Lucan, and Jayna were in right now. Not to mention the reason she was stuck out here with a man who would probably kill her as soon as they found it.

CHAPTER THIRTY-ONE

After the rope had fallen down in a figure eight around him, Lucan had seen the gun barrel poking over the edge with barely enough time to slam himself against the rock wall for cover. As the echoes of the shots died away, Lucan waited ten seconds, then ten more, before daring to inch back from the wall. He eased out onto the ledge of the crevice and ran his hands along his body. No wounds.

Thank you, Lord for letting me see the danger coming and for protecting me, but now I need to get out of here.

The rope. Where did it go?

He searched around frantically. Not here. He peered down into the dark fissure. In his scramble to get to cover, he must have kicked it down.

Fantastic. Now what?

He stared up at the massive wall of weathered rock. Thirty feet straight up with few handholds. Not ideal, but no other option presented itself. He'd have to climb out freehand.

Digging through the pack, he found spikes and gloves. Thank goodness, Hellerman was prepared for everything. Lucan slipped on the one-size-too-small gloves and turned to the rock wall. He'd completed almost a hundred hours of free climbing, but not on anything this rugged and not without a rope to back him up.

Finding a foothold at about knee height, he dug his boot in, then searched above his head for a place to pound in a spike. Weathering had stripped the clay minerals from the granite, leaving a crumbling structure of tiny quartz nodules. He scraped away the loose material to get to stable rock. Once he'd embedded the spike, he hauled himself up. He searched for another handhold while keeping his core muscles tight to ease the weight on the spikes.

He repeated the procedure over and over to get halfway up where he took a rest. Clinging to the rock like Spider-Man, he stretched out his weary muscles one by one. Afterward, he peered between his feet. If he fell now, he'd probably fall right onto the same ledge that had held Garrick captive, or worse he might fall farther down into the crevice.

Turning back to the rock, he reached out and discovered another handhold nearby. A luxury. Only one foothold and handhold were necessary, but when he could get more, it eased his aching muscles.

He stretched to dig the spike in about a foot above his head, pounding it in with his fist. It dug in and held. He transferred his weight to his right hand.

The spike shuddered, then slipped free.

Gravity pulled at him. Pebbles dropped into his face. His arm swung out wide. He was going to fall if he didn't grab onto something.

Clawing at the cliff side, he twisted his body, desperately searching for something to support his weight. The side of his hand found a small crack down by his feet. He bent down, smashed the side of his palm into it and clung to the rock face, his chest heaving. That was a close one.

It took a full minute for his heartbeat to return to a manageable level. Only then, did he realize it shouldn't have been so easy to double over at the waist as he had. The gun had slipped out of his jeans. Peering down, he saw it lying near the edge of the crevice. It was useless now. There was no way he could go back for it.

He wiped dirt and sweat off his face with his free hand, then searched for a higher handhold. The climbing got harder as the rock became more weathered. Adrenaline swarmed through his muscles, giving him plenty of strength to reach the top, as long as he kept from falling.

What would he find there? A few minutes before the rope had fallen down, he'd seen the rifle rocket off the edge of the cliff twenty feet away. It fell to the desert below, and from the sound of the impact, it smashed into pieces. The three of them on top had no protection. A morbid image flew through his head—Elery and Jayna lying shot on the ground, Garrick slowly dying of shock. He grimaced and focused instead on each movement of his limbs.

At the edge of the cliff, he swung his arm over in an arc to spike into the flat ground. The first time it didn't hold and his hand slipped back down. The second time, the spike dug in. He pulled himself over to lie face down on the loose rock, taking in huge gulps of air.

When he'd caught his breath, he lifted himself up on his elbows and cautiously looked around.

No Elery. It should have been good news, but his gut tightened at the sight of Jayna and Garrick lying motionless nearby.

He crawled over to them. Garrick was nonresponsive— the same condition as before—but Jayna was in greater danger. A dark red stain covered the top right section of her yellow T-shirt. She must have been shot. With two fingers, he checked her neck for a pulse. Strong and steady.

Digging through Hellerman's pack, he found an old T-shirt. He knelt down and pressed it against Jayna's wound to slow the flow of blood, while he scanned the area for Elery.

She was gone. His relief over not finding her body morphed into a jagged fear. She would never have left her brother by choice. Someone had taken her. Probably Ron, but where did they go?

He searched the ground until he found a smooth, flat rock. He placed it on Jayna's wound to keep up the pressure. Wiping his bloody hands on his jeans, he got up and examined the ground in a wide circle. Disturbed dirt, smashed scrub brush. A clear trail headed down to the valley. He could track them.

The pull of dual responsibilities threatened to tear him apart. Too many people were in immediate danger. Should he go after Elery or get the help Garrick and Jayna needed?

***

Ron kept a tight grip on her arm as he tugged her over to the granite boulder with the rough heart carved on it. She pulled back, but her resistance didn't seem to bother him a bit. His eyes remained completely locked onto the rock. If he'd just let go of her, she could make a run for it.

When they reached the rock, he released her to trace the carving with his fingers. "Definitely man-made."

She slid her feet backward.

He didn't notice. But just as she was about to turn around and sprint down the mountain, he turned his head. He took a step and grabbed her arm again. "Where is the heart pointing?"

She followed the line of the heart, looking at it sideways. It led to another granite boulder on the edge of a sharp cliff, slightly below their position. *Please, not another cliff. I have to get back to help the others.*

The thought of Lucan lying dead at the bottom of the other cliff tore her heart to pieces. But she couldn't afford a breakdown. Garrick still had a chance, maybe Jayna did too. They needed her.

Ron pulled on her arm again. "Let's go see."

Slipping and sliding, he dragged her down the slope to the boulder. She wrapped her arms around it and clung to it for fear he might decide to throw her over the edge.

He stretched out his neck and peered around the boulder. When he turned back to her, his eyes were wide. Clutching her arm, he pulled her to the other side of the rock. She struggled to keep her balance on the loose rock underfoot, while clinging to the boulder.

On the other side, her feet came down onto a narrow ledge, slick with crumbly rock. She caught a glimpse of the extent of the ledge over his shoulder. It ran for more than twenty feet, skirting the edge of the cliff. At half the distance, opening onto the ledge, the mouth of a small cave yawned.

Ron put a hand over his heart. "This has to be it."

Reaching back, he grabbed her wrist and forced her to the entrance. After a shaky exhaled breath, he ducked inside, yanking her along with him.

Darkness swallowed them for a brief moment. Her eyes adjusted quickly, thanks to a yellowish glow coming from an inner cavern. Still, she couldn't see much because of Ron's crouched form in front of her. Noise echoed through the cave. Was there somebody else in here? Or was it the sound of their movements bouncing back?

He passed through the small tunnel and into a larger cavern. As his figure moved out of her way, light showered her from above. Sunlight. The light cascaded down from a hole in the roof. Was it a natural skylight or man-made? Without a long ladder, she couldn't be sure, but the rough edges made it look natural.

Ron dropped her arm. Mouth agape, eyes fixed, he drifted toward a white stripe high on the far wall.

Her pulse raced at the sight. A seam of milky white, glossy rock dotted with chunks of dark mustard.

Gold ore.

And lots of it. The gold continued along the whole of the quartz vein, as if someone had squirted an entire bottle of mustard in one stripe on the walls. At the back of the cavern, the seam disappeared down another cave opening. Did it continue through there?

Pick marks gouged the walls. In the corner lay the remains of an old arrastra, a gold recovery machine used in the 1800s.

They'd actually found it! This was the Lost Dutchman Mine. A mine that could make dreams come true. Or at least pay her father's medical bills. She gazed around the cavern taking it all in. So much gold hidden in the crevices of this mountain.

Her awe was slowly replaced by dread. What would Ron do now that he didn't need her? How could she defend herself?

Near the arrastra sat a small pile of scrap quartz. The miners would use the arrastra to grind up the chunks of quartz with gold on it, but they wouldn't waste their efforts on rock with no gold in it. They used rock picks to break out the thick ore, then they discarded the less valuable mineral in a heap. A chunk of quartz could be a weapon, but Ron kept her in view out of the corner of his eye at all times. Unless she distracted him, she'd never be able to pick one up unnoticed.

Lord, give me something here. I need help. It had been so long since she'd dared to ask the Lord to work in her life. Would he answer? She waited a few seconds. The only thing that came to mind was her discussion with Ron about the curse. Might as well go with it. "Are you sure you want to mine this vein? What about the curse? Maybe we'll both disappear out here. One more statistic for Dutch Hunters to quote."

He ignored her, continuing to swivel his head from one side of the seam to the other.

"Aren't you afraid?" she tried again.

He shot her an annoyed glance. "I told you, I'm a descendant."

"Oh, yes, I remember. You're worthy." She folded her arms across her chest, faking indifference. "What if you're wrong? What if the curse kills descendants as well?"

He turned to her, irritation raising his eyebrows. "Gold tends to outweigh fear. But what about you, Elery? What are you afraid of?" He drew closer to explore the length of the seam, even though it was out of reach. Her distraction was working. When she talked to him, he didn't worry about what she was doing. He tapped a finger on his temple. "Oh, I almost forgot, you're afraid of Garrick."

She slid her feet backward toward the quartz pile. "I'm not afraid of my own brother."

He cocked his head, looking at her with one eye. "You're afraid Garrick will never forgive you."

She coughed out a breath. That was a road she didn't want to travel down again. "Don't talk to me about him."

He shrugged and turned back to the rock, spreading his arms wide. "You know, Garrick would love all this."

Sliding her feet one last time brought her directly over the quartz pile. She ducked down, grabbed the biggest chunk of rock she could fit in her palm, and stood up, hiding the quartz behind her back.

"Maybe if he saw all this, then he'd forgive you." Ron glanced back at her with a half grin. "Oh, that's right. He won't live to see it."

Her heart seized at the thought of Garrick dying slowly on the edge of the cliff. He needed help, and she couldn't get to him. With one hand, she brushed stray curls from her eyes. Who was she kidding? If she didn't do something to stop Ron, she might die first.

With his back turned, Elery slid her feet stealthily toward him, the chunk of quartz gripped tightly in her fist like a baseball. The gold vein sucked in all of his attention. When just a few feet separated them, she raised the rock over her head with both hands. Her hand shook. She fought to steady it. If she hit him, it might kill him. She focused her mind on survival and swung her arms down, aiming for his head.

In one motion, he twisted around, stepped back and caught her arms. They stood there for a moment, arms locked in place, staring at each other. Ron closed his eyes as if holding back a wave of disappointment. What had he been thinking? That they would somehow become partners? It didn't matter. What mattered was getting out of here.

She dug her feet in and pushed. If she could throw him off balance, she'd run. Ron stepped back, staggering his legs to get a stronger stance. A low rumbling echoed through the cavern and the rock beneath their feet vibrated.

Behind Ron, the ground slid away and a deep pit opened up. A trap.

His back foot slipped down, and he fell backward, dragging her with him. She wrenched one arm free. His hand flailed for a second before it latched onto the front of her T-shirt. He swung his other hand over to grab more of her shirt. She leaned her weight back to counteract his pull.

Light glinted off something close to his head. Something razor thin and stretched out, anchored to the walls of the chamber.

A nearly invisible wire. The evil intent made her stomach turn. If Ron fell back into the pit, the wire would decapitate him, and he wouldn't see it coming. Could she stand here and let it happen?

Her heart beat erratically in her ears. After what he'd

done, he deserved worse than decapitation. But what would she deserve for what she'd done? She'd crippled Garrick for life.

Ron slipped deeper into the pit. His eyes went wide with panic. His forearms bulged as he strained to hold onto her.

The cotton fabric of her shirt started to tear. As much as she'd like to be done with him, she couldn't do nothing and watch him die. God would want her to show mercy. She grabbed his hands and ducked, throwing all her weight down on her rear end.

The impact jolted her and pitched Ron forward. His feet slipped all the way down the side of the pit. The crown of his head skimmed the wire.

It sliced through his hair and scalp, shearing off a little of both. He howled and let go of her shirt.

Bringing his hands to the back of his head, he pressed on the small wound. A thin stream of blood trickled down by his ear. It would hurt, but it wasn't fatal.

He glared at her, eyes full of anger and pain. Why was he mad at her? She hadn't put the wire there.

His jaw clenched. He grabbed the front of her shirt again. She tried to scoot away, but standing in the deep hole put him at the perfect height to seize her and hold her still.

She needed a weapon again. The chunk of quartz sat a few feet from her right hand. She snatched it up and brought it down onto his arm. He screamed and loosened his grip.

Not enough. He held her tighter, leaving her no choice. She switched the rock to her other hand and wound up like throwing a baseball. On the upswing, she slammed it into his forehead. He released his hold on her.

She didn't wait to see what damage she'd inflicted. She jumped to her feet and ran for the cave entrance.

CHAPTER THIRTY-TWO

Lucan crept into the entrance of the cavern. A gruff yell came from the interior. Was it Ron? The time for stealth had passed. *Please, Lord, help me protect Elery.*

As he rushed into the first chamber, he ran smack into someone. Instinctively, he grabbed the person to keep them both from falling over, then he looked down.

"Elery." He smoothed the hair from her face.

She blinked several times and touched his cheek. "You're alive. How did you get out?" She shot a fearful glance down the tunnel. "We have to go."

"Ron is still back there?"

She nodded and took a step toward the outside entrance.

He put both hands on her shoulders. "Go. I'll be right behind you."

She flattened her lips and shook her head at him. "Come with me."

Her pleading eyes almost convinced him. He should leave Ron to the police, but then Ron would probably just disappear into the mountains. No, Lucan wouldn't miss the chance to confront him. "Go, please. Get help for the others. I need to keep you safe." She opened her mouth to protest again, but he shook her shoulders. "No time for stubbornness." He raised his voice. "If you care about me, then go!"

He pushed her toward the opening. This time, she didn't resist. She had just passed through to the outside when he heard Ron's voice echo from the chamber. "You really climbed up that cliff? Unbelievable."

Lucan spun around. Ron stood with his feet spread, a half-smile on his face. Smeared blood colored his jaw line like war paint.

"I suppose this is the part where I say, 'You're a hard man to kill.'" Ron laughed at his own joke. "But, man, look at you. A survivor to the core. Like me." Lucan cringed as Ron lifted a loose piece of hair and scalp off the back of his head, then gently laid it back down. "I guess it's in our DNA. Although on your side of the family it skipped your father's generation."

"Why did you kill him?" The rational part of his brain knew Ron was trying to stir up emotions, trying to weaken him. It was working. Anger raged through him like a forest fire.

"Technically, Hellerman did." Ron put a finger to his chin. "But, yeah, I told him to. Your father got too close to my mine."

His dad had underestimated Ron's greed. Lucan had done the same. He clenched his teeth. Ron would never give up this mine. If he didn't get rid of Ron, Elery would pay the price. Lucan rushed at him in a football tackle. Ron sidestepped out of the way.

Putting his hands up at the last second, Lucan narrowly avoided head-butting the wall.

A fist slammed into his kidney from behind. The pain stole his breath. He twisted away just as Ron let another punch fly. Ron's fist slammed into the rock, showering pebbles onto the ground.

Lucan's breath came in shallow gasps. Adrenaline made his limbs shaky. He needed to calm down and fight smarter. He needed to draw on his police training.

Ron grunted and shook his hand out. The blow had probably broken bones, but Ron didn't look ready to concede. He tightened up his fist, ready to deliver another blow.

When Ron threw a right hook, Lucan waited half a second until all of Ron's momentum was committed, then dodged left. As he had guessed, it was too hard for Ron to correct in that direction. Ron missed.

Lucan slammed his fist into Ron's stomach.

Doubling over, Ron gasped for air.

Lucan raised his leg and kicked Ron in the chest, sending him sprawling backward. But Ron didn't fall. Instead, he put his hands to his knees and kept his head up, his gaze darting to the cave entrance. The only way to keep him from going after Elery would be to kill him. Could Lucan do that? He'd die for Elery, but could he kill for her?

"Why didn't you give up the mine rather than kill Dad? We're family."

Ron stood to his full height. "Don't ask me to shed any tears for your father."

"He was my dad, but he was *your* uncle."

Ron snorted. A drop of blood went up his nose, and he sputtered a little. "Your side of the family treated us like inbred misfits. Your father kept the secret of the journal pages from us for years. He didn't deem us worthy."

Lucan remembered the huge fight between their two families when Chad had accidentally mentioned the pages to Ron. Ron's father threatened to sue to get the pages. That was when Lucan's father got the idea to find the mine and stake a claim on it. "So, you proved Dad right. He shouldn't have trusted your family."

Ron pursed his lips. "Interesting question. Was it a self-fulfilling prophecy? Would I have killed your dad if he'd trusted us? I guess we'll never know." He shrugged. "Just water under the bridge now. Or rather, dirt over the grave."

In a quick motion, Ron darted for the cave entrance.

Lucan cut him off with another tackle. They both landed on the ground. Ron was on the bottom, but his taller stature gave him more leverage. He pushed against Lucan and rolled him onto his back.

Lucan tried to flip Ron back over, but Ron sat on his chest, leaving only Lucan's arms free. He pushed at Ron's legs to no avail. Ron grabbed him by the hair and smashed his head into the hard rock floor. Searing pain erupted up the back of his scalp.

Ron squeezed his legs, cutting off Lucan's air supply. Lucan squirmed and shifted, unable to throw Ron off. Ron smashed his head down again. The world spun, flickering at the edges.

Then, the weight on his chest abruptly left. Air rushed into his lungs. Ron had jumped off of him.

Lucan rolled over to see Ron racing out of the cave entrance in pursuit of Elery. "No!"

***

Elery bolted out into the sunshine, stopping her momentum a fraction of a second before she would fall over the edge. Nowhere to go but up. She flattened herself against the rock wall and slid her feet along the ledge.

At the large boulder, she hesitated. Her thrumming heartbeat pounded in her ears.

Lucan's insistence had driven her outside, but she shouldn't have left him. Ron didn't have a gun anymore, so she and Lucan together could overpower him. She turned to go back.

Ron bolted out of the cave at full speed. He backpedaled at the edge, too late. One foot slipped into thin air. He was going over. The desire to push him burned her insides with shame.

His other foot went over. He leaned back and

slammed his backside into the ground. It was the only thing he could have done to stop his fall. His feet swung in a downward arc, but the bulk of him landed with a thud on the ledge.

She stared, shocked he hadn't fallen. At the sight of her, anger fired in his eyes. She took off up the mountain while he struggled to get his feet back on solid ground. Straining her thighs and calves, she climbed as fast as she could. She stumbled on the loose rock, caught herself before she fell, and kept struggling to go up.

The sound of crunching rock behind told her he was closing in. She shouldn't have left the cave without Lucan. She should have stayed and helped fight. What had Ron done to him?

God knows. The thought nearly brought her to her knees. God did know. And He knew how this would turn out. With no time for prayer, her soul cried the same words over and over. *Help, Lord. Help, Lord.*

A hand encircled her ankle and yanked her down.

She fell, landing on her stomach. Sharp rocks broke through her palms and cut through her T-shirt. She pushed at the ground, trying to crawl away from him.

He stood over her, dragging her backward by one leg. She wouldn't go that easy. Flipping over, she looked down, cocked her other leg and kicked at his knee.

Howling in pain, he let go of her and cradled his kneecap. She'd inflicted damage, but it hadn't brought him down like she'd hoped. She scrambled away on all fours.

He followed, grabbing both her feet, then her knees, so she couldn't kick him. He flipped her over, moving up her body until he straddled her hips. She thrashed and struggled, but couldn't throw him off.

He wrapped his hands around her neck. His fingers compressed her windpipe, squeezing and cutting off her air.

"You can be so frustrating. You always fight me." Ron's words came out in a gravelly whisper. His calm veneer had crumbled to pieces. The locked box of emotions had exploded to splinters.

He focused on her neck, all his concentration fixed on squeezing the life out of her. She clawed at his fingers. They were locked on, immovable. Her mind slowed. She had to do something. A weapon. She needed a weapon.

Flinging both arms out, she desperately searched around with her hands. Nothing, except bits of rock and dust. She gagged, but the bile had nowhere to go.

Her lungs burned. The dull thump of her heartbeat slowed in her ears. If she didn't do something now, she wouldn't have the energy left.

Dust. That was it. She grabbed a handful and flung it into his eyes, keeping hers tightly closed.

"Aggh!" He let go of her neck.

She rolled to the side, coughing and gasping for breath. The skin around her throat burned as if circled by a necklace made of fire. Ron staggered away as he wiped streams of tears from his eyes.

She pulled herself to her feet and backed away. Get away or fight?

Ron wouldn't let her go. As soon as he cleared his eyes, he'd be on her again.

This time, she wouldn't run. If she was going to die, she'd fight to the end. Enough oxygen had returned to her body for one more assault. Then, a random neuron kicked into overdrive. A plan took shape, but it would only work if she could trust her sense of direction.

She scanned the ground for anomalies. There, an uneven shadowed patch of ground a few feet behind him. No way to be sure from this angle, but it was her best chance.

Ron wiped the last of his tears on his shirtsleeve and looked up at her with red-rimmed eyes. A tremor of fear quaked in her stomach at the fury in his gaze. He walked toward her, but for her plan to work, she couldn't let him move too far.

Scrunching her face into a similar mask of rage, she rushed at him. He stopped, his brow furrowed. He hadn't expected her show of bravery. His fists clenched into tight balls.

She wouldn't get close enough to worry about his fists. Three feet away, she jumped and raised her leg in the air. She kicked at his hip with every molecule of reserve energy she had. Her foot connected, sending him sprawling backward. She landed hard on her left side. Her ribs pounded into solid rock. Her shirt pulled up, gravel scraping the tender skin underneath.

Ron's arms flailed as he tried to regain his balance. For a second, he hovered in a strange crane-like pose, but then gravity won out. His torso twisted around and he fell.

Except he didn't stop at ground level.

He disappeared head first ... down into the skylight of the cave below.

His muffled scream echoed in her ears, followed by a loud thud.

An icy chill crept over her. It had worked. But was he dead? On her knees, she crept toward the hole. Ron lay thirty feet below on the floor of the cave. His eyes were open. Blood seeped out in a semicircle around the back of his head.

CHAPTER THIRTY-THREE

"Elery!" Lucan called to her from halfway up the slope.

Relief washed over her. Tears burned her eyes and poured down her face. *Thank you, God, for keeping him safe.*

She crawled away from the skylight, got to her feet and rushed down. He met her with a smothering bear hug. She melted into his strong arms. When he pulled back, she had to fight the urge to throw herself at him again. He put his hands on both of her cheeks. "Thank you."

"For what? I left you like a scared little girl to face Ron alone."

He shook his head. "For listening to me. I couldn't fight him and worry about you, too."

What could she say to that? Apparently, she'd pushed against him on so many things that he thought she wouldn't do anything he asked. It wasn't him she'd meant to fight, just her feelings for him.

He leaned closer. One thumb swept away a tear, the other traced her bottom lip. How was forgiveness so easy for him? Ron might have lowered the stabilizer to kill Chad, but she'd still been the one to risk the miners' lives with an old machine. The fact Lucan wanted to be this close to her was a miracle. A God-sized one. Maybe it was time to start trusting in miracles for herself.

She pulled his mouth to hers, kissing him fast and rough. They didn't have much time, so she made it count. She let him go within seconds, but a wave of shivers still rushed through her body. If only she could stay in that place forever where everything felt right. Where nothing bad could touch her, only his sweet lips.

She reached up to a dark spot under his hairline. Her fingertips came back blood red. "Are you hurt?"

He blew out a slow breath and gave a rueful smile. "Maybe a little."

Reality hit her like a sudden rockslide. He was injured. And so were the others. "We need to get help."

Lucan took her hand and led her quickly down the slope. "I checked both of them before I left. Jayna has a gunshot wound. Thankfully, it's in the right shoulder, away from her heart."

Not mentioning Garrick was probably for her benefit. His condition was probably more grave than Jayna's.

They scrambled and slid down the rocky slope. The previously two-hour climb took only an hour with gravity as their ally.

As they drew close, the sunny yellow of Jayna's shirt popped into view first. She lay next to Garrick, her hand resting on his chest. She must have been checking his pulse, but now she lay motionless, her eyes closed.

Lucan knelt beside her. "Jayna?"

She moaned and shifted against the rocky ground. "Mark?"

Who was Mark? Elery dropped down on the other side of her. "No, it's Elery and Lucan."

Jayna's eyes flew open. "Oh, Elery. Garrick still has a pulse, but he's ..." She sucked in a pained breath. "He's in bad shape."

Lucan slipped the backpack off his shoulders. "I'm going to get help right now." He handed Elery a water bottle and several energy bars, then swung the pack over his shoulder again. Leaning over Jayna, he pressed his lips to Elery's forehead. "I'll see you, soon."

Her eyes followed him down the slope. He looked

back once, giving her a crooked grin, then continued. When he disappeared over a distant ridge, her heart felt like it had gone into a deep valley with him. Now, there was nothing to do except watch her brother and her friend suffer. *Lord, protect him and us as we wait.*

A gentle touch landed on her hand. She looked down. A weak smile spread across Jayna's face. "You know that man loves you, right?"

Even with the adrenaline still elevating her blood pressure, Elery felt herself blush like a schoolgirl. Certainly, he was attracted to her. She'd never been kissed with such passion. But love? She wasn't so sure. "Do you think so?"

Jayna rolled her eyes. "Duh."

Despite the circumstances, Elery let excitement turn her insides into molten lava. Lucan had forgiven her when he thought she'd killed Chad. He'd looked beyond the sins of her past and never given up on her. She didn't deserve him, but then who did deserve love? It was a gift from God, no different from her health or the mine or any of the other things God gave her. But the most important thing God offered her was forgiveness. For so many years, she'd turned her back on it. Thankfully, God could forgive her for that, as well.

She took Jayna's hand in both of hers. "So, who's Mark?"

CHAPTER THIRTY-FOUR

Garrick woke to the familiar ache in his leg. He opened his eyes to bright light, expecting to see piles of crumbling rock. Instead, the white light temporarily blinded his vision. As his eyes adjusted, he took in the hospital bed, the blanket wrapped tightly around his legs, the blinking machines next to him and an IV in his arm. In a chair beside the bed, Elery slept with her arm curled around a book.

His head pounded. He rubbed his temples. The crevice. He remembered falling and then days of being trapped. He'd been waiting for someone to help him. But Angela hadn't come back. Where was she?

He shifted in the bed and cleared his throat. It had the desired effect. Elery stretched and opened her eyes. When she glanced at the bed and saw him, she sat bolt upright. Her curls stuck out in all directions. Her eyes were lined by dark circles. "Garrick! How long have you been awake?"

"Not long. Can you open up the blinds, please?" The additional light would hurt his eyes and his head, but after a week of sleeping outside, he now felt claustrophobic in this small room.

She smoothed her hair a bit, then did as he asked with a smile on her face. A swell of gratitude ballooned up inside him. He thought he would never see his sister's smile again. Had Angela told Elery to come to the mountain to save him? He remembered hearing her voice, but thought it was an auditory hallucination.

"Dad and I have taken turns waiting in here for you to wake up. He's just outside."

"How long have I been here?"

"Only a day. You were severely dehydrated."

He glanced at the open door. "Where's Angela?"

Elery returned to the chair and sat heavily. The smile gone, she tugged on her lower lip. This couldn't be good. "Here's what we've been able to piece together. Angela got mixed up with Ron somehow."

"Ron? The supervisor at the mine? I don't understand."

Elery explained about Ron's involvement in an illegal mine and his ruthlessness in trying to find the Lost Dutchman Mine.

"Maybe Ron told Angela that he would help you if she cooperated or maybe he threatened her. I don't know. What I do know is she made it to her apartment, probably four days after you fell into the crevice." Elery licked her lips before continuing. "She showed the original map to Ron. But when her map turned out to be useless, Ron had her killed."

"Angela's dead? How?"

Elery shifted in the chair. "She was shot in the chest."

Guilt pierced his heart. He should have protected her, should never have taken her out there in the first place. She hadn't been cut out for it.

Not that he'd fared much better. He could have died too, but apparently God had different plans. He glanced down at the bed. Much different plans. The white blanket followed the contours of his thighs, flattening out completely below the knee of his left leg. The missing skin and bone should have been a shock, but it wasn't. He'd known there was no way doctors could have saved his leg. Getting around without it would be difficult, but maybe now Elery could let go of her guilt for what happened to the same leg so long ago. He swept a hand toward it. "At least this wasn't your fault."

Elery turned her eyes to the floor. He hadn't meant for it to sound so flippant. "I didn't mean ..."

"I know what you meant, but I'm still sad about your leg."

"Me, too." Having no one else to blame for it though would be a welcome change. It would be his cross to bear alone. He grabbed a cup of water from a tray by the bed. His throat felt raw and scratchy, although it didn't hurt, not like Elery's probably did. The band of bruised skin encircling her neck stood out as a deep purple tattoo.

He gestured to the area. "What happened?"

"I'll fill you in later." Her smile reached her eyes with an excitement he hadn't seen for a while. "I have something else to tell you about."

More? He took a deep breath. "Go ahead."

She left the chair to sit on the edge of his bed. Lifting his hand, she gently rubbed his cracked skin. "We found the lost mine."

His heart pounded double time. The machine next to him protested with its own set of beeps. "The Dutchman Mine." He pressed his other hand to his forehead. "You found it? You're sure?"

"Positive. I'll take you to see it."

The offer brought a turbulent storm of emotions. He should have been the one to find the mine, not Elery, who had never thought it was real. But then again, the mine wasn't lost anymore, which meant he'd been proved right for believing in it. He dropped his hand to the bed again. "I'd like to go." He gestured at his left leg. "But we might have to play it by ear."

She gave him a sad smile. "If this whole experience should have taught you one thing ..."

"I know, don't go off all crazy on my own."

She shook her head. "That wasn't what I was going to

say. This whole experience should have taught you that you're persistent. When you set your mind to something, you never give up. And I mean never." She tilted her head. "Seems to be a family trait, actually."

She was right. Thankfully, Elery and their dad were very similar. No matter Garrick's physical condition, both of them would stick by him. "Yeah, maybe."

He rubbed the front of the hospital gown. "So, will you transfer Hearst Stone to the Lost Dutchman Mine?"

She crossed her legs and wiped her hands on the fabric of her jeans. "Probably not. It's on private property. The owners haven't been informed yet, but even if they want to sell, Hearst Stone doesn't have the capital to buy the property." She tapped her kneecap with her index finger. "Dad and I have talked. The accident investigation couldn't prove whether the machine failed or was tampered with, but because the machine caused the accident, the mine will have to pay a hefty fine. Plus, the vein will be tapped out in a couple of months. Any profit the mine makes above the fine will go to Chad's family. Then, we've decided it will be time to close the doors."

"You don't want to try to revive tunnel C?"

"Tunnel C was a long shot. Even if it panned out, I don't think I can be responsible for an entire mine again."

Her lips tilted down into a frown. He knew how hard it was for her to admit she couldn't do something. He squeezed her hand. "I understand."

"Besides, I've got a better offer."

"What do you mean?"

"One of the people who helped to rescue you, Jayna Rowan, has asked me to work with her consulting firm." Elery's eyes sparkled. "It means I can help other mine owners without having to run a mine myself. And I get to travel. The work might come slow at first because Jayna is just getting her business started, but it sounds like the perfect combination of freedom and responsibility."

He smiled. "I'm happy for you. Really."

Taking a deep breath, he held it in as long as he could. The story of his life had changed in one torturous week. The chapter entitled "The Lost Dutchman" was coming to an end. Other than wanting to solve the puzzle of the lost mine and find the treasure, he'd never been all that interested in mining. "Since we won't have the mine anymore, what would you think if I changed my major?"

"You have to decide what you want to do, Garrick. Don't study mining because of me or Dad."

What did he want? He'd wanted the Lost Dutchman Mine. Beyond that, he'd never given it much thought. Now, somehow, he'd have to find a purpose for his life without Jacob Waltz.

***

In the hallway, Elery found her father slumped in a chair across from the nurse's station. She slipped into the chair next to him and bumped his elbow to wake him.

His eyes flew open and searched around wildly before focusing on her. "Elery, is everything okay?"

"Yes. Good news, actually. Garrick is awake if you want to talk to him."

"Of course." He leaned forward to stand, then hesitated, peering at her. "Is everything okay with you?"

She tugged at one of her curls, wrapping it around her finger. "Well, I need to talk to you about something. I've been putting it off because you won't be happy."

"Both of my kids are alive and safe. Nothing else matters."

Easy for him to say before he knew what it was. A few weeks ago, this news would have devastated him. But maybe they had all gained a bit of perspective through this ordeal. "Pastor Arroyo found out about your cancer. Because we kept it from him, he believes we are deceitful people."

Her father twisted his lips to the side. "I suppose he's not wrong since it was a planned deception."

"I tried to reason with him, but ..." She dropped her hands to her lap. "But he kicked us out of the church."

"Oh." He sat up straight in the chair as if the change in posture would help him process her words. Christ's Body Church had been his church home for more than thirty years. Pastor Arroyo had baptized both her and Garrick.

She shifted in the plush chair. "I honestly don't know who told him."

"I do." Her father paused for a few seconds as a nurse rolled a young girl in a wheelchair down the hall. After they had passed, he turned back to her and met her gaze. "It was Candace. She was the only other person I told. A few days ago, she said she accidentally let it slip while talking to the pastor. I just never thought he'd kick us out of the church for it."

"I'm sorry."

"I'm not." He squared his shoulders and nodded. "I think it's about time we found a different place to worship."

"You're sure?"

He patted her leg. "God doesn't care where we worship Him. Just as long as we do."

She smiled, leaned over and gave him a hug. "Sounds great."

He got up and walked across the hall. At Garrick's door, he looked over his shoulder at her. "Elery, it was my fault we were kicked out of church. I forgot something important."

She tilted her head and waited for him to tell her what he meant.

"Our pain, our problems, they aren't meant to be hidden. They're like little cracks in the surface of our lives. They need to be filled in by God, so that eventually we are completely covered in His grace and all anyone can see is Him."

Her father was right, but learning to embrace her brokenness would take time and a lot of prayer. As he disappeared inside Garrick's room, she stood to stretch her legs. The Dutchman and his lost mine had brought tragedy to many people. Finally, the search was over, but the potential of the mine was not fulfilled. She had one more thing to do.

***

Elery wiped her sweaty palms on her jeans and took slow steps up to the royal-blue front door. The house was an older ranch style, gray with curtained windows and similar royal-blue shutters. On the tiny porch, she stopped and fanned herself with the papers she'd brought.

Standing beside her, Lucan put a comforting hand on her shoulder. Thank goodness he'd come. Earlier in the day, she'd gone with him to put a stone grave marker at the place his murdered father had been buried. Rather than move the remains to a cemetery, he and his mother had decided his father would prefer to stay close to the mine. "Are you ready?"

She nodded, then winced. The inflamed tissue around her neck still burned with every movement, a constant, but temporary, reminder of Ron's betrayal.

Lucan let go of her shoulder and gave her an encouraging smile. "You're doing the right thing."

She knocked on the door. A few seconds later, a woman with a deeply lined face answered. She was dressed in jeans and a flowered pink sweatshirt. "Can I help you?"

"I hope so. Are you Inga Cresky, wife of Edgar Cresky?"

The woman raised her eyebrows, stretching out the wrinkles on her face. "Yes, what do you want?"

Elery pushed her shoulders back. "I'd like to come in and talk to you for a moment."

"What about?"

"It's about something I found on your property."

Inga scanned her up and down, then did the same for Lucan. She smiled at them, and Elery realized the wrinkles were laugh lines. "Okay. You two seem harmless enough. Come in."

She followed Inga into a sparsely furnished living room. A small floral love seat rested against one wall, an ornate metal cross hanging above it. Two side-by-side recliners were on the other wall, angled toward the television. In one of the chairs, a bearded man sat fully reclined with a colostomy bag hanging off to one side. Inga grabbed a blanket and covered it. "Sorry. Edgar needs reconstruction of his innards, but we haven't yet been able to afford the deductible on our medical plan." She spoke matter-of-factly with no trace of shame.

Elery opened her mouth to speak, but nothing came out. She tugged on her lower lip instead. Pastor Arroyo would question whether this man had asked God for healing, but Elery was filled with a deep certainty that helping Edgar was God's plan all along.

She cleared her throat. "As I said, we found something on your property."

Inga motioned for them to sit on the love seat, while she took a seat in the recliner next to Edgar. "We own a lot of property out here still. Most of it isn't good for much beside a beautiful view. Eventually, we'll probably sell some of it to pay for Edgar's surgery. So, if you've found some Indian graveyard or something that would cause us to not be able to sell it, please don't tell us."

"No, it's not that. And if you want to sell it, you won't have any problems." Elery hesitated. Most people would think of the mine as a blessing, but it had caused havoc in many lives. What would these two think? She presented the top piece of paper to Inga. A computer-printout map with GPS coordinates on it. "In the northwest corner of your property, about two miles from here, we found a gold mine."

Inga took the paper, then turned to stare at Edgar. His wide-eyed stare matched hers. Neither of them said anything for a full minute.

When Inga spoke, her mouth was stiff. "Is this a college prank? You know, see if the old folks will have a heart attack when you tell them they won the lottery?"

Elery gave her the most sober face she could. "This isn't a prank. And we didn't find just any mine. It's the Lost Dutchman Gold Mine."

"Now, I know you're faking. That mine has been lost for a hundred years."

"Believe me, you don't want to know how we found it, but it's not lost anymore. The two of us, plus the sheriff, are the only people who know its location."

Inga glanced down at the paper, holding it with two fingers as if it might bite her.

"We found it, but it's located on your property. The mine is yours, not ours."

Inga finally took the map in both hands and examined it. When she looked up, her eyes were wide with understanding. "This isn't far from where those hikers were rescued. We knew that was on our land somewhere. Was that you?"

Elery swallowed past the lump in her throat. "Yes."

"How is that boy doing? The one who's still in the hospital?"

"He's going to be okay. He lost part of his leg, but he's dealing with it very well. Thanks for asking."

Lucan took her hand and squeezed it. "We're all going to be okay," he added.

She squeezed his hand in return. Finally, the mine would do more than bring death. It would bring Edgar a new kind of life, and God would get the credit.

They left the GPS coordinates with the Creskys, along with an affidavit detailing what had been found. She told them to contact the sheriff to stake their claim to the mineral rights of the mine. On the walk down the driveway, fatigue settled into Elery's bones. She sank down on a large block of granite edging the gravel drive and gazed at the massive mountains in front of her.

Lucan sat next to her and pulled her close. "Tired?"

"Yes, but glad this is all over." The only wild card left was their relationship. Where did Lucan see this going, now that he knew everything about her past? He might have forgiven her for what she'd done, but what about what she would do in the future? She had to ask. "Is any part of you afraid of me?"

At first, he blinked at the out-of-the-blue question, then he shook her shoulders gently. "No. You're a strong woman, but you don't scare me."

"I'm serious. You know what I'm capable of." Even though the prosecutor had ruled Ron's death as justified, she'd still killed a man.

Lucan turned her to face him. She looked deep into his eyes, their amber depths calming her fears. Too often, she'd fought against him when she should have listened. Whatever he said next, she'd accept it.

Only he didn't speak. Instead, one finger traced along her jaw line, then tilted her head up. He leaned down, gently kissing the damaged skin on her neck. Tingles swarmed through her body as if a thousand fireflies had been let loose inside.

His lips slowly moved to her ear. He whispered her name and goose bumps broke out along her arms. As his lips traveled along her cheek, she grabbed the front of his shirt, tugging him closer. He entwined his fingers in her curls and pulled her mouth to his, drawing her into a deep kiss. She wrapped her arms around his neck, never wanting to let go.

When he finally pulled back, he cradled her cheek in his palm. "Elery, I see you as God does." His voice was low and husky.

She took slow, even breaths to calm her racing pulse. "How's that?"

He gave her a beaming smile that almost knocked the heart right out of her chest. "Flawless."

AUTHOR'S NOTE

Dear Reader,

This was my first attempt at fictionalizing the life of a historical person, and I had amazing fun with it. I became so engrossed in researching the Lost Dutchman Mine and Jacob Waltz that I came to understand the obsession many people have for the legends. But of course you can't find everything you want to know about a person's life, which leaves room for my imagination to take over. Whenever I read books with a historical thread, I love to know what's real and where the author took artistic license. In the spirit of full disclosure, much of Jacob Waltz's story in this novel is fictional because not much is known about his life, but here is what I discovered in my research.

Jacob Waltz was a real person who had large amounts of gold from an unknown source. He was not Dutch, but actually German, born in Germany around 1808, or maybe 1810 (scholars disagree, although his gravestone says 1808). The name Dutchman arose from people calling him Deutsch (German) man. Most people believe he had a partner named Jacob Weiser (sometimes spelled Wiser) who died, although some will dispute even this. Many stories of Weiser's death have circulated around, including one in which Jacob Waltz killed Jacob Weiser for the gold. Obviously, that wasn't the position I took in the book, but such is attributed to my imagination.

Jacob Waltz came to America in 1846, landing in New York. He left there and traveled through Mississippi, and probably the Arizona territory, all the way to California, where he filed papers to become a naturalized U.S. citizen in Los Angeles in 1861. In 1863, Waltz returned to the Arizona territory, staking several claims in the Bradshaw Mountains northwest of Phoenix.

By 1868, Waltz had settled onto a homestead with a farm on the Salt River (modern day Phoenix). The details of Jacob Waltz dying in 1891 are essentially true. He escaped the flooding of his house by clinging to a tree, then contracted pneumonia shortly after. Julia Thomas and her adopted son, Rhinehart, did care for him as he lay dying, at which time he reportedly gave them clues to the location of the mine. After Waltz's death, Julia discovered a box of gold ore under his bed. Some of this gold has survived and has been tested against samples of gold from mines in the area—no match has been found. Julia and Rhinehart spent many years looking for the mine with no success. Eventually, Julia gave up and settled down with her second husband, Albert Schaffer. During this time, she sold copies of her version of the Lost Dutchman Mine map to recoup the money she spent looking for the mine.

The ancestral connections to the lost mine used in this novel were completely fictional. As far as I could determine, Julia and Rhinehart had no living heirs when they died, but Julia's second husband, Albert Schaffer, had some brothers who survived, hence Angela's ancestral connection to the mine. As for Lucan and Chad being descendants of Jacob Waltz, I found information that Waltz had a sister living in Kansas when he died, but I am not sure if any of those descendants are still living.

Thank you, dear reader, for sharing this adventure with Elery and Lucan, and Jacob Waltz. I pray you enjoyed their journey as much as I enjoyed writing it. And I would ask you to please consider taking a brief moment to leave a review on the website where you purchased this book. We authors appreciate reviews (even negative ones) more than you know.

May God grant you much grace and peace for the adventures in your future.

Blessings,
Janice

ACKNOWLEDGMENTS

Authors may seem like a solitary bunch, sequestered alone with only a computer for company, but that's not completely accurate. No one publishes a novel without a literal army behind the scenes supporting them. Here, I salute some of the voluntary members of my writing army. As far as I'm concerned, all of you deserve the Medal of Honor.

To my amazing husband, Todd. Many people don't realize how hard it is to handle us writers. You could give a college-credit course on it. Whether I'm on top of the world in love with my story or an insecure little ball of fluff, you remind me why I'm doing this—because I'm living out my dream by creating stories. I appreciate, more than you know, how you work faithfully at your day job, so that I can pursue this dream. And in your off-time, you traipse (very manly traipsing, of course) around the rain forest or the desert mountains, even random graveyards, all for the sake of my stories. Thank you for all you do to help keep my crazy imagination satisfied. Oh, and also for keeping our kids fed during nightmare edits.

To my wonderful kids, Zach, Jenna and Riley. Thank you for believing I will be the next best-selling author. Even if it doesn't happen, you have always made me feel like the best and that matters more to me than any number of books sold.

To my wonderful critique partner, Crystal Joy. You bring a level of emotion out in my work that always makes the story more powerful. Plus, you never let me kill a character off just for fun—you insist on a good reason for bloodshed. I couldn't ask for a more supportive critique partner. I'm so happy God brought us together, dear friend.

To the incomparable Katie Ganshert. You were the first actual author to encourage me, and encourage you did, over and over again. When you read my first few pages and said I was a great writer, I bawled for an entire hour (out of happiness). Thank you for taking the time to come alongside me early in my writing journey and for pushing me to continue.

To my early readers who've had to read through some agonizingly raw stuff. Donna Feld, Sue Muszalski, Mary Johnson, Kara Hunt, and Paula Rutkowski (the best sister God ever made). And to Ramona Richards and Mary Kay Wayman, both amazing editors, for their insightful developmental edits. Thank you all for making my work rise to a higher standard.

To all of my supportive friends who have asked when I was getting published about a hundred times, and yet still believed this day would come. Amy Farrey, Stacey Ickes, Sarah Forgrave, Jill Kemerer, Jeannie Campbell, Mikka Appel, Amy Leigh Simpson, everyone in the Quad Cities Scribblers group, and all my ACFW friends, especially my fun conference roommates.

To the hard-working professionals at WildBlue Press, Ashley Butler, Steve Jackson, Michael Cordova, and others who touched this book, including Kim Mesman for an amazing cover. Thank you all for taking a chance on a new author like me and for making this book the best it could be (all mistakes lie solely with me). Your dedication to authors and to readers is an inspiration.

To my precious reader. If not for you, these words would be as lost as the Dutchman's Mine. Thank you for being here, for spending your valuable minutes engrossed in this story, and for supporting the art of writing. We authors covet your support, especially in the form of reviews. Positive reviews help other readers to find a good book and negative ones help authors to improve in the craft of writing, so if you have another one of your valuable minutes to spare, please review this book. And if you'd like to know when the next book is this series is coming out, please visit my website and sign up to receive my newsletter.

Blessings,
Janice

Get Book Two In The Earth Hunters Series. On Sale Now!

"CREATED has everything—suspense, romance, adventure, and an age-old theme that resonates with us all..." (Katie Ganshert, award-winning author of The Gifting Series and Life After) When Paleontology Professor Travis Perego's fragile new faith leads him to question evolutionary theory, the dean tells him to get it together soon, or he's fired. So when he learns of an experiment designed to prove evolution, he searches the Costa Rican jungle for the result—a mysterious creature. But tracking down the truth could cost his life."Strong, skillful and engrossing." (E.E. Kennedy, author of the Miss Prentice cozy mystery series)

http://wbp.bz/created

See even more at:
http://wbp.bz/cf

More Crime Fiction You'll Love From WildBlue Press

LOCKOUT by John J. Nance

The newest aviation thriller from New York Times bestselling author John J. Nance. *"A wild ride in the night sky."* (Capt. "Sully" Sullenberger, author of New York Times bestseller Sully). Whoever electronically disconnected the flight controls of Pangia Flight 10 as it streaks toward the volatile Middle East may be trying to provoke a nuclear war. With time and fuel running out, the pilots risk everything to wrest control from the electronic ghost holding them on a course to disaster. *"As good or better than any of his previous works. Hop aboard Pangia flight 10 - if you dare."* (Charles Gibson, former anchor ABC World News)

wbp.bz/lockout

SAVAGE HIGHWAY by Richard Godwin

From an internationally acclaimed author of noir thrillers comes *"the road novel from hell"* (Castle Freeman Jr., author of The Devil In The Valley). Women are disappearing on the highway, a drifter hunts the men who raped her, and a journalist discovers the law has broken down. An *"irresistible hard-boiled read that's reminiscent of old school black and white noir."* (Vincent Zandri, New York Times bestselling author).

wbp.bz/savagehighway

WHEN FALL FADES by Amy Leigh Simpson

A *"Must-Read Romance of 2015"* (USA Today). Hunky FBI Agent Archer Hayes reluctantly enlists the lovely and beguiling Sadie Carson to solve the mystery of her elderly neighbor's death and its connection to a conspiracy dating back to WWII. Results in fiery romance and chilling murder plot. *"Simpson swung for the fences."* (Anthony Flacco, New York Times bestselling author). The first book in up-and-comer Simpson's The Girl Next Door romantic mystery series. Compares to New York Times bestselling romance author Julie Garwood.

wbp.bz/whenfallfades

9 781942 266549